THE B[...]

I heard Patrick i[...] [...]eep them warm. He was [...] go in.

But I was too curious to turn around. I was shivering, but not only from the cold.

The shadow I'd seen wasn't a deer.

In the moonlight I saw a man's body face down in the snow. He was wearing a black and white patterned sweater, jeans, and cowboy boots. A darker shadow was under his head, and parts of his body were lightly covered with recent snow. I knelt to check his pulse.

There wasn't one.

"What're you doing? Let's get back to the house!" Patrick called again.

"Just a minute," I yelled back. I pulled out my cellphone, snapped several pictures, and walked back toward Patrick.

"There's a body," I said as calmly as I could. "We need to call the police."

This was not the beginning of a Merry Christmas . . .

Books by Lea Wait

TWISTED THREADS

THREADS OF EVIDENCE

THREAD AND GONE

DANGLING BY A THREAD

TIGHTENING THE THREADS

THREAD THE HALLS

Published by Kensington Publishing Corporation

Thread
the Halls

Lea Wait

KENSINGTON PUBLISHING CORP.

http://www.kensingtonbooks.com

KENSINGTON BOOKS are published by

Kensington Publishing Corp.
119 West 40th Street
New York, NY 10018

All Kensington Titles, Imprints, and Distributed Lines are available at special quantity discounts for bulk purchases for sales promotions, premiums, fund-raising, and educational or institutional use. Special book excerpts or customized printings can also be created to fit specific needs. For details, write or phone the office of the Kensington special sales manager: Kensington Publishing Corp., 119 West 40th Street, New York, NY 10018, attn: Special Sales Department, Phone: 1-800-221-2647.

Kensington and the K logo Reg. U.S. Pat & TM Off.

ISBN-13: 978-1-4967-0630-0
ISBN-10: 1-4967-0630-7
First Kensington Mass Market Edition: November 2017

eISBN-13: 978-1-4967-0631-7
eISBN-10: 1-4967-0631-5
First Kensington Electronic Edition: November 2017

10 9 8 7 6 5 4 3 2 1

Printed in the United States of America

Chapter 1

"As some fair violet, loveliest of the glade
Sheds its mild fragrance on the lovely shade
Withdraws its modest head from public sight
Covets not the sun nor seeks the glare of light,
So woman born to dignify, retreat, and be unseen,
Fearful of fame, unwilling to be known,
Should seek but Heaven's applause, and her own."

—Stitched by Eliza Ely in 1881, somewhere in
   New England.

After ten years of not celebrating December 25 other than
by listening to carols on my car radio during surveillance
gigs, I was determined this Christmas would be perfect. It
wouldn't be magical, like it was when I was a child. But I
needed it to come close.

When I was young, Christmas had always made up for

the other 364 days of the year that, despite Gram's efforts, had been memorable in other ways.

"Gram, where's my star?" I called to her. "It has to go on the tree first."

"It's in a gold box, Angel," she answered from the dining room, where she and Reverend Tom (I still had trouble calling her new husband "Tom," no matter how often he told me to drop the Reverend) were adding to the bowl of eggnog.

Gram was the only one who called me "Angel." I liked the old nickname.

"It's probably in the same carton as the lights," she added.

Boxes of red and blue and gold Christmas balls were stacked near the fireplace, next to ornaments I'd made in elementary school, and a few needlepointed ones I'd added to the collection this year.

This tree was my first as a grown-up, on my own. I hadn't bothered to have a tree in my Arizona apartment. Life there had been temporary. Last Christmas had meant white lights twinkling on saguaro cactuses and dinner with my boss in a Mexican food diner.

As usual, Gram was right. The gold box was under a string of colored lights.

I opened it carefully, hoping my star would be the way I remembered it.

I'd made the large, lopsided ornament in kindergarten, covering coat hanger wire with aluminum foil. I'd proudly brought it home and given it to Mama. Her perfume had mixed with the scent of pine as she lifted me up so I could put my star on the very top of our tree.

Sometimes I imagined the star still held a trace of her fragrance.

When I was a teenager I'd talked about replacing my star

with something more elegant. But, secretly, I loved it and the years it represented: Christmases with Mama.

I stared into the box. In the past ten years the star's silver foil had crackled, and pieces had fallen off.

Gram saw me looking at it. "Nothing lasts forever, Angel. Maybe you can cover it with fresh foil."

She didn't understand. "I want it the way it was," I said.

I'm twenty-eight. I knew I was being silly. But I wanted this Christmas to be the same as the Christmases I remembered as a child. After all, Christmas meant tradition. Even if not every Christmas was traditional.

I climbed the paint-spattered stepladder and wound the now-rusted wire around the base of my star and the top of the tree.

Curtis family traditions in Haven Harbor, Maine, meant Santas on the mantel, a tree that touched the ceiling, and wreaths on every door and window.

I secretly believed one of my Victorian ancestors had added our bay window to frame their Christmas tree. Yesterday, Patrick, the new man in my life, and I had donned our blaze orange (hunting season was over and his land was posted, but you never knew), cut my tree in his woods, and then stood it in the Christmas tree stand Mama and Gram had used before me.

Sharing the holiday with a special man was one change I welcomed.

Other changes were harder to accept. I remembered the excitement and anticipation of early Christmas mornings in a flannel nightgown, nibbling ribbon candy before breakfast while Gram made blueberry pancakes in the kitchen. Now Gram was married and living down the street in the rectory with Reverend Tom. They'd invited me to spend Christmas morning with them, but they were finding new ways to celebrate together.

Most of their plans didn't involve me. They were part of his ministerial duties and were shared with the rest of his church family.

Gram was taking their first Christmas as a married couple in stride.

I wasn't.

But I was trying. Today I'd invited my friends from Gram's (now my) Mainely Needlepoint business to a tree-trimming party. I hoped new traditions would keep me from missing old ones.

When I was seventeen, hating Maine and all it stood for, and hating Mama for disappearing when I was ten, leaving me to deal with rumors and pity, I never could have imagined someday my life would be like this. After ten years of working for a private investigator in Phoenix, learning to handle a gun and "follow and photo," I'd come home.

Mama's body had been found, and I'd found her killer. I'd finally answered the questions I'd lived with for seventeen years.

Tonight I was surrounded by friends: Patrick West, the guy who wasn't perfect, but who made me smile; Sarah Byrne, who'd moved to Maine from Australia, had a rocky few months recently, but had become my closest friend; Dave Percy, who taught high school biology and whose poison garden intrigued me; Captain Ob and his wife, Anna, who'd had a difficult summer, but were now ready to ring in a new year; Ruth Hopkins, who did needlepoint when her arthritis allowed, and wrote books when it didn't; Katie Titicomb and Dr. Gus, parents of one of my high school friends; Clem Walker, a high school friend who lived in Portland and worked for Channel 7, but was now home for the holidays with her family; and, of course, Gram and Reverend Tom.

And Trixi. As the tree began to shake I realized I'd been lost in the past and hadn't seen her for a few minutes.

I reached through the wide branches and caught her, one small black kitten, on her way to the top. She jumped from my arms and skittered to her favorite hiding spot behind the couch.

As I climbed down from the ladder Patrick's arm went around me. "Penny for your thoughts? You look as though you left us for a while."

"I'm here," I said, smiling into his eyes. "Very happy to be right here right now." I stood on my toes and kissed his cheek. Who needed a kissing ball or mistletoe when I had Patrick?

He looked around the room, took a deep breath, and announced, "This is as good a time as any for me to invite all of you to Aurora for a dinner party Christmas Eve."

Aurora was Patrick's mother's estate. She was an actress, making a movie in Scotland.

"Skye will be back for Christmas?" I asked.

"She thought she'd have to work through Christmas, but they've had weather delays and script problems. Last night she called to tell me they'd decided to close the set for the holidays. She's coming here with some of the others working on the film."

"Really?" Clem asked. "Anyone famous?"

Clem was the only one of us who'd never met Patrick's mother, who'd bought Aurora as a retreat, far from the pressures of Hollywood. We'd all made it an unwritten rule that Skye should have the privacy she valued.

Patrick looked at Clem. He'd remembered my old friend

was also a part of the media. By issuing a general invitation to his mother's party, he'd included her. "Paul Carmichael is coming, and an actress I don't know, Blaze Buchanan. And Thomas and Marie O'Day, the screenwriters, will be here re-working the end of the script with Marv Mason, who's directing."

"Wow!" Clem breathed. "I'm a real Paul Carmichael fan. He's gorgeous. And Marv Mason's won two Oscars!"

"Sounds like a working holiday," Ruth Hopkins pointed out.

"Exactly. Mom said besides the script, they've had personnel problems on the set they hope to work out while they're here. She sounded distracted. And here's my challenge. She wants me to decorate the house in what she termed 'traditional Maine Christmas fashion,' so all is 'as she dreamed' when she arrives." Patrick smiled, but looked tense. "Her plane gets in December twentieth."

"She wants you to decorate the whole house in two days?" I gasped. Skye's home was enormous.

Reverend Tom shook his head. "Sounds as though she's been watching old Christmas movies. This is Haven Harbor. Not a movie set."

"Exactly," Patrick agreed glumly. "She even rattled off a list of what she wants—garlands everywhere and an enormous tree, of course. And that's just the beginning. She wants a horse-drawn sleigh and carolers. And an elegant buffet dinner Christmas Eve, including lobster."

Silence. A horse-drawn sleigh? Did Patrick's mother think Maine was still in the nineteenth century?

Captain Ob Winslow was the first to speak. "I'll help with the tree, Patrick. What are neighbors for? But Anna and I've planned a quiet Christmas this year, just the two of us. I'm afraid we'll have to pass on the invite to your fancy party."

"Gus and I'll be heading to Blue Hill for Christmas with the grandkids," said Katie. "We won't be in town Christmas Eve."

"I'd be happy to come," Sarah said quickly. "And you'll be here then, right, Dave?"

"I'd planned to spend the holidays in Boston. But, sure. I can come Christmas Eve." Dave looked cornered.

"I'll come," said Ruth, quietly.

"I'll be there for sure," Clem put in.

Patrick glanced at her and then me, and shrugged.

"I'll help decorate," I put in. Like Ob and Anna, I'd looked forward to a quiet Christmas day, mine with Gram and Tom. And Patrick, of course. But I could manage Christmas Eve. I'd miss the children's pageant at the church, but I could do that. I glanced at Patrick's hands. Last June they'd been badly burned in an accident. The delicate task of hanging ornaments would be hard for him.

"I'll bet I can find some sophomores from my bio class who could use extra spending money over the holidays. School's out already. You get the tree and ornaments, and I'll find decorators," Dave suggested.

"I'd really appreciate that," Patrick said with relief, squeezing my hand. "Thank you, Dave." He looked around the room. "I have to warn all of you. I know most of Mom's friends in the movie business. I'm afraid there may be more drama at Aurora this Christmas than Haven Harbor's used to."

"As long as any dramas stay at Aurora," said Reverend Tom quietly. "Here in town we're pretty set in our ways of celebrating. After all, Christmas is a religious holiday. A time for families to be together. Not a spectacle."

"I understand." Patrick nodded. "I do."

His hand tightened on mine.

He might understand. But did his mom and her Hollywood friends? My dream of a quiet, perfect, Maine Christmas was fading fast.

But Skye seemed to picture Haven Harbor as a Currier and Ives scene. And nothing bad ever happened in a Currier and Ives print. Right?

Chapter 2

"Sacred to the memory of Jonathan Prat,
Born July 14, 1801, Died August 22, 1803, Aged 2 years."

—Silk embroidery in metallic thread stitched
by Harriet Pratt (1797–1880) of Oxford,
Massachusetts, at Abby Wright's School in
South Hadley. Harriet's picture depicts a marble
memorial to her brother. Her father (aged thirty-
three), her mother (aged thirty), her younger
sister (aged four), and Harriet herself (aged six)
are weeping next to it. Harriet married William
Dana on July 12, 1812, and on August 30 their
son Jonathan was born.

"I have a children's pageant and a candlelight service
scheduled for Christmas Eve," said Reverend Tom. "But I
could probably get some of the choir members to go to
Aurora and sing a few carols between the services." He

looked at Patrick. "We've been needing some new choir robes."

I liked Reverend Tom. He treated Gram with love and kindness. It might sound crass to take advantage of the Wests' wealth, but it was practical. And he'd be asking the choir to interrupt their Christmas Eve to sing for a group of people from away.

Patrick didn't blink. He got the message. "Mom would be happy to make a donation to the church," he assured Tom. He and Skye were used to paying for what they wanted. And getting it.

Carolers were taken care of. "What else can we help with?" I put in, before anyone else found a reason they couldn't come to Skye's party.

Patrick looked embarrassed. Then he hit us with another of his mother's requests. "I hope some of you have a little time between now and Christmas. Mom would like to give each of her colleagues—all five of them—small balsam fir pillows embroidered with a Christmas tree and their names."

No one said anything. We Mainely Needlepointers looked at one another. Skye and Patrick had no idea how long needlepointing took.

Anna was the first to speak. "I'm the newest needle-pointer, but if they're small, I'll try to do one. Time is tight this time of year."

"Small is fine," Patrick assured her.

Sarah shrugged. "Count me in. I'll be at my shop hoping for Christmas shoppers between now and Christmas. What about you, Dave?"

"Sure," he said, reluctantly. "School's already out for the holiday, so I don't have lesson plans or papers to grade."

Ruth shook her head. "My arthritis is acting up. I couldn't finish one in—what is it? Six days?"

"And I'm booked with church activities. Sorry," said Gram.

I swallowed. "I'll do my best." I had other plans for the next week. Needlepoint was new to me, too, and I'd already volunteered to give up at least one day to help Patrick decorate. Plus, I had a little more to do on the pillow I was stitching for him as a Christmas surprise. The threads matched the vibrant colors and design of the painting hanging in his living room that he'd completed before he'd burned his hands. I'd been working on the pillow all fall, but it wasn't quite finished.

I hoped my gift would encourage Patrick to paint again. Recently he'd spent most of his time at the gallery he'd bought on Main Street. His studio stood empty.

"That's four pillows," said Patrick, looking at all of us hopefully.

"Okay," Ob sighed reluctantly. "If Anna can do one, I can, too. Your mother's worked wonders with Aurora. It'll be good to see a Christmas tree up at the place this year." Ob and Anna lived across the street from Aurora.

"Thank you all so much," said Patrick. "That's a relief. Mom will pay you all well, I promise, for the fast turnaround involved."

"I'll get back to those of you who volunteered. Patrick and I will talk." I sent him a glance I hoped he'd find meaningful. "First thing in the morning I'll call the four of you who volunteered to stitch and let you know the colors and dimensions of the pillows and whose name to stitch. We'll use our usual pattern for the tree."

But Patrick wasn't finished asking for help. "Do any of

you have suggestions for a caterer?" he asked. "I called the lobster bake place in Camden Mom used last summer, but they don't do bakes in December. And every caterer I could find online was already booked for Christmas events."

A lobster bake in December? Not exactly. Patrick was out of his depth.

Maine's restaurants and caterers were famous for their gourmet delights in the summer, but many of them closed in the off-season. Those still open were sure to be booked.

Gram came to the rescue. "What about Bev Clifford? Her Wild Rose Inn is closed for the winter, and she's a good cook. She's a widow, and her son won't be home for Christmas. Recently she told me she was dreading the holidays. Too many memories. Tom and I invited her for Christmas dinner, but as long as you want lobsters and good Maine food she might be willing to help you out."

In other words, nothing fancy. And Bev Clifford could use the money. Winters were tough for Mainers who ran businesses for summer visitors.

"I'll call her," said Patrick gratefully. He wrote down her name. "Mom isn't looking for French cuisine. She used the words *authentic* and *local* when I talked with her. And, of course, seafood."

"Some French food *is* authentic Maine cuisine," Anna put in. "Think of the patisserie downtown, and all our French-Canadian neighbors."

"Right," said Patrick, who clearly hadn't thought about Quebecois cuisine at all. "I should talk to Bev Clifford about that."

"I'm sure she could make up some *tourtières,*" suggested Gram.

"What?" Patrick asked, blankly.

"Spicy pork pies. A traditional Christmas dish from Quebec. A lot of Maine folks bake them this time of year. And you'll want local oysters as well as lobster," Dave suggested.

"And local wines and beers," Patrick said, taking more notes.

"Local distillers make spirits," I added. "The only libation you may have to buy from away is champagne."

"You could always introduce these folks to Moxie," Captain Ob said, a glint in his eye.

"There are Maine fruit sparkling wines," agreed Reverend Tom, with a smile. "Charlotte and I can suggest some."

Patrick looked overwhelmed. "I only thought I had to worry about a tree and wreaths!"

"I have a cousin who has a horse," said Ob, getting into the spirit. "And a wagon. Wouldn't be a sleigh, like Skye wanted, but it'd be better than nothing. Most of us drive trucks and snow plows these days."

"And snow mobiles. I know. I do know. I'm sorry. Mom spent time here, but she hasn't lived here. And this is our first winter. We both still have a lot to learn about Maine." Patrick smiled at everyone. "I'm throwing myself on your mercy. I really appreciate all this help."

I touched his arm. "You can do it, Patrick. It may not be exactly what your mother has in mind. But she has to be flexible. This isn't a movie set. Haven Harbor is a real town, and we all have real lives."

Real lives that had been planning Christmas for months. I'd looked forward to joining Gram and Tom for Christmas morning and having Patrick join us for Christmas dinner. Now he'd be spending Christmas Day with his mother and her Hollywood friends at Aurora.

He was the man in my life, at least for now. I was willing to help him arrange his mother's house for her guests.

But I didn't want to sacrifice family time for the amusement of people I'd probably never see again.

Patrick might be used to doing that. I wasn't.

Chapter 3

"Liberty in the Form of the Goddess of Youth Giving Support to the Bald Eagle."

—Silk embroidery stitched by Louisa Bushnell (1799–1887) in Essex, Connecticut, depicting the goddess reaching up to the eagle, an American flag on her right, and the scene surrounded by a garland of flowers.

Patrick excused himself to call Bev Clifford.

The rest of us looked after him as he headed for the quiet of the kitchen. Reverend Tom shook his head.

I expected a few comments from the needlepointers about folks from away who expect too much from locals, but everyone held their tongues. Maybe on my behalf. They'd all accepted that, at least for now, Patrick was my guy. (He didn't know it, but that gave him a little more leverage around Haven Harbor, especially with my friends.) Or maybe they'd been willing to help because of the promised donation to the church, or because it was Christmas.

I poured myself a glass of egg nog and was silently grateful.

Quiet carols were playing on my computer (the living room, minus the Christmas tree and decorations, was also my Mainely Needlepoint office). Captain Ob added two logs to feed the flames on the hearth. Everyone else was eating, drinking, or needlepointing. Clem, who didn't know the others as well as I did, was chatting quietly with Sarah. I hoped Sarah was filling her in on how Skye and Patrick would expect us to keep news about the famous guests quiet.

"Time to put on the ornaments!" I announced.

"I'll pass on hanging balls, but I'll supervise. Let you all know if you're overloading the tree on either side," Ruth suggested. Her arthritis was keeping her close to her walker these days.

The rest of my guests each took a box of ornaments and went to work.

Patrick rejoined us in a few minutes. "Thanks for recommending Bev Clifford, Mrs. McCully," he said to Gram. "She's on board. I'm going to meet her tomorrow afternoon at Aurora."

"Good," I said. "Now, here's a box of ornaments for you to hang."

"Yes, ma'am," he said, smiling.

I handed him ornaments I'd made as a child—gold-painted starfish tied with red ribbon and papier-mâché shapes of uncertain intent. The attached pieces of string or wire would be easier for him to hang than the small hooks on the balls.

He picked up a glittery picture frame made of Popsicle sticks holding a picture of eight-year-old me. "Pretty cute kid," he grinned as he hung the ornament on a nearby branch.

With everyone helping, decorating took less time than I'd imagined.

After we'd found places for every gold or red ball and lumpy ornament we sat to admire our handiwork. Katie and Dave picked up their needlepoint. Most of us sipped more eggnog.

"I haven't told you all," Sarah shared. "Last Saturday I went to an auction up in Thomaston and bought an amazing collection of antique needlework tools. You should all come to my antiques shop to look. I'm afraid they're expensive, but I'd love you to see them before they sell. They're the sort I'd only seen in museums."

"Tools?" I asked. Unlike most of the others, I was still learning about needlework. I had no idea what "antique needlework tools" would be.

"An elegant lady in the eighteenth or nineteenth century would have a personal set of everything she needed for needlepointing or sewing—needles, needle cases, scissors, thimbles, stilettos, tape measures, shuttles . . . everything you can imagine. Her tools were made of elaborately carved bone or ivory or mother-of-pearl or silver or even gold, sometimes set with gemstones. They'd fit in an inlaid sewing box, or an etui—a tabletop holder for tools—or sometimes hang on a chatelaine . . . a series of chains she'd wear around her waist to hold the gadgets, almost like charms on a bracelet. Chatelaines were for the wealthy; they're expensive. But some pieces in the collection are affordable. I've already decided to keep a wooden needle case decorated with a Blue Wren—it's from Australia, from the nineteen forties or fifties, and reminds me of a case my grandmum used."

"Then it's meant for you, Sarah," agreed Dave. "I once saw scrimshaw needle cases and thimble holders at an exhibit of mariner carvings. Sailors didn't just carve pictures on whales' teeth and walrus tusks. Do you have any tools like those?"

"I do. Gifts made on long voyages to be given to a mother or wife or sweetheart when the mariner returned home. And there's a set in a tartan ware case, from Scotland, and silver cases with Art Nouveau designs, and needle cases from China for the export trade. You have to come and look! Some of the carvings and etchings and inlays are wonderful."

"Whose collection was it?" Katie asked. "It sounds fantastic."

"Hinting for a Christmas gift?" her husband, Dr. Gus, put in.

"Might be," Katie said, nudging him with her elbow.

Sarah had said "expensive." I suspected the tools were out of my reach, although Dr. Gus would have the money. Too bad. I could use another gift to put under Gram's tree. She'd given me so much, for so many years.

"The collection was started years ago by the grandmother of a woman in Waldoboro. She inherited it and then added to it. It's being sold since none of her heirs were interested in carrying on the tradition." Sarah shook her head sadly. "'I had some things that I called mine—And God, that he called his.'" I'd gotten used to Sarah's quoting Emily Dickinson at odd moments, but Clem looked puzzled. It could be confusing.

"Sad," said Ruth.

Sarah shrugged. "It is. All the items were well cared for. The scissors and needles are still sharp! Most antiques auctions today are full of furnishings or collections being de-accessioned by people downsizing, or by their children, who don't want to polish family silver and think mahogany furniture is old-fashioned. Most of the pieces in this collection are from England or France. Here in the States women did needlework, but most couldn't afford the accessories upper-class British women in the eighteenth and nineteenth centuries prized."

"I'd like to look at the collection," Patrick put in. "My mother's not a needlepointer, but you all restored those needlepoint pictures in her dining room, and it might be nice to have something to display near them. Mom's impossible to buy for—she buys everything she wants herself."

"Do stop in, then," encouraged Sarah. "One of the elaborately carved stands would fit in Aurora. Or an inlaid box of tools. Your gallery is nearby. I'd keep my shop open a little late if I knew you were coming."

"When I learned Mom and her friends were flying in I decided to close the gallery until Christmas," Patrick said. "I'll put a 'call for appointment' sign up. I have too much to do now to gallery-sit. But I can fit in a trip to your shop. I'm intrigued."

"Me too," I said. "You'll be open your regular hours?"

"Until four in the afternoon Christmas Eve," she promised. "Oh, and, Angie? I almost forgot to tell you. A woman from Texas was in my shop yesterday. She asked lots of questions about Haven Harbor. A nuisance. But she may turn out to be a good customer. She was fascinated by all the old needleworking tools and is looking for someone to needlepoint some chair covers. I didn't get the whole story—I had other customers—but I gave her your name."

"Thanks. That might be a big order. As long as she doesn't want the work done by Christmas!"

"I don't think so," said Sarah. "Although she didn't say."

Captain Ob stood, reaching a hand to Anna. "We've enjoyed this evening, Angie. Thanks for inviting us. But Anna and I have some Christmas preparations of our own to do. We're going to take off." He turned to Patrick. "Shall I come over with my saw tomorrow morning to help you with a tree and extra branches for decorating?"

"I'd appreciate that. About eight?"

"Sounds good," said Ob. "No major snow's predicted tonight, so we should be able to get what you need in an hour or two. I'll bring a sled we can use."

"After you get the tree up you'll need ornaments," I put it. "There's a Christmas shop in Portland that has all the lights and tree decorations you need. Don't forget electric candles for all the windows, and call me when you're ready to decorate."

"Put me on your call list, Patrick," Dave added. "I'll see what students I can convince to help you out. I'll be at home tomorrow morning. Angie, let me know about those needle-point pillows, too."

I gave Patrick a special hug as he and the others left.

"Now it's you and me and the dirty dishes," I said to Trixi, who'd come out of hiding and was batting at a low-hanging red glass ball. "I should rearrange the ornaments so the unbreakable ones are on the bottom branches."

I started piling up the ornament and light cartons.

My dream of a cozy Christmas at home now seemed un-likely. But my tree was beautiful, Gram and Tom didn't live far away, and tomorrow I'd be helping Patrick decorate the Victorian mansion his mother called home.

Even if she was expecting guests for the holidays, and I'd go to her Christmas Eve dinner, I'd still have Christmas Day with my family.

I focused on the positives. I had a lovely tree, my family—Gram—was here, and I was in Haven Harbor. Home.

Even with last-minute changes, it would still be my best Christmas in years.

I texted Clem to caution her that all she'd heard tonight about Skye West and her friends was confidential.

Then I extricated Trixi from the branch she was climbing. "I may have to put a fence around that tree," I scolded. "Merry Christmas, Trixi! We're home for the holidays."

Chapter 4

"To labour and to be content with that a man hath
Is a sweet life.
There is nothing so much worth as a mind well
*   instructed."*

—Unsigned (as was most British needlework) and
    stitched in an elaborate gold-threaded sampler
    about 1800. The words are between two large
    gold birds. Below them is a pastoral scene of a
    shepherd with sheep, and the entire sampler is
    bordered in wildflowers.

My friends had agreed to stitch the pillows Skye wanted
for her guests, but I know none of them were looking forward to the task.

It was December 19. Everyone already had plans for the
next week, even if those plans were to bake cookies and eat
them all themselves. (Sarah's plan.) No one was happy about

dropping other Christmas preparations to fill what they saw as a rich woman's whim.

I called Patrick. He reluctantly agreed the "needlepoint pillows" could be more like balsam sachets, about five by six inches, with plain green backs and red fronts as background for a green tree and a name. The struggle would be fitting the names on them. I won another battle when I convinced him first names alone would be all right—and even more personal.

Gram had already called to say she thought Paul Carmichael was the handsomest young actor in Hollywood. Sometimes she amazed me. Or the magazines she read at the hair salon did. Sarah would stitch the pillow for Marv, the director. Anna and Ob agreed to cover the screenwriting team Thomas and Marie, and I assigned Dave Percy the pillow for "Blaze," which I assumed was her stage name. I'd stitch Paul's gift myself.

I was already sorting through my stash of threads and canvases, pulling out what I'd need for the new project, when I glanced through the bay window. A woman I didn't recognize was standing on my porch. She was probably in her mid-fifties, but her makeup and teased hair (neither commonly seen on the coast of Maine) said she was trying to look younger.

I hoped she wasn't selling anything or asking for a donation. I hated saying no, especially at the holiday season. Reluctantly, I opened my door.

"Are you Angie Curtis?"

"Yes," I answered, tentatively.

"I'm Carly Tremont. Did the nice lady with the Australian accent call to say I was coming?"

The "nice lady" could only be Sarah. I opened my door a little wider.

"She was so busy with all those customers yesterday I wasn't sure she'd remember to call you. I met her at her little antiques shop on Main Street," she explained.

Where had Sarah said this woman was from? Then I remembered.

"Of course. She told me someone from Texas might be calling." Not stopping in, for sure. I would have remembered that.

"I was admiring the needlework accessories collection she has, and she told me you were the one to see if I wanted to have some needlepointing done."

I gestured that she should come in. "You've come to the right place. My office is in the living room, although right now it's also decorated for the holidays."

She walked to the mantel and admired the needlepoint stockings hanging there. "Two stockings. How sweet. One for you and one for the man in your life?" She winked.

I didn't tell her the second stocking was for my cat.

She turned back toward me and put out her hand. "Call me Carly. I hail from Houston. I hope I wasn't too personal. We Texans have our own way of talking."

I shook her hand, then indicated two chairs where we could sit. "Visiting Maine for the holidays, Carly?"

"In a matter of speaking," she said. "And last week I bought six lovely mahogany dining room chairs at an auction. They have cushioned seats, but the seat covers are an ugly orange and yellow plaid. I saw a dining room set in *Southern Living* a few months ago that had cushioned seats embroidered with different spring flowers. Cushions like those would be perfectly elegant for my dining room. I've been told your business can design and embroider seat covers."

I took a breath. "We can. But to design six seat covers and

needlepoint them will take a while, and cost quite a bit. I have a machine that helps design the patterns we use, but all our Mainely Needlepoint work is stitched by hand."

She didn't look concerned. "I understand. Quality work is expensive. If I brought you one of the chairs so you could measure it, could you have the designs done by mid-February, so I could approve them, and then have the chair seats finished by the end of June?"

I did some fast calculations. Winter was our slow season, when most of the needlepointers had extra time to work on large projects. "We could," I agreed. "I'd need a deposit of one thousand dollars when you bring in the chair, to cover the design work. When you've approved the designs and colors, I'd need fifty percent of the total cost of the project. I can't tell you exactly how much that would be until I see the chairs and we decide on the designs."

"That sounds reasonable," she said without hesitation. "I could bring you a chair this afternoon."

"I'm afraid I have an appointment this afternoon," I told her, remembering my promise to help Patrick decorate.

"What about tomorrow morning?"

"That would be fine." I stood.

"By the way," she added, "I heard on *Show Business Daily* that Skye West has a home in Haven Harbor."

"Really?" I said.

"I'm a big, big fan of hers," she said, still sitting. "Huge. Have been for years. It's such a thrill to be in the town where she lives!"

I nodded. Skye's privacy was important to her. Fans asking about her wasn't uncommon. But details about Skye's life weren't for public consumption.

"Your friend Sarah told me you know the West family. That,

in fact, you're dating Skye's son!" She glanced significantly toward the two stockings hanging above the fireplace.

"Sarah told you that?" I needed to have a serious talk with Sarah.

"What's Skye West really like? Is she as glamorous in person as she is in her movies? She always looks perfect— like someone who never has smeared lipstick or a hair out of place," Carly rattled on. "But on the television they said she'd been having problems on the set of the movie she's doing now. That it might be canceled, and the studio could lose millions of dollars—millions, can you believe?—if she and her costar, that handsome Paul Carmichael, don't stop fighting."

"You heard all that on television?"

"I never miss *Show Business Daily,*" Carly continued. "I follow several stars, but Skye West is my favorite."

"I've never seen *Show Business Daily,*" I admitted, proudly.

"But do you know how her movie is doing? I was so looking forward to seeing it next year. *Pride of Years.* Isn't that a great name? But maybe the television had it all wrong. You're an insider. I can't believe I'm talking with someone who knows Skye West personally. So—give me the scoop." She leaned forward. "What's happening on that movie set in Scotland? I promise, cross my heart, I won't breathe a word to anyone. I've been so concerned about those reports."

"I couldn't tell you," I said, heading toward the door. "Even if I knew. Which I don't. I haven't spoken to Skye in months." Not since September.

Carly got up and followed me as I headed to the front door. "And what's her son like? Does he look like Skye? If he does, he must be handsome!" She smiled at me as though we were girlfriends sharing secrets. "What a catch.

To be dating someone rich and handsome who's also Skye West's son!"

"I'll be here tomorrow morning about nine, if you bring your chair by," I said. "I'm sorry, but I have another appointment now."

"Of course. I apologize. I burst in here, I was so excited about my chairs. But if you see that man of yours, you tell him you met one of his mother's biggest fans. I'd give anything to meet her," she was saying as I closed the door.

Fans! If Carly Tremont hadn't had the potential to be a very good Mainely Needlepoint customer I would have ignored her. But we could use a few big orders about this time of year. Orders slowed after Christmas, although winter was the time to prepare inventory for next summer.

And I hadn't told Carly anything about Skye or Patrick. What harm would it do to take an order from a fan?

I reminded myself to tell Sarah to keep her mouth closed in the future, though.

Mainely Needlepoint was not the Maine office of Skye's fan club.

Chapter 5

*"A time to learn my Parents give,
I'll ne'er forget it while I live."*

—Verse stitched on a sampler by 12-year-old Fanny
  Mosley of Westfield, Massachusetts, in August
  1784. Fanny's sampler features a filled-in black
  background, two alphabets, a geometric border,
  strawberries, a basket of flowers, and two trees.

I had plenty of time to get the needlepointers lined up and
the ornament boxes stowed before Patrick called. He sounded
relieved. "Mom's tree is up! Ob had all the right equipment,"
he said, "and he brought two friends. I couldn't have cut and
hauled and set up a sixteen-foot tree by myself, even if my
hands were still good. Wait until you see it in the front hall.
We cut pine branches for the tops of the downstairs doors
and mantels, and I called that shop in Portland you told me
about and they're delivering lights and ornaments this afternoon. Dave's going to have four young people here to

decorate at five, while I'm meeting with Bev Clifford. But I still need wreaths and garlands. Do you have time now to help?"

"Sounds like you made a great start," I said. "I'll come over and show you where you can get everything else you need."

Patrick must have placed an enormous order with that Christmas shop in Portland if they were going to personally deliver everything in a few hours.

I bundled up, boots and scarf and parka, and drove out to Patrick's carriage house, on the grounds of his mother's home.

"Let's use my car," Patrick suggested, looking at my Honda. "Mine is bigger."

"Your car will be littered with pine needles," I warned. "But that's up to you. Head out to Route 1," I instructed as we got into his car. "When we get back I want to see that enormous tree you found for your mom."

"It was up in the woods behind the back field, so we didn't have to bring it far," he said. "Ob knows Aurora's land and buildings better than Mom and I do. He knew just where to find the right tree."

"He was the caretaker there for years," I reminded Patrick.

Snow was lightly covering the windshield. He turned on the wipers. "How far do we have to go?"

"Not far. Beyond the used car dealership. Do you know the space on the side of the road there where cars can pull over?"

"Last June I bought strawberries and rhubarb from a car parked in that spot."

"That's the place. I'm pretty sure Arvin and Alice Fraser will be there today."

"Do I know them?"

"Not yet. But they're a nice young couple." And they could use the money Patrick had to spend. "Arvin lobsters in the summer, but this time of year they make and sell wreaths." The Frasers were a young family steeped in Maine ways, including finding an assortment of ways to support themselves.

Arvin scouted pine trees for the tips needed for wreaths, and Alice assembled them in the evening and while their baby napped. Wreaths were a cottage industry in Maine. People hung them on all their windows and doors, and sometimes left them up until spring. And each year Maine sent thousands of wreaths south to be placed on veterans' graves in Arlington National Cemetery as part of Wreaths Across America.

We pulled over a few minutes later.

"Angie! Good to see you again. I thought you'd bought what you needed last week."

Arvin was taking fresh wreaths from the back of his truck to fill empty spaces on a large display frame.

"My doors and windows are covered, thanks to you," I answered. "But I've brought you a new customer." I pushed Patrick forward. "Today Patrick's looking for wreaths."

"Ours are wicked good," Alice assured him, knocking snow off some of the hanging wreaths and then clapping her gloved hands together to remove the icy particles. "Fresh made. Last for months. Choose your size from those on the easel or leaning against the truck. We have more of every size, with red bows or without. But adding a bow means another two dollars each," she cautioned.

Patrick shook his head. He hadn't expected the wide selection of sizes he'd been offered. "I'll need two for the carriage house doors."

"You'll need wreaths for your windows," I reminded him. "At least for the front of your house and the windows facing the street. Mainers hang a lot of wreaths."

He nodded, doubtfully. "You know the territory." He walked along the side of Arvin's truck, looking at the sizes.

"Wreaths are a Maine tradition," I assured him. "Wreaths. Plural."

Patrick looked down at me and touched the end of my nose with his gloved hand. "Angie. My consultant on all things authentic Maine." Then he turned to Arvin. "I'd like two twenty-inch ones and seven fourteen-inch." He smiled. "Complete with ribbons. Let's go for it."

I hid a smile as Alice pulled out a bag of ribbons and started attaching them. That large a sale would make her day.

"Shall we put them all in your car?" Arvin asked, looking at Patrick's BMW. "Do you have a cloth to put under them? Otherwise you'll have pine needles in your car for months."

"And it will smell like Christmas," Patrick agreed. "No problem. Inside my car's fine."

Whatever the customer wanted.

"I saw your *Little Lady*'s still in the water," I said. "Are you decorating it for the parade?"

"Wouldn't miss it," he said. "Alice and Jake are sailing with me this year. We have a tree for the deck all picked out and lights for the boat. After the parade I'll be dry-docking it so I can caulk and paint it this winter. But we wouldn't miss the parade."

"Parade?" Patrick asked.

"Lobstermen in Haven Harbor decorate and light their boats for Christmas and accompany Santa as he circles the harbor and arrives at the town dock," I explained. "Then the high school band and Y kids and other town groups accompany him and his moose assistant to the Haven Harbor Town Hall, where he's available for photo ops and there's a town Carol Sing."

"When does all this take place?"

"The twenty-second," said Arvin as he shook the snow off Patrick's wreaths and piled them into his trunk. "It's called the Christmas Cheer festival. Anything else?" He grinned at me. "A kissing ball?"

Patrick looked confused.

"It's a ball made of pine or holly to hold your mistletoe," I explained. Didn't they have kissing balls in southern California?

"Sure." He winked. "Better have one of those. Maybe it'll help me find someone to kiss." He nudged me.

"Okay, then," said Arvin, adding a kissing ball to the pile of wreaths. "That it?"

"Actually, no," Patrick said. "Those wreaths are for my house. Now I'd like your largest wreath—a four-footer, right? And twenty-six two-footers for my mother's house. You'd better add another kissing ball, too." He was getting into the spirit of the afternoon.

"Yes, sir!" said Arvin. "Coming up!"

Alice was trying not to look gleeful.

"Do you have garlands?" I asked.

"In the truck," he assured me.

"Then, about sixty feet of pine," I ordered.

"No bows on the garland; bows on the wreaths, though," Patrick instructed.

Arvin and Alice were grinning as they almost emptied their truck for Patrick. They'd have to go home and make more wreaths. And home was warmer than standing by the side of their truck on Route 1 hoping for customers. "How's the baby?" I asked.

"Shush. Napping," Alice said. "He's sleeping through the night now, thank goodness. Had a colicky first six months, but now he's fine. We're looking forward to his first Christmas. He loves to stare at the lights on the tree in our living room."

I brushed a few snowflakes off their truck window and peeked inside. Jake was sleeping snugly in his car seat with wreaths and garlands stacked behind him. In a few years he, too, would be constructing the wreaths that helped his family make it through the dark winter.

Making a living from land and sea wasn't a bad way to live. But it wasn't easy, either.

Would I ever have children? I glanced back at Patrick, who was helping Arvin stack wreaths in the back seat of his car, since the trunk was already full. Then he peeled bills off the stack he carried in his pocket. He'd given up using a wallet. His swollen hands couldn't remove bills or credit cards easily.

Patrick had grown up attending private schools and Hollywood parties and smiling with his mother in magazine spreads and publicity pictures. I suspected by the time he was twelve he'd owned a tux to wear at movie premieres.

I glanced through the truck window at little Jake.

His life would be very different from Patrick's.

Money had made Patrick's life easier. Had it been a better life than Jake's would be?

I wasn't sure, as Alice finished attaching bows to wreaths and Arvin thanked Patrick for choosing his stand to buy wreaths.

No simple answers.

Chapter 6

"Abby Wright 'called in Springfield (Massachusetts) to see a piece of needlework lately executed at a celebrated school in Boston,' adding, 'the expense of the limner in drawing and painting was $8 and six months were spent in Boston working on it.'"

—From *Journal of Abigail Brackett Lyman,*
    March 23, 1800.

Back at the estate I told Patrick I loved to hang wreaths, but needed him to hold the ladder steady for me.

It was a white lie.

I volunteered because I was afraid his hands would make it difficult to hold the nails steady.

He'd learned to manage most day-to-day tasks, but he hadn't gone back to painting. Picking up small items, like paperclips or brushes or nails, was still difficult. He didn't talk about his hands, but I'd noticed he avoided displaying them to others. He'd added a high front to his desk at the gallery so customers didn't see him struggling to pick up papers and writing invoices. His new cell phone had larger buttons. I was beginning to doubt his hands would ever again be "normal." I was used to the way they looked, but people who didn't know Patrick stared.

Today's light snow freshened Haven Harbor's roads and buildings but made hammering nails a challenge even for me. I took my gloves off after hanging the second wreath (which included dropping five nails into the snow below the ladder) and decided frigid fingers and half an hour were a small price to pay for making the carriage house look like Christmas was really coming.

Aurora, his mother's house, was another story.

Three stories, to be exact.

I was secretly relieved when Captain Ob appeared from his home across the street with a longer ladder. And more relieved when Dave Percy's high school students showed up early to help decorate. They hung the wreaths on the second- and third-floor windows. Patrick and I managed the first floor and, inside, added electric candles to every window in the house.

"Perfect," Patrick pronounced, stepping to the road in front on the property and admiring our work. We'd finished just before dark; most of the lights were on, the candles glowed, and the outlines of the wreaths were clear. Aurora shone.

Skye could have no complaints about the outside decorations.

Now for the inside.

Patrick supervised as the students enthusiastically climbed ladders, wound lights around the tree in the front hall, and hung the ornaments the Christmas shop had delivered. They weren't personal ornaments, like the ones on my tree, but they gleamed.

I spent the next hour weaving garlands around the staircase railing from the first to the third floor, and then, with Patrick's help, adding shorter pine branches to mantels, tops of bookcases and cabinets, and above first-floor doorways.

I was tempted to discard the kissing ball Patrick had bought, but ended up hanging it in the doorway between the dining room and front hall. That invited a few impudent remarks from the teenagers, which Patrick and I ignored after one chaste kiss to demonstrate the ball's power.

Bev Clifford arrived while the boys were finishing the tree. She looked as sturdy and dependable as she was, and she was wheeling a small suitcase and carrying a box of pans and other cooking gear. She and Patrick retreated to the kitchen to plan the next week's menu. Patrick had even talked her into "living in" for the duration. As always, he and his checkbook were very convincing.

Sometimes I wondered what he'd be like if he didn't have his mother's money to depend on.

"'Kissing don't last: Cookery do.'" Gram had often repeated when she (unsuccessfully) tried to teach me to cook as a teenager. George Meredith wrote that. I should have taken it seriously. I was finally learning the basics of cooking, but I was a little late to the party. Bev Clifford was known locally as an excellent cook. She could capitalize on opportunities like the temporary job Patrick had offered.

The tree was decorated and lights sparkling (every time I looked at those red and green and yellow lights, my mind said, "Caution!"), and the teenagers and I were piling up empty ornament and Christmas light cartons when we heard the beeping of a truck backing up.

Was Patrick expecting more deliveries?

I looked out one of the front windows.

To my horror, a Channel 7 News van was parked outside the gate to Aurora (which we'd left open), and several men were setting up lights focused on a short blond figure carrying a microphone.

It was Clem. Hadn't I made it clear Skye and Patrick were off-limits?

Patrick joined me at the window. "What's happening?"

I sighed. "I'm afraid your mom's house is going to be on Portland's local news tonight." I glanced at my phone. "Late news. She's not in time for the early edition."

"But . . . why?"

I shook my head. "I'm not sure. But one of Skye's fans came to see me this morning about a needlepoint job. She said *Show Business Daily* has been reporting there've been problems on the set of Skye's movie."

"So? What has that to do with the truck out front? The movie isn't being filmed here."

"No, but that woman with the microphone?" I pointed. "That's my friend Clem. Remember—she was at my house when you told us Skye and some of her colleagues were coming here for Christmas. I'll bet she's trying to scoop the national entertainment news."

Patrick headed for the door. "Well, she's no friend of mine. I'm going to tell her this is private property."

I followed him, shivering in the cold and snow. "She's not on your property," I pointed out. "She and her crew are in the street."

"Enough!" Patrick called toward the news crew. "There's no story here. Leave us alone! This is a private residence!"

"And here's Skye West's son, Patrick. Is it true your mother and the stars of her new movie will be spending Christmas here in Haven Harbor?"

I flinched as the lights and camera turned on Patrick.

"That's none of your business," he said. "Now, leave. You've got a picture of the house, and that's more than enough."

"We're doing a segment on how homes on the coast of Maine are decorated for the holidays," said Clem, sweetly. "This home is a lovely one."

"Out! Turn off those lights and the microphone!" Patrick yelled. "Get out of here!"

"Clem, he's serious," I said. "I told you not to say anything about Skye." To my horror I saw the camera light was still on. "Patrick, let's get out of here."

I took his arm and turned him around. We headed back to the house, where our teenaged decorating helpers were standing on the front steps, cheering us on.

It was a circus.

I was embarrassed on behalf of the whole state.

The cameras were my fault.

Clem had been my high school friend.

How had I imagined this would be a cozy and calm traditional Christmas?

Chapter 7

"Not Land but Learning
Makes a man complete
Not Birth but Breeding
Makes him truly Great
Not Wealth but Wisdom
Does adorn the State
Virtue not Honor
Makes him Fortunate.
Learning, Breeding, Wisdom
Got these three
Then Wealth and Honor
Will attend on thee."

—Sampler worked by Harriet Taylor, aged seven,
in 1813. She surrounded her words with four
flying angels, a wreathed arch, and columns
holding vases of flowering plants. This sampler
may be seen at the South Kensington Museum
in England.

After apologizing too many times to Patrick for Clem's behavior, to the amusement of the high school kids, I volunteered to drive them all home.

Patrick didn't need me for anything more today.

Bev and Patrick were going to finalize the menu for the next few days and make out a shopping list for tomorrow morning.

"You go along now, Angie. You've been a big help to Patrick. Let me take it from here," she said quietly, patting me on the shoulder. "He needs time alone before the mob comes crashing in tomorrow."

I assumed she meant Skye and her guests—not more media or fans. But maybe not.

"What time are they arriving?" I asked.

"He says they've a plane all to themselves." She looked up toward the ceiling. "'The studio provided one.' Not like us, these folks coming. They're flying into the executive airport at Brunswick. Patrick's going to meet them while I get the kitchen stocked and some chowder on to warm for when they get here."

"Which is?"

"Noon, or thereabouts, he says. Depends on weather between here and Scotland, I'd guess."

Naturally. I should have thought of that.

"Patrick!" I called to where he was stacking the ornament boxes in the cellar. "I'm going to take the guys home now."

"Thanks, Angie! I'll call you later."

I herded the young men out to my little red Honda (at least it was a seasonal color). Haven Harbor covered a fair number of acres outside downtown. It took almost an hour to deliver my passengers, who were happily counting the fifty-dollar bills Patrick had handed out. They'd already agreed to come back and remove all the ornaments and the tree after the holidays.

Driving back to town alone, I admired the sparkling white lights on homes and businesses. Arizona could be lovely, especially after the rains, but I'd missed fall colors, the sound of frosted snow crunching under my boots, and the emergence of snowdrops in the spring.

But I was still getting used to living alone, without Gram. I should have left the Christmas lights on before I'd left.

I was more relieved than I wanted to admit when Trixi met me at the door and then ran to her empty food dish. She looked from it to me. Is that what psychologists call "passive-aggressive"? I'd only taken a couple of courses at Arizona State, and I didn't remember much from any of them. But I was glad to be needed.

I obeyed her clear (if unspoken) command, filling her dish and refreshing her water. Then I walked through the house, turning on the window candles and tree lights, and most of the lights on the first floor. Light made the house feel less empty.

Despite the moments of missing the house the way it used to be, full of bustle and smells of supper cooking and Gram's lavender cologne, most days I enjoyed living alone. My home was my sanctuary, filled with memories reminding me of good and bad parts of the past. Gradually I was rearranging furniture and ornaments and pictures to reflect who I was now, or, I admitted to myself, who I wanted to be.

Tonight, taking advantage of my status as an independent single adult, I decided not to cook dinner or eat anything virtuous. Instead, I nibbled Christmas cookies left from my tree-trimming party, poured a glass of wine, and picked up my needlepoint. Hanging the wreaths and decorating Aurora had tired me more than I'd thought.

Now I had to make up for the time I'd lost. I'd planned to finish Patrick's pillow today, and that stitching alone would take most of the evening. Trixi joined me in the living room, making herself comfortable on top of a bag of yarn. By some miracle she hadn't yet figured out how to pull the skeins apart.

She'd had a busy afternoon while I'd been with Patrick. Several ornaments were now under the tree. Luckily only two had broken. I checked her paws; no glass shards or fragments. I should have bought unbreakable ornaments for this year.

I'd been working on Patrick's pillow since early October. After I finished the stitching I'd still have to assemble it— I'd needlepointed a plain back and bought a pillow to fit inside. All fall I'd been imagining how surprised and pleased Patrick would be when he saw it. Now, selfishly, I hoped he wouldn't be too distracted by the excitement at Aurora to appreciate my hours of work.

Plus, now I had to stitch a balsam pillow for Paul Carmichael. The actor Gram (and Carly from Texas) seemed to know all about.

Out of curiosity, I Googled him. Gram was right. He was good looking. Thirty-three . . . about Patrick's age. Tall, a former college soccer player, wavy dark hair that hung over his forehead. Not bad. He'd been the romantic interest in three recent films I hadn't seen, been arrested for drunk driving in Nevada two years ago, and was linked to several young actresses, including, I noted, Blaze Buchanan. Was that for publicity, or was it more? Based purely on what I was reading I didn't think he'd value a Maine balsam pillow, even a personalized one. But who was I to decide? I was just a Mainer who ran a custom needlepoint business.

I glanced at the search options once more—and stopped.

According to two fanzines and a newspaper in Edinburgh, Paul Carmichael has been kicked out of the Three Goats pub there for throwing a glass of whiskey at a bartender who'd refused to keep serving him. The article was unclear about what happened after that, but Carmichael had ended up in a local hospital for stitches after the police broke up what sounded like a small riot.

No one else working on the *Pride of Years* set was mentioned.

Maybe Paul's behavior and injuries were why the movie "had problems," as Patrick had said.

In any case, Paul would have healed by now—the event had occurred a couple of weeks ago—and with his director and writers and Skye (and Blaze, if she was his current love, as the fanzines said) in attendance, he'd probably be on his best behavior in Haven Harbor.

I hoped.

But I decided not to work on his pillow tonight. It was getting late. Instead, I wrapped a couple of gifts for Gram and Reverend Tom: a bottle of Maine's Cold River Vodka, made from Maine's potatoes, two bottles of sparkling blueberry wine, and a locally handwoven red and green scarf for Gram I'd bought at a holiday craft fair the week before.

It was only December nineteenth. Patrick would be busy with Skye and her guests for the next few days. That would give me time to finish my pillows for both Patrick and Paul, and make a loaf of orange nut bread to contribute to Gram's Christmas breakfast.

I was ready to call it a day, but first I called Clem. She had to hear how upset I was at her showing up at Aurora with a video crew.

She didn't answer, of course. She was probably in the studio in Portland right now, editing her footage of Patrick and me

yelling at her. I left a message for her to call me. I doubted
she would. I hoped I was wrong about where she was.

I put the last stitch in Patrick's pillow at 10:29. Moments
later he called.

"Thanks for your help this afternoon. Mrs. Clifford is a
treasure! She understood exactly what had to be done with
the house as well as the food. She's made the beds, put
towels in each room, and added tissues, paper, and pens. She
even took pine sprigs left over from the garlands and filled
small vases for each of the guest rooms. I'll admit I was feeling overwhelmed with all that had to be done. She calmed
me down and convinced me of one thing for sure: I'm never
going to run an inn!"

I laughed as I turned off the room lights and headed up to
my bedroom, phone at my ear, Trixi at my heels.

Patrick would be great at the hosting part, but I couldn't
imagine him taking care of—or even supervising—the
day-to-day maintenance of an inn.

"Just as well," I assured him. "You're an artist and a gal-
lerist. That's plenty." I collapsed on my bed, the holiday
lights from Haven Harbor's Green shining in my windows
and making patterns on the walls. I'd forgotten they did that
at Christmastime.

"Today I felt like a set decorator," he admitted. "But it
worked, thank goodness. Mom will be pleased."

"She'd better be," I said lightly, but I meant it. "Bev told
me Skye and her guests would be arriving about noon
tomorrow."

"A little later than that," said Patrick. "I got a text from
Mom about an hour ago. Their departure from Edinburgh
was delayed. Haar, she called it. She's estimating they'll
arrive in Brunswick at about two o'clock tomorrow afternoon. Could you be free in the morning? I'd like to look

at Sarah's needlepoint tools and have an early lunch before I leave for the airport."

"Don't you have to help Mrs. Clifford with groceries?"

"Told you she was a treasure! She figured out exactly what we'd need, called a butcher and a fishmonger (I didn't know they still called them that!) tonight to place orders, and she'll be at the local supermarket first thing in the morning. She's also called a local winery and a farm that makes cheese, and placed orders so all she has to do is pick them up. She said she wouldn't need me. I suspect she can work faster without my asking questions."

"I assume you gave her a credit card?" I said, smiling at Patrick's easy solutions to what I would have thought major logistical challenges.

"Right. So . . . Sarah opens her shop about ten?"

"Nine in the morning this week, for the Christmas traffic," I told him. "And I'd love to join you for lunch. But a needlepoint customer is bringing a chair over tomorrow morning at nine so I can measure it and take pictures. She's talking about ordering six seat cushions, so that's a big order. I have to be here."

"Understood. What about meeting me at the Harbor Haunts a little past eleven?" he asked.

"See you then," I agreed. "And you can fill me in on the needlepoint tools. I'd love to get something special for Gram for Christmas. I could use an extra gift for under her tree."

We said our good nights, and I glanced at the clock. Almost eleven. I turned on the local news. I hoped we weren't expecting any heavy snow in the next couple of days.

Maine doesn't always have snow for Christmas, especially along the coast, where temperatures are warmer than inland or in the mountains. But this year it snowed on Thanksgiving, and despite a little melting and a lot of drifting, I hadn't seen the ground since then. About half a foot was in most places, and drifts were considerably higher. Almost every day another inch or two fell; enough to keep the white world sparkling and clean. Temperatures had already been low enough to freeze the ocean spray on ledges near the lighthouse and rocks framing Pocket Cove Beach.

I loved this time of year. The snow was fresh and clean. It covered up the good, the bad, and the ugly.

The Channel 7 weatherman assured us that the possible nor'easter he'd been tracking wouldn't affect Maine "for at least a few days. No guarantees after that. Better finish your Christmas shopping now." He ended his broadcast with a collage of the brightly lit Portland Christmas tree across from the library, surrounded by shoppers listening to a local chorus singing carols.

I reached for the remote, to turn the television off, when the picture changed.

"In exclusive entertainment news," the anchor was saying, "Channel 7 has learned that Hollywood actress Skye West, who earlier this year bought a home in Haven Harbor, and whose current movie project, *Pride of Years,* is rumored to be in major trouble, will be spending the holidays in Maine with her son and several close friends from the movie world." The picture changed. There was Clem, dressed in her Channel 7 ski jacket and striped wool hat, microphone in hand.

"Tonight, Skye West's Haven Harbor home is decorated for her arrival" (cut to shot of the house, with Patrick and me leaving it and striding toward Clem and her crew). "Maine is buzzing about which show business luminaries may be celebrating Christmas here. And, perhaps even more interesting, why? What new project is Ms. West planning at her estate, known locally as Aurora? Details when we know them. Clem Walker, reporting from Haven Harbor."

The picture cut out before Patrick and I got to Clem. Back to the studio. "We welcome Skye West and all holiday visitors to Maine, and wish them a very happy stay in the Pine Tree State. What better place to be at this time of year?"

I clicked the TV off. What better place? Lots of places. Places that would allow Skye and her friends some privacy.

Damn Clem.

At least she hadn't mentioned the names of Skye's guests.

Who in town might have seen the broadcast? In a state traditionally populated by farmers and fishermen, where some diners opened at five or five-thirty in the morning and closed at two-thirty in the afternoon, few people except retirees from away regularly stayed up for the late news. But this time of year people might be preparing for the holiday, or checking the weather because of friends and family traveling.

I hoped Patrick hadn't seen the broadcast.

This was just the beginning. If one local channel covered Skye's visit, other local channels would, too. And the New England network. And that *Show Business Daily* program. And . . . I turned off my bedside lamp and snuggled under my quilts.

I needed to get a good night's sleep.

Skye was arriving tomorrow. And I had to meet with that fan of hers, Carly, have lunch with Patrick, and then, I hoped, work on Paul Carmichael's balsam pillow.

But all I could think about was Skye, who'd bought her house here at least partially because of Maine's reputation for respecting the privacy of well-known residents and visitors.

I hit my pillow again.

Why had I impetuously invited Clem to my Christmas

decorating party? Why hadn't I left the past—and past friends—in the past?

This was all my fault. But what could I do now?

I visualized social media spreading the word from Maine to the rest of the world, as Skye's plane left Scotland and headed for Brunswick.

At least Clem hadn't said when they were arriving. Or where.

But anyone checking local airports could find that out.

Trixi jumped up, purring and kneading my shoulder. Tonight I didn't find her amusing.

I pulled my pillow over my head.

If only hiding from the press was as simple as hiding from my kitten.

"Damn," I muttered as Trixi snuggled her way under the pillow to find me.

Turned out I couldn't even hide from a four-pound black kitten.

Chapter 8

*"An attractive sachet may be made of old-gold plush,
embroidered with rosebuds and leaves, and trimmed
with lace and bows of ribbon."*

—From *The Farm and Household Cyclopedia:
A Complete Reference Library for Farmers,
Gardeners, Fruit Growers, Stockmen and
Housekeepers,* Published by F.M. Lupton, 1885.

No mention of Skye West or Haven Harbor or anything else
I cared about on the morning news. Good.

Skipping dinner the night before had been a mistake. I
was starving. I made myself an onion and cheese omelet,
toasted an English muffin, and drank two cups of coffee
before pulling on my down vest and boots and filling the
birdfeeders, to the delight of the chickadees and cardinals
and nut hatches that appeared immediately. Trixi was torn
between sitting at one of her two window perches and watching the activity outdoors, or playing with the felt catnip

Christmas ball I'd bought her at last week's craft show. It was a hard decision, but the birds won out.

At nine o'clock on the dot Carly Tremont was at my front door, stomping her unbooted feet on the wire mat.

"Come in," I said, opening the door. "Don't worry about the snow. The rug in the hall is indoor/outdoor carpet."

She picked up the heavy armless side chair she'd been carrying and lugged it in with her, plopping it near the entrance to the living room and kicking off her snowy sneakers. "I'm not worried about the snow on your rug. My feet are freezing! How do you people stand this weather?"

I tried not to laugh as she wiggled her toes. "We wear boots," I said. "While you're here you should check out L.L. Bean's rubber boots. They're the best."

She wrinkled her nose. "I looked. Ugly. We'd never wear boots like that in Texas."

I resisted pointing out that Texas wasn't known for its frequent blizzards. "You've brought the chair," I said, stating the obvious.

"Yes, I have six, just like that one," she said, as I picked up the chair and put it next to my desk in the living room.

The chair was badly stained and the seat cover was ripped where it wasn't worn. I hoped she hadn't paid a lot for the set. "Are all six chairs exactly like this one?" I asked.

"Of course. Why wouldn't they be?"

"Some dining room sets include one or two chairs with arms," I said calmly.

"Not this set," she assured me.

I suspected the other two chairs had disappeared through the years, or been sold separately. But six identical seat cushions would be easier to plan for.

I pulled out my tape measure. "You said you wanted bright flowers, am I right?"

"Texas flowers. Like bluebonnets."

"I'll have to do a little research, but that shouldn't be a problem." Thank goodness for the Internet. "Any special colors?"

"I'd like the background to be navy blue," she specified. "And different flowers on each chair. Reds and whites and yellows would look pretty. My dining room walls are pale yellow."

I nodded, taking notes.

"I saw Skye West's house on the news! Was that you in the background, with that man? Was that Skye's son?" Carly asked. She sat on my couch.

Not everyone had gone to bed early last night.

"Yes, that was me." I focused on staying calm. This was a customer. Potentially, a valuable customer.

"I'm sorry you didn't get to be on the broadcast. They cut away much too fast."

"It was fine," I said. "We'll have to replace the cushions on the chairs. Is this thickness about right, or would you like something a little deeper?"

Carly Tremont waved her hand as if dismissing the question. "Whatever would look best. I'm going to have the chairs refinished while you're working on the cushions."

"That would be good," I said, smiling. "Refinished chairs with new cushions should look lovely."

"Elegant," she pronounced. "That's what I want. I'm a very elegant person."

I glanced at her hair, wet and disheveled from being out in the snow, her bare feet (no wonder they were cold!) bedecked with smudged red toenail polish, and the red and green sequined Christmas sweater she was wearing. "I can see that. As I told you yesterday, I'll need some time to design the cushions. After you've approved the designs it will take five or six months to complete the needlepoint."

"Not a problem. Does Skye have needlepointed cushions in her house?"

"A few," I admitted. "Shall I send you the designs by e-mail, or will you still be in Maine at the end of January or beginning of February?"

"I don't know exactly," she answered. "Do I have to decide now? I've taken a leave of absence and don't have a definite return date."

"What do you do?" I asked, to be polite.

"Work for a company that makes jewelry."

She wasn't wearing any jewelry. Maybe she didn't like taking her work home. "You don't have to set a specific date to see the designs today," I assured her. "But I'd like you to fill out this contract to make sure it says what we've agreed to. Make sure you include your contact telephone numbers and e-mail address so I can get in touch with you when the designs are ready. And, as I mentioned yesterday, I'd like a nonrefundable deposit to cover my design work."

"Fine," said Carly, glancing through the contract I'd prepared. For any large needlepoint job I required a contract. I didn't want any misunderstandings with clients. That was one of the things I'd learned when I worked for a private investigator. Make sure everyone understood deliverables and expectations and costs and time frames. Carly filled out her contact information quickly and handed me a credit card. "You can take a card, I assume?"

"I can." Who could do business today without taking credit cards?

Her card went through easily.

"So when will Skye be arriving?" she asked. "And who's coming with her? I'm dying to know!" She leaned toward me. "I still can't believe I'm in the same town with her!"

"She's not here yet. I'm not exactly sure when she'll be arriving," I said, standing. "I'll call you when I have the seat designs finished. Do you need any help taking your chair back out to your car?"

"I can do it," she answered, bending to put her soaked sneakers back on. "I'm fine. Only I wish we'd have one day without snow."

"That could happen," I agreed. "It's unusual to have snow every day, even in Maine."

"You couldn't prove that from the past week." Carly stood and pulled on her pink fleece jacket. "Maybe I'll see you around town. I'm not sure how long I'll be in Haven Harbor, but I'll be in town for the holidays for sure."

I opened the front door for her and her chair. "Have a Merry Christmas, then!" I said as she carefully descended my porch steps, carrying her chair. "I look forward to working with you."

And, I thought as I closed my door, I'll look forward to spending the money you spend with Mainely Needlepoint.

Chapter 9

"Let us count all things loss
That Jesus we may win
Let's glory in his cross
And leave the paths of sin."

—Susannah Wearing stitched this silk on linen
sampler in England in 1833. She embroidered
her words in an oval that included a chipmunk,
a bird, and a scene of a farmhouse and barns,
then stitched this center work onto dark fabric
and embroidered a dramatic floral border in
shaded silks.

My meeting with Carly Tremont had taken longer than I'd
thought. It was almost ten-thirty. I quickly brushed my hair,
slipped on my (warm and dry) Bean boots, put on my ski
jacket (which I never skied in), and headed downtown to
meet Patrick for lunch at the Harbor Haunts. As usual, the

only jewelry I wore was the gold necklace with a small gold angel Mama had given to me for my First Communion. I'd worn it off and on for years, but it meant more now that I knew Mama was gone forever.

Snow was falling lightly, dusting everything with a new layer of white. I stuck out my tongue, hoping to catch a snowflake or two. As my friend Sergeant Pete Lambert of the local police department passed me, waving from his car, I pulled my tongue in. No, I wasn't a child anymore. But snow always made me feel like tossing a snowball, or making a snow angel, or building a snowman (or woman) or fort. I couldn't remember when I'd last done any of those things.

Who cared what I looked like?

I stuck my tongue out again.

It was back in my mouth before I got to Main Street, where smiling Christmas shoppers were buying gifts at The Book Nook and Hubbel Clothing and, I hoped, at Sarah's antiques shop, From Here and There. Even the Harbor Lights Gift Shop was open. Unless they'd changed their schedule in the past ten years, the owners would be closing at the end of the month and heading for Florida until March.

Portland, Camden, Damariscotta, and Yarmouth, among others, were year-round towns. College towns, like Brunswick and Waterville, were active in the winter. Towns like Haven Harbor shuttered after Christmas and hunkered down until spring. The shrimping season, which started in December and was shorter every year, kept the town wharf open. But most restaurants and gift shops closed for at least a couple of months.

Would Patrick keep his new art gallery open all winter?

The patisserie stayed open, and so did The Book Nook (readers needed books to get them through long, dark nights). The Harbor Haunts Café, my current destination, stayed open seven days a week, twelve months of the year, and was cherished by locals and rewarded by their patronage.

Patrick had already claimed a table by the window by the time I got there. Eleven o'clock was early for lunch, even in Haven Harbor. I'd had a big breakfast. I wasn't even hungry. But I was glad I'd come. Patrick stood and hugged me before I sat down. I noticed a shopping bag between his seat and the wall.

"You found something for your mom at Sarah's shop?"

"I did. You have to check out what she has! I can't show you what I bought—Sarah wrapped all the little pieces in tissue paper and even Christmas-wrapped the whole package for me. I bought one of those eighteenth-century things—etuis—she told us about, the kind inlaid with patterns of wood and mother-of-pearl. It sits on a table and holds needles and scissors and hooks and stilettos and all sorts of other sewing tools. It'll look great on the sideboard in Mom's dining room, near the needlepointed pictures of Haven Harbor." He paused. "It was so cool I also bought a large brass spool holder with ivory finials. I figure the two would balance each other on the sideboard. Mom won't get anything like them from anyone else."

I nodded.

"I'm going to give her a painting for Christmas, too," Patrick added.

Maybe his hands were getting better!

"Not one of mine," he said quickly. "One of Ted Lawrence's. He left a stack of his local scenes in the storeroom at the gallery. Mom liked Ted when she met him last summer, and she's pleased I've taken over his gallery, even if the circumstances weren't ideal. I think she'd like to have one of his paintings. I chose one of the lighthouse and the boats in the harbor that's close to the view Mom has from her bedroom at Aurora."

"She'll like that," I agreed. Would Patrick give me something for Christmas? If he did, I hoped it would be sentimental, and not extravagant. After all, I was going to give him a needlepointed pillow. Holidays were difficult for new couples. If a gift was too small, or too large, or too personal, or too impersonal, it could ruin a romance. Knowing that, I was nervous about gifts. And, I admitted to myself, curious about how Patrick felt about them. Ours was still a new relationship. We'd never discussed gifts.

"The painting sounds perfect, and the needlepoint tools unique." Sarah was probably really happy about those sales, too. "I'm planning to stop in to see Sarah after lunch and see if I can find something for Gram." Something a lot less expensive than what Patrick had bought.

"Do you have to do that today?" asked Patrick. "I was hoping you'd go with me to the airport."

"I don't know any of those people," I said. "And I have other things I have to do before Christmas."

"You know Mom, and she knows we've been seeing each other. She's asked about ten times whether you'll be coming with me."

Skye'd always seemed to like me. I'd liked her, too, when I'd worked with her last summer. But I hadn't been dating her son then.

"Please, Angie?"

The waitress stood by our table. Her earrings were flashing Christmas bulbs. "Specials for today are oysters on the half shell, an oyster poor boy sandwich, and oysters Rockefeller," she announced.

"Must be an *r* month," Patrick said drily. "Aren't you only supposed to eat oysters in months including an *r*?"

"The chef got carried away when the Damariscotta Oyster Company came by to take orders," the young woman explained.

"I'll have a half dozen of the half shells," I decided. "And a cup of onion soup."

"Might as well go with the flow," Patrick said. "The oyster poor boy and some sweet potato fries."

"And to drink?"

"Water," I said.

Patrick reluctantly agreed. "Same for me. We have to drive."

"YOU have to drive. I'm not coming with you, Patrick. Helping you decorate was fun yesterday, but I can't take more time now. Besides, your mom and her friends will be tired after their long flight. They'll want to rest. I'll have plenty of time to see her while she's here. I've agreed to come Christmas Eve."

"Are you sure? I'd really like your company. And you know where the airport in Brunswick is."

"So does your GPS. She's your mother, Patrick. Not mine." That might have been strong, but I meant it. "You haven't seen her in a couple of months. The two of you should have some private time together before you get involved in holiday events and she begins the work she brought with her from Edinburgh."

"You're right. Go ahead with your plans. I'll call you when I get back from the airport."

Neither of us said much during the rest of our meal. The

oysters were fresh and delicious, and for dessert we both ordered cups of cocoa with whipped cream.

It was Christmas, after all.

It was snowing a little heavier than usual when Patrick got in his car and headed for the airport. I waved good-bye and walked up the street to Sarah's shop.

Chapter 10

*"The dearest man in the world must not be left out of
your Christmas list. And if, perchance, your purse is
too slender to give him what you would like, make
him a 'daisy' shaving pad: a circle of gray linen,
on which you embroider tinted pink daisies and
the words 'A Daisy Shave.' The latter may have a
suggestion of slang, but the new woman occasionally
indulges in that."*

—From an article titled "Christmas Novelties" in
   The Modern Priscilla magazine, November 1905.

The wide windows at From Here and There were lit with red
and green lights. Sarah had hung Victorian ornaments on a
small artificial tree, and surrounded the tree with vintage
Santas, old dolls, toy soldiers, and nineteenth-century board
games. Framed prints of Christmases past hung on the side
walls, and a large brass star hung over the whole scene.

I wished I knew someone who would appreciate antiques.

I was learning more about them all the time, and found some fascinating.

Sarah was alone, doing needlework behind the counter. She'd started the balsam pillow for the director, Marv, and finished stitching most of the tree.

"I'm impressed!" I said, pointing at her work.

She shrugged. "I stitch when I'm not selling. Only certain people shop for gifts at an antiques shop."

"I hear you made at least one good sale this morning, though."

"Patrick said he was going to have lunch with you. Yes, his check will cover a lot of my expenses this month. I had to go into overdraft checking to buy all those needlework tools at the auction, but I'm already sure I made a good investment."

"I came to look."

"Everything is on those four tables." Sarah pointed at the left side of her store. "The ones covered with red, to be seasonal, and the shelves above them. Looking for something in particular?"

"Browsing," I said, heading for the red tables. Sarah's shelves were laced with pinecones and vases and antique floral tea cups holding holly. More Christmas ornaments like those on the tree in the window were on many shelves, and china and glass with holiday patterns were prominently displayed.

"I didn't know you had so many Christmas items!" I said, looking around.

"I gather them all year. Collectors of Christmas memorabilia look for it all year, so I always have a few things out. But most I save for December."

I stopped at a table filled with Santa Clauses made of wood, china, pottery, cloth, wax, and some more recent ones of plastic. One plastic Santa about a foot tall was equipped with an electric cord and glowed. "Let me guess. There's a Christmas tree bulb inside?"

"Exactly," said Sarah. "He's from the nineteen fifties."

I wondered how he would look on a table in my living room. I had Mama's collection of Santas—only seven or eight of them—on the mantel, but hadn't thought of adding to it.

But today I wasn't shopping for myself.

"I'm looking for something for Gram," I explained. "I have a couple of things for her already, but I'd love to add a package to her pile." I hesitated. "A small package."

I looked over Sarah's tables of needleworking tools. "Wow. Some of these are gorgeous." I pointed at a group of needle cases and thimbles. The gold and silver ones were simple; the fancier ones were enameled and inlaid and engraved. I glanced at one price tag. Way above my budget.

"What's this?" I asked, picking up what looked like a white stone painted with gold flowers.

"Isn't that interesting? It's an alabaster hand cooler."

"What?"

"If your hands holding your needlework got hot and sweaty, they'd leave a mark on your sewing. You could pick up the hand cooler to cool your hands."

I shook my head. "I'll bet that didn't come from Maine."

"France, I'm pretty sure."

"And these are pin cushions?" They'd be more practical. And less expensive. About two dozen soft shapes, from apples to shoes, were in one group. But would Gram use a pin cushion?

"This is fun," said Sarah, handing me a silver and blue enameled thimble.

It had a "D" on it. "Too bad Gram's name is Charlotte," I

said, handing it back to her. "That would be perfect for someone whose name started with a D."

"It's modern—the Thimble Society had it made as a memorial to Princess Diana," said Sarah. "So many of these things have history. Some of them came with information, but I've been doing a lot of research, too."

The elaborate boxes of needlework tools and spool holders were the sort of pricey antiques Patrick had bought for his mother. They weren't in my price range.

"Charlotte stopped in yesterday," Sarah said. "If I wanted to be a Christmas elf I could show you something she admired, but didn't buy."

"Please!"

She picked up a white oval china box painted with a floral border and a bee on the top. "This is a Limoges needle case. See?" She opened it. "It's lined inside. There's also a matching thimble case." She pointed. "They're not old—maybe nineteen eighties. But because of that, they're not terribly expensive."

I held the needle case. "It's beautiful," I admitted. "And elegant, with the gold hinge. And Gram liked it?"

"She did. She said she might come back after the holidays to see if it was still here."

"How much?" I hesitated. "For both the thimble case and the needle case."

Sarah looked at me for a moment. "For a friend? One hundred dollars should cover both of them."

I gulped. More than I'd planned to spend. But in this collection, a bargain. And Gram had liked them. "Sold!"

"Good!" she said. "Charlotte will be surprised—and pleased! Would you like me to gift-wrap them?"

She'd gift wrapped Patrick's gifts. Why not? "Absolutely. You're coming to the rectory for Christmas dinner, right?"

"Wouldn't miss it," she said. "I told Charlotte I'd bring some Anzac biscuits—cookies. My Grandmum always made them at Christmastime. And a sausage dish she served then, too."

"Sounds good," I said. "Gram usually has a big turkey, and a smoked salmon and potato casserole. And vegetables, of course. And pies."

"You can never have too much good food at the holidays," Sarah agreed. "And if you have enough, you can enjoy left-overs for a week afterward."

"True," I agreed, already thinking of Gram's salmon and potato casserole.

"I'm going to make cookies tonight. Want to come over?"

Reluctantly, I shook my head. "I have to finish Patrick's Christmas gift—and work on Paul Carmichael's balsam pillow."

Sarah handed me a bag holding my (now-wrapped and beautifully bowed) gifts for Gram.

"I'll see you Christmas Eve, though, at Skye's," she said.

"Probably before that! I don't want to miss the Christmas parade on the twenty-second," I said.

"I'll be in my shop. Maybe people will be intrigued by my window and stop in," she said, raising crossed fingers.

"Good luck!" I said. "And thank you for your advice." I raised the bag in her direction as I headed for the door. "And for making the pillow for Marv."

"It's kind of cool," she called after me. "My work could end up tucked in the sweater drawer of an Oscar-winning director."

I waved as I left the store and headed home.

The snow was falling harder than it had been earlier.

I hoped Skye's plane wouldn't be delayed, and that Patrick would be able to cope with driving in the snow.

He'd grown up near Los Angeles. Not a place anyone learned to drive on ice and snow. I pulled the hood of my jacket over my head.

In Maine, driving in snow and ice was Driving 101.

Chapter 11

"On Earth Let My Example Shine
And When I Leave This State
May Heaven Receive This Soul of Mine
To Bliss Divinely Great."

—In 1765, Sarah Doubt of Boston,
   Massachusetts, embroidered this verse
   in silk threads on linen. She included a
   scene of a man and woman holding
   hands, standing between two trees.
   Five dogs are sitting on the ground near
   them, and a bird is flying above them.

I walked home, full of food and happy about the gifts I'd
gotten for Gram. A win-win—a sale for Sarah and perfect
gifts to put under the tree.

I wondered again what Patrick would give me. *If* he gave
me anything. If he didn't, giving him the pillow I'd made
could be embarrassing. But I'd spent weeks on it. I was

going to give it to him, anyway. If he was embarrassed—
tough.

Jed had plowed my driveway. It *had* been snowing a little
more today than usual.

I wasn't planning to go out again, anyway. I stomped on
the mat outside my door to shake the snow off my boots, and
went in and turned the tree lights on.

My tree was beautiful. Perfect. Just the way I wanted it.
I touched the angel Mama had given me, for luck and re-
membrance.

Now all I had to do was figure out the rest of my life. And
I wasn't going to worry about that tonight.

Trixi was sound asleep in the armchair near the fireplace.
She had the right idea even though I was depending on my
furnace today. For a moment I thought about lighting a fire.
But, no. It would need tending.

I needed to stitch.

I turned on Christmas music, poured myself a cup of tea,
added a little brandy (for warmth), and settled in on the
couch across from the tree.

Several hours passed easily.

I was focusing so much on my work that the telephone's
ring startled me.

"Angie! We're home."

"Patrick?" I glanced at the clock. It was almost five
o'clock. "You just got home now? I thought the plane was
getting in about two."

"It was delayed because of the snow, and I drove home
pretty slowly. There's some ice under that snow out there."

Not unusual. "But you're back, safe and sound. How's
your mom?"

"Weary. But she loved all the decorations and the tree,

and was delighted to find Mrs. Clifford in residence and a pot of chowder on the stove."

"Good."

"The only one not delighted was Blaze—the young actress? You should have seen her walking across the snowy airport runway in three-inch heels. She bitched the whole way home. And then she wouldn't eat the chowder. Turns out she's a vegetarian."

"She sounds charming."

"Mrs. Clifford made her a peanut butter sandwich. I figured that was good—after all, we'll be having supper later tonight. But Blaze complained the peanut butter was too oily for her complexion."

"Really?"

"I didn't pay much attention, to tell the truth. I was too busy schlepping luggage."

"So you're both the chauffeur and the bellboy?" I almost laughed, thinking of Patrick, who was used to having people take care of him, in those roles.

"I'm whatever they need. Except cook. Mrs. Clifford has that job in hand, thank goodness. Which is why I'm calling you now. Mom is dying to see you. She wanted me to invite you for supper."

"Tonight? I don't know any of her friends. And doesn't she want some time with you alone?"

"We talked a little in the car, although I was focusing on the road, not on her. I suspect she wants you to assure her I'm taking care of myself even when she's across the pond."

"Does she remember you're thirty-two years old? Old enough to take care of yourself?" I thought of the ten years I'd lived in Arizona. As far as I knew, Gram hadn't been worried about me. If she had been, she hadn't told me.

"She got very maternal last summer, when I was burned. But I know she wants you to come for supper."

"You get Maine native points for not calling it dinner." I sighed and stretched my legs. Maybe it would be good to get out. Although I didn't look forward to meeting all of Skye's luminary friends. "What time is this meal?"

"Eight. But the bar will open at six-thirty."

"Let me guess—you're the bartender, too?"

"Bonus points for guessing what supper will be."

"I have no clue."

"Mrs. Clifford had planned salmon for dinner. But since Blaze doesn't eat fish . . ."

"Yes?"

"It's a casual evening. Nothing fancy. She's making individual pizzas—pick your own toppings. That way Blaze can have all the vegetables she wants, and everyone else can have local sausage or bacon on theirs."

"Mmmm. Sounds creative and good. I'd go for the sausages."

"Woman after my own heart. So—you'll come? Early? So we can have a little time at the carriage house before I open the bar?"

"It's about five now," I reminded him.

"Then move that lovely rear end, lady! I turned the outside lights on, and the candles are glowing."

"I'll feed Trixi and be on my way."

Feeding Trixi didn't take long.

But deciding what I'd wear was a challenge. I stared into my closet. Patrick had said supper at Aurora was casual. But what did Hollywood folks consider casual? Were individual pizzas considered worthy of a skirt? I didn't even own a skirt.

I glanced out the window. Members of the Chamber of

Commerce had set small potted pine trees around the edges of the Green and wound their branches with hundreds of tiny white lights. The lights were reflected on the snow. It had snowed most of the day, although right now it was only flirting, as Gram would say.

Christmas in Haven Harbor looked the way it always had.

It was my town. I decided to dress as though I was going to have dinner at, say, Dave Percy's house. If the others were more dressed up, they could consider me local color. It was a cold, snowy night, and I was going to be comfortable.

Navy wool socks, jeans lined with red flannel, a red plaid flannel shirt, topped with a navy wool fisherman's sweater. I looked in the mirror. I could have been in an L.L. Bean ad.

But—okay. I'd add my Bean boots and make it official. Only Patrick would care who I was or what I was wearing, anyway. And he'd seen me in considerably less coordinated attire.

My car was in the barn. I didn't even have to brush the snow off the windshield.

The roads were clear, if white. Maine road crews kept streets clear in all but blizzard conditions.

He opened the door of the carriage house before I had a chance to knock.

"I wasn't sure what to wear," I admitted.

"You look beautiful as you are," Patrick assured me. "You're authentic."

Authentic? Was that like "an authentic Maine woman," who lived in a "classically Maine home" decorated for a "traditional Maine Christmas"? I decided not to ask.

Patrick looked up at the sky, which had suddenly cleared and was full of stars. "Tonight is beautiful. Don't take your jacket off. I'll get mine and let's go for a walk."

Stars lit the sky, and the moon was full. He was right. It was a beautiful night.

I loved when Patrick got excited about Maine—especially Maine winters. I'd been hoping he'd love them as I did, and not long for the warmth of southern California. So far his reactions had left no room for doubt.

He reappeared in a few moments, fully equipped in a down jacket and his own L.L. Bean boots. He held out a gloved hand to me. "Let's go over to the field in back of Aurora. Without trees nearby we should be able to really see the sky."

I squeezed his hand. "Don't tell me you're an amateur astronomer?"

"Took a couple of courses in college. That's all. I always loved the stars. They're not just in Maine, you know. You can see them over the Pacific Ocean as well."

"They even had stars in Arizona," I assured him as we headed toward the field. I squeezed his hand. "I'm glad you called me." We walked a little farther. "I'll admit, I'm nervous about this evening."

"Why? You know Mom. You've always gotten along with her."

"True enough. But these friends of hers . . . help me, Patrick. Cue me in so I know what to expect."

He sighed. "They're people, Angie. Just people."

"People whose pictures are on television and in movies. People with fan clubs. Not people like me."

"Maybe not," he admitted. "But I'd rather be with you than with any of them." He tweaked my nose. "Except Mom. I like my mom."

"I do, too," I agreed. "That's why I want her to have a relaxing Christmas."

"I suspect that's not going to happen. She doesn't bring

colleagues home with her unless it's a special occasion. But
this group of people? I'm guessing she hopes getting them
into a different environment will ease tensions and let
them resolve whatever their issues are."

"Doesn't sound like a fun vacation."

"It doesn't. I agree. All we can do is keep life flowing so
Mom doesn't have to worry about organizing anything, and
stay out of the way if anything gets tense."

"Wonderful."

"It'll be fine. I'm sure," Patrick said again.

Was he trying to convince himself?

"So . . . tell me about these people. I Googled Paul Carmichael. According to fan magazines he's handsome and
charming, and was arrested for starting a small riot at an
Edinburgh pub a couple of weeks ago. He also has a reputation as a ladies' man."

"So . . . you've got the goods on him." Patrick smiled. "I'd
only met him a few times before today. I don't remember he
and Mom working together before, but the producer wanted
him in this film. Last summer she told me he'd insisted
Blaze Buchanan also be hired, as a condition of his employment. I assume she's his latest lady friend."

"He must be a great actor, and really popular, to be able
to sway the producers."

"He's had several hits recently. Romantic suspense and
action movies." He glanced at me. "I don't keep up with the
fan magazines or show business news. Movies are Mom's
business, not mine."

"Okay. What about Thomas and Marie O'Day?"

"Married. Writers. Not always a smooth marriage. Been
divorced and remarried a couple of times, but always end up
together, probably because they write well as a team. Mom's

been in their films before. I don't remember any special problems. Nice people."

"And the director? Marv Mason?"

Patrick hesitated. "Short. Stubby. A perfectionist; not easy to deal with. Mom's always said he was full of ideas, some of which are crazy, but some of which are genius. He and she had a 'close relationship' once. Only temporary. Romances on movie sets can be intense. People are away from home and working together ten, twelve hours a day"

"I'll meet them all soon."

"You will. Mom and Blaze said they were going to nap, Paul and Marv were making phone calls, and the O'Days were in their room when I left the house. And, thanks to you and the other Mainely Needlepointers, the house looks great, the food should be plentiful, and we'll even have carolers unexpectedly arriving on Christmas Eve."

"Reverend Tom called you to confirm that?"

"First thing this morning. The Haven Harbor Congregational Church choir will have new robes in January."

I shook my head. "Everyone has something to trade. It's an old Maine tradition."

"Not unknown in Hollywood, either," said Patrick. "Although this may be the first time the deal involves choir robes."

His shoulder touched mine. My nose was brittle with the cold, but I felt warm next to him.

"Didn't you once say you liked the snow because it covered all the dirt and grime, and made the world sparkle?"

"I did," I agreed.

"Then you'll be pleased to know that the next few days will really sparkle. It's going to snow again. And I heard there might be a nor'easter heading this way." He grinned. "I hope it hits; it'll be my first serious Maine storm."

I shook my head and smiled. It wouldn't be my first.

"Don't worry," he assured me. "Mom's friends won't be a problem."

He was probably right. After all, I liked Skye.

I didn't know what dealing with his "just people" meant. Or even what would happen in the next few minutes.

Chapter 12

"Diligence, Industry, And proper improvement of time are material duties of the young and the acquisition of Knowledge is one of the most honourable occupations of youth."

—Stitched by Catharine Willsey Van Cleve in 1829 at Mrs. Haywood's School in Hackensack, New Jersey. Catharine was born May 30, 1819.

The temperature was dropping. Patrick and my steps crunched into the thin layer of ice now covering the new snow. When we reached the highest point of the field behind Aurora, we stopped.

Every room in the estate was lit, and the lights were reflected on the snow and nearby trees. A year ago Aurora had been a broken-down, deserted, Victorian house Haven Harbor considered an eyesore. Thanks to Skye West it had now been restored to its earlier glory.

My personal plans might be discombobulated because

Skye was here with her friends, but it *was* her home (or at least one of them), she was Patrick's mom, and it was good to see Aurora welcoming guests, as it had for generations before being abandoned.

On summer days you could see boats coming in and out of Haven Harbor from the field. This December night the view was of the Christmas lights on buildings downtown that ringed the harbor itself. Haven Harbor Light stood alone on the southern end of the C-shaped village, its blinking lights warning ships off the high ledges protecting the harbor.

Patrick put his arm around me. "I can't imagine anyplace more beautiful than here. Or anyone else I'd want to share it with."

I didn't quibble. I was the one sharing; this was the town where I'd grown up, after all. Patrick had only been here six months.

But when I turned to kiss him, it didn't seem important that I was a native and he was from away.

We walked a little farther, toward the woods that ringed the sides of the property. The woods where we'd cut our Christmas trees.

Patrick stopped, looking from the scene in front of us to the house.

"It's time to go in and see Mom and the others. I have to set up the bar." He turned back.

He was right. We'd have to go in. But I needed a few more minutes.

The snow was six or seven inches deep except where the winds had blown deeper drifts near the house and trees. "I love the designs the wind draws in the snow." I pointed farther down the hill, where the snow lay in semicircular patterns. "They remind me of quiet waves heading inland at

Pocket Cove Beach." Our footsteps marked the snow like drops of ink on a white sheet of paper. The only other tracks were those of two deer that must have passed by earlier; their tracks were almost covered by more recent snow. Occasionally a car or truck passed by on the road in front of the house and a snowplow's blade hit the pavement. Other than that, the night was silent.

As Patrick turned back, I stayed, silently enjoying the peace. Then, about thirty feet ahead, I saw a change in the shadows.

"Did you and Ob leave any trees or branches on the field when you brought your mom's tree to the house?" I called to Patrick.

Patrick turned and shook his head. "We piled the tree and the smaller branches we'd cut on top of Ob's sled. He and one of his friends pulled it, and his other friend and I walked alongside to make sure nothing slid off. It's snowed enough so the traces we made are gone. Com'on Angie. Time to go in."

"Something's on the snow ahead." I pointed to the shadow.

Patrick shrugged. "Can't imagine what. Nothing was there yesterday."

"I want to see." I started toward the shadow "Maybe someone else was cutting trees in your woods."

"Don't worry about that tonight. I've posted NO HUNTING OR TRESPASSING signs," Patrick called after me. "We should be heading inside. Mom will be waiting for us."

"No one's lived here for years," I called back. "Could be someone's gotten into the habit of using the land." I'd seen a lot of snow, and shadows, in my life. Something about this one wasn't right. "You go ahead. I'll be there in a minute."

"Forget it, Angie! Whatever it is isn't important."

Something was in the snow. A deer someone had decided could fill their freezer this winter? That wouldn't be unusual. But deer hunting season was over. And no hunter would leave a deer they needed for meat.

The snow near the shadow had drifted. It filled my boots. I heard Patrick impatiently stomping his feet to keep them warm. He was right; we should go in.

But I was too curious to turn around. I was shivering, but not only from the cold.

The shadow I'd seen wasn't a deer.

In the moonlight I saw a man's body facedown in the snow. He was wearing a black and white patterned sweater, jeans, and cowboy boots. A darker shadow was under his head, and parts of his body were lightly covered with recent snow. I knelt to check his pulse.

There wasn't one.

"What're you doing? Let's get back to the house!" Patrick called again, less patiently now.

"Just a minute!" I yelled back. I pulled out my cell phone, snapped several pictures, and walked back toward Patrick.

"There's a body," I said as calmly as I could. "We need to call the police."

"A body?" Patrick looked confused. "How could there be a body?" He walked toward it.

"Don't get any closer," I told him, as I called 911. "It might be a crime scene. I checked. He's dead."

Patrick turned back toward me. "There's a dead man in our back field?" he repeated.

I nodded, holding my cell. "Police department? This is Angie Curtis. I'm out at Aurora, the Wests' estate. Right. We need an officer. A detective, if one is on call. I just found a body in the back field."

Patrick looked as pale as the snow. "Who was it?"

I shook my head. "I don't know. I'd never seen him. And most of his face was in the snow."

Patrick shuddered.

I held up my phone with the picture I'd taken. I'd used a flash, but it wasn't clear.

Patrick squinted at the small screen. "I can't say for sure. But Paul Carmichael was wearing a sweater like that this afternoon."

"I thought it might be him. But I've only seen his picture online. Com'on. We need to let your mother know what happened. And we should wait for the police out front."

"But . . . Paul's dead? He said he was going to make phone calls. How could he be dead? And how can you be so calm?" Now Patrick was the one hesitating, and I was the one striding through the snow.

"We don't know what happened to him," I said. "If we get frazzled we'll get in the way of the police investigation." Besides, I thought, unfortunately, this wasn't the first body I'd seen. Since I'd been back in Haven Harbor, a lot had happened.

I might look calm. But for sure, I wasn't happy.

This was not the beginning of a Merry Christmas.

Chapter 13

"The best and most correct designs in embroidered flowers are made from natural plants. The tints are easily matched in silk, and even in beads various colors may be found. Great taste can be displayed in selecting appropriate flower patterns for an embroidered design. Double and single hyacinths, combined with a tulip, give a lovely effect, and show to splendid advantage on black velvet or deep brown satin."

—From *The Farm and Household Cyclopedia: A Complete Reference Library for Farmers, Gardeners, Fruit Growers, Stockmen and Housekeepers,* Published by F.M. Lupton, 1885.

"You shouldn't say anything to your mom or the others about who we think it is," I cautioned Patrick as we headed toward the front of Aurora. "It might not be Paul. Maybe someone else was out for a walk in the snow and had a heart attack."

"You don't need a detective for a heart attack."

"Had a heart attack, fell, and hit his head on a rock under the snow?" I tried to imagine possibilities. "The police need to investigate any unattended death," I said, wishing I didn't know as much as I did about such events. "Did Paul have a heart condition?"

"I have no idea. But it must be him. He bragged about getting a bargain on that sweater in Scotland. Who else could it be? People don't wander around on our land. I've lived here full-time since I got back from Boston and I've never seen anyone but the guy who mows the grass or people working on the house. And they finished months ago."

"Still. We didn't see his face. It's up to the police to identify the body."

"The body . . ." he repeated softly.

As we rounded the house and entered the circular drive at the front, we heard sirens. The police would be here before we'd told anyone in the house what had happened. They must have been close by.

The squad car turned into the drive. I raised my hand as it skidded to a stop.

"Pete!" I said, walking toward the car. It was Sergeant Pete Lambert, the one and only Haven Harbor detective. I'd gotten to know him in the six months I'd been back in town, and he'd been out to Aurora several times.

"Good evening, Angie, Patrick. What's happened?"

"Patrick and I were taking a walk in the field in back of the house."

"But the message I got said . . ."

"We found a body in the snow. I checked; no pulse. But even in the snow, he wasn't stiff."

"So he died recently. Could have been a seizure. Or a stroke. Did either of you touch anything?"

"I touched his wrist. Patrick didn't come near him." I hesitated. "I'm not a medical examiner. Maybe he fell. But I don't think he had a heart attack. There's blood on the snow."

"What's going on?" Skye waved from her front door. She was wearing a long blue and white tartan scarf over a matching pale blue sweater and slacks, and looked more elegant than she had last summer in her jeans and T-shirt.

The young woman who followed her out, clutching the stair railing, was skinny and gorgeous, wearing three-inch heels that slipped in the snow, a short black skirt that left nothing to the imagination, and a low-cut red sweater. Seasonal color, perhaps. Practical? No way.

But she did get Pete's attention.

He walked toward the doorway, giving a whistle so low only Patrick and I heard it. "Ms. West?" He walked toward the door. "Sorry to bother you. Sergeant Lambert. We met last summer."

"I remember," said Skye, hugging herself. One sweater and a scarf weren't enough to keep anyone warm tonight. "What can I help you with? Is there a problem? Would you like to come in?"

"Stay where you are," he said, looking at the woman beside her I assumed was Blaze Buchanan. "And keep everyone in the house until I tell you it's all right. We had a nine-one-one call from Angie and Patrick here." He gestured toward us. "Seems they found something in your back field I need to check out."

"Good to see you, Angie!" Skye waved at me.

"And you," I called. "Glad you could make it for Christmas."

"That's Blaze, behind her," Patrick said softly.

"I guessed," I whispered back.

"I'm going to go check the back field," said Pete. "Angie, would you go with me? And, Patrick, why don't you stay with your mother and her . . . friend. We'll be back in a few minutes and let you know what's happening," he assured the shivering women on the doorstep.

Patrick went toward the door, glancing back at me hesitantly, but following his mother and Blaze into the house.

"A guest?" Pete asked, looking toward the closed door.

"Skye brought several movie colleagues back with her for the holidays," I said. "That's Blaze Buchanan."

"Interesting," said Pete. He glanced back at the house. Then he was all business. "Okay. Now show me where you found the body."

I led him back behind the house. "Any clue as to who it is?" Pete asked as we followed Patrick's and my footprints in the snow.

"I took a couple of pictures. Patrick thought it was Paul Carmichael."

Pete stopped. "The actor, Paul Carmichael?"

"Right. He's a guest here."

"My wife will have a fit if that's right. She's made me sit through a ton of romantic movies with that guy in them," said Pete. "If it's him, that'll be wicked big news."

"True enough," I agreed. I pointed ahead. "You can follow my footprints." I didn't need to see the body again. Seeing it once was enough.

It didn't take Pete long to find the body. He bent to get a close look and then straightened up. "Looks like a job for Ethan," he said. "The ME will say for sure, but it looks to me like he was shot."

I shivered. Who would shoot a famous actor?

Pete and I both looked around. Where had the shot come

from? Why was Paul wandering around the back field in the dark? Was it an accident? Could the shooter still be around?

"Is Ethan in town?" I asked. How long would they leave a body in the snow?

Ethan Trask was the Maine State Trooper who handled homicides for Haven Harbor. He'd grown up here, but now lived near Augusta. In Maine, only police in Portland and Bangor handled homicides in their areas. Troopers took care of the rest of the state.

"I heard he and his little girl were staying with his parents in town for Christmas," Pete said. He knew Ethan and I'd known each other in high school. "His wife's unit's supposed to be back in early January."

"From Afghanistan?"

"She's been gone near a year," Pete said. "Figure he'll be mighty relieved when she gets home safely."

"So. What now?"

"Now I call Ethan and tell him we have a job for him. He'll call the medical examiner. Let's hope we can get this taken care of before his Laura gets home."

I stomped my feet while Pete called Ethan. That snow in my boots was freezing my toes. The call didn't take long.

"He's on his way. I was right—he's in town, lucky for us. If we've got a dead celebrity on our hands, we'll have a circus here if it isn't handled right." He hesitated. "I'll stay with the body until he gets here. You mind telling Ms. West and her friends we're investigating a possible crime out here? Don't tell them who it may be. Until he's officially identified, we won't know for sure." He looked around. "Thick woods over there, at the edge of the field. Someone could've been trying to get some extra venison for the winter and made a major mistake. If so, we should be able to find footprints if we get a team out here before more snow falls.

No one ever wants to see anything like this. But around the holidays, somehow it's worse."

Kind of thing that would mess up a Christmas party, I thought. Or filming that wasn't finished.

"Who else is at Aurora now, anyway? I saw Ms. West, and you and Patrick, and that other young woman. Blaze Buchanan."

"Bev Clifford is cooking for them this week. Skye's other guests are Thomas and Marie O'Day and Marv Mason." I paused. "And Paul Carmichael."

Pete shrugged. Those names didn't mean anything to him. "I know Bev and Ms. West, and I've seen Carmichael in the movies. The others are Hollywood types, too?"

"Right."

"I told Ethan not to use any sirens. We'll keep this as quiet as we can until we know for sure whether that guy was killed, and if he was, how." Pete sighed. "I don't envy Ethan. Deaths are never fun. I have a feeling this one could get especially messy."

I agreed.

"Time of death and cause is up to the ME and crime scene folks. But I only saw one set of footprints. Yours." Pete's smile was ironic. "The heels on those cowboy boots he was wearing were high enough so he could've slipped on an icy spot. No rubber soles. So let's hope I'm wrong about his being shot."

I'd thought the same thing. How could an actor who began the day in Scotland end up dead in the snow in Maine? It didn't make sense. But, then, accidents . . . or murders . . . never did. "I'll go inside," I said. "They'll be wondering what's happening. Especially after Ethan gets here."

As I said those words he pulled into the drive. I waved,

pointed at the trail of footsteps Patrick and I and Pete had left in the snow, and headed for Aurora's front door.

Someone had to talk to Patrick and his mom, and her guests. By now they'd probably connected that Paul Carmichael, last year's "Stud of the Year," was not inside the house.

It hadn't been confirmed, of course. But I was pretty sure Paul wouldn't be celebrating the holiday in Haven Harbor.

He'd be spending Christmas at the Medical Examiner's office in Augusta.

Chapter 14

"When death dissolves the dearest ties
And Love stands mourning o'er the bier
What luster shines in Beauty's eyes
Formed by Lily's sparkling tear."

—Dolly Hariot Stone stitched this sampler
    in Middlesex County, Massachusetts,
    when she was fourteen years old, in
    1819. Her needlework on linen features
    a wide border of grapevines and a house
    and landscape, in addition to two
    alphabets.

Skye came to the door as soon as I knocked. She must have
been waiting in the front hall.

Behind her, the Christmas tree, bright with lights and ornaments, stretched from the first floor to above the balcony
surrounding the second-floor rooms. Skye was five feet nine

or ten and she was wearing heels. The tree dwarfed her. I'd
forgotten how spectacular it looked.

"So good to see you, Angie," she said, giving me a quick
hug. "Patrick told me how you helped him get this place
ready for Christmas so quickly. I really appreciate it." She
winked. "And Patrick does, too."

"It was fun," I said lamely, as people I didn't recognize
gathered in the doorway to the living room.

"So," she said, linking my arm in hers. "Patrick says
there's a bit of a mystery outside. What's happening?" Skye's
voice was calm, but forced, and she held my arm so tightly
I wondered if it would bruise.

She was acting, I realized. Putting on a positive, brave
face for her guests. I scanned the group, looking for Patrick.

"Patrick went to help Mrs. Clifford in the kitchen for a
few minutes," Skye explained without my asking. "He'll be
right back. Come and meet my friends who've joined me for
the holidays." She gestured toward the doorway.

They were all holding glasses. Patrick had opened the bar.

"This is our friend Angie Curtis," Skye introduced me.
"Angie, I'd like you to meet Blaze Buchanan, and Thomas
and Marie O'Day, and Marv Mason. We've been working
together all fall."

Blaze was teetering on her heels. She glanced at my outfit
and plainly dismissed me, turning her back on the group and
heading into the living room. Marv Mason, whose hairpiece
was a shade darker than his eyebrows, reached over to shake
my hand firmly. "Nice to meet you, Ms. Curtis."

"Angie," I replied.

"Patrick told us you used to be a private detective," said
Thomas. He was tall and good looking for a man in his
fifties, and his shock of gray hair looked as though he'd
grown it himself.

"That must have been exciting work," added his wife, Marie. She looked a little younger than Thomas, and, like Skye, she was wearing a tartan scarf around her shoulders. Edinburgh shopping, no doubt. Marie's scarf was interwoven green and yellow, and matched her yellow wool slacks and sweater.

I felt underdressed in my jeans. But there wasn't anything I could do about that now. I didn't even own a matching sweater and slacks set.

"Sometimes," I said, not adding that I'd only been the assistant to a private investigator. That detail didn't seem important. What was important was what was happening behind the house right now. The reason there were two police cars in the driveway. Would anyone ask me about that?

"Maine is as cold as Skye warned us," said Thomas, with a smile. "Is it like this all winter?"

"Depends. The temperature can be ten degrees below, or go up into the forties," I said. "Today is about average."

"I turned the furnace up yesterday, and there's wood for the living room fireplace," Patrick said as he joined us from the kitchen.

"We're comfortable and warm," Marie said. "Or—most of us are." She glanced obviously at Blaze, who was standing as close as she could get to the fire screen in front of the blazing fire in the living room fireplace.

"My feet will never be the same after having to walk through that snow at the airport this afternoon. What kind of a place is this? Iceland? I could get frostbite and lose my toes, and no one would care!" Blaze said plaintively. "Thomas, would you massage my feet?"

Thomas ignored her.

"I told you not to wear those stupid heels," said Marv, glancing at her.

"But I always wear heels," pouted Blaze. "That's what I do. It's my signature. I'm a girlie girl. And besides, Paul loves me to wear them. He says they make my legs look sexier."

She stretched out one of her legs, as though to demonstrate. She looked around. "Where is Paul, anyway? He slept on the plane. He shouldn't still be napping."

Should I say anything? Patrick glanced at me. I shook my head slightly.

"Maybe he was more tired than you thought," Thomas put in. "He'll join us when he's ready. He's never missed an opportunity to have a cocktail, and Skye told him the bar was opening at six-thirty."

"Bartender at your pleasure," Patrick put in.

"I want to know what's happening outside," said Skye, firmly. "You know the local police, Angie. Why are they here? What are they looking for?"

Everyone turned to look at me.

"There may have been an . . . accident . . . in your back field. The police are checking."

"Accident? Was anyone hurt?" Skye asked. "Can we help?" She moved toward the door.

"No." I stepped to block her. "I mean, they asked me to tell you they didn't want anyone leaving the house until they investigate. More people would mess up the scene."

"The scene?" Thomas stepped toward me. "What scene?"

"Scene" meant one thing to a screenwriter and something quite different to a homicide investigator. "Where the accident happened," I started to explain.

Patrick couldn't keep quiet any longer. "We found a body in the back field," he blurted. "They're calling the medical examiner and crime scene technicians."

"Ohhhhh." Blaze turned and collapsed dramatically in an armchair by the hearth.

I sent Patrick a "shut up" look. "The police aren't saying anything officially now," I said. "When they know something definite, they'll let us know."

"I could use a double martini," said Marv, following Patrick to the bar set up on a corner table in the large dining room. "This holiday is shaping up to be more exciting than I anticipated."

Skye took my arm and pulled me into the back of the front hall. "Angie, what really happened? I saw that state police car. They suspect murder, don't they?"

"Nothing is official until the medical examiner rules," I said.

"But murder is a possibility, right?"

"Afraid so. Pete Lambert and Ethan Trask are out there. You met them both last summer. They don't want anyone to worry until they know for sure. But, yes, murder is a possibility."

Skye's shoulders sagged. "You don't need to know the details. But although officially I'm home for the holidays to see Patrick, and show off my new home to friends, we've been having a rough couple of months in Edinburgh. We all needed a peaceful time to make some script changes and rest and reconnoiter. Maine is one of the safest states in the country. I never dreamed anything like this would happen. And in my own backyard!"

I tried to smile, but couldn't. "This isn't what anyone wants. At Christmas or any other time."

The rest of her guests had gathered in the dining room. Blaze's voice rose above the rest. "Oh, my God, look out that window! They're carrying a body bag like the one we used in my last film!"

Skye and I looked at each other.

Since I'd been outside an ambulance had pulled into the drive. It was still snowing, but lightly. The EMTs had worked quickly. They must have gotten permission from the medical examiner to move the body, maybe because of the snow. Pete had once stayed with a body all night because the ME couldn't get to it quickly enough.

"Who would have been wandering around the back field in this weather?" Skye said, almost under her breath.

Marv Mason finished his drink and handed it back to Patrick for a refill.

We all heard the knock on the door.

Chapter 15

*"May virtue mark my footsteps here
And point the way to Heaven."*

—In 1801 Sally Champney stitched two
alphabets in French knot, stem, and
cross-stitch. She included a scrolled
border, a fence, flowers, trees, and birds
surrounding a large urn of flowers,
flanked by two baskets of flowers. Sally
lived in Ipswich (sic), New Hampshire.

For a moment, no one answered the door.

Then Patrick dropped the lemon he'd been squeezing for
Blaze's mineral water and walked into the front hall.

He opened it as Ethan was about to raise the brass
knocker again. "We saw . . . out the window," Patrick started
to say.

"Pete and I would like to come in," Ethan said.

Patrick opened the door wider.

We all gathered next to the Christmas tree in the hallway. The newcomers to Maine stared at Ethan's state trooper jacket and badge, as Ethan and Pete stomped the snow off their boots and came in.

"Good afternoon, Ms. West," said Ethan. "Sorry to see you again under such circumstances. I assume Angie told you someone had an accident in your back field?"

"She did," Skye answered. "Do you want to talk with everyone?"

"I would," he agreed.

"Why don't we all go into the living room?"

Skye was gracious, as always, but her right hand, holding her wineglass, was shaking. "Can I offer you something to drink?" she asked Ethan and Pete.

"No, thanks," Pete said. "We're on duty."

"What about coffee?"

Ethan smiled. "Coffee would be appreciated. Thank you."

"Two blacks," Pete said.

"I'll go tell Bev," I said, heading for the kitchen. I didn't want to miss anything, but I suspected Ethan and Pete wouldn't want anyone else to leave the room.

The warm kitchen was filled with the rich smells of haddock chowder and baking bread, maybe the bases for the pizzas. I wished I could stay there and not deal with what was happening in the living room.

Bev Clifford, wearing a long apron over her jeans and flannel shirt, was sitting at the large pine kitchen table. She looked up as I came in. "Police are here. I saw them."

Of course. The wide kitchen windows, like those in the living room, looked out on the field beyond. How much had she seen?

"They're with the Wests and their guests in the living

room. Do you have any hot coffee? Two cups? They've been outside."

"Coffee should help warm 'em, even if their news is grim. How do they want 'em?"

"Both black," I said, looking around and admiring the immaculate room. "Your chowder smells delicious."

Bev got up and poured coffee into two large Edgecomb Potters mugs decorated with lupine.

"Brought some of my own lobster broth from home as a starter," she said, handing me the mugs. "Lobster broth makes all the difference."

"Gram says the same," I agreed. "Thank you."

"Angie? Let me know what happens?" she said as I turned to go.

She'd been crying. What did she know?

"I will. I promise." I hesitated a moment. I didn't want to be heartless, but why was Bev Clifford so upset? Although death would be upsetting to anyone.

She sat again, hard, on one of the red painted chairs around the table. Skye had designed a new kitchen for the old house that was bigger than three rooms at my house. The custom cabinet makers had fit modern appliances into the Victorian house without making them look out of place. How much cooking would Skye be doing here herself? I wasn't sure. But Bev Clifford would be taking advantage of the two stoves (not counting the microwaves), two sinks, and a walk-in refrigerator. A wine refrigerator was hidden behind one of the panels.

After Skye and her friends went back to Scotland, those conveniences would sit, unused, possibly for months.

I'd almost gotten to the door to the hall when a woman screamed.

Chapter 16

*"America Greeting Clio and Liberty. Monument, listing
patriots Washington, Montgomery, Green, Franklin,
Warren, Adams, Mercer, Putnam, Jay, Clinton, Gates,
Morris, Fayette."*

—Seventeen-year-old Chloe McCray of Ellington,
   Connecticut, stitched this in silk and metallic
   thread on silk, most likely at Lydia Bull Royse's
   school in Hartford, Connecticut, in 1814. Her
   patriotic scene depicts Liberty and America
   (holding the Constitution), meeting Clio, the
   muse of history, who is kneeling with an
   open book.

I ran toward the living room, the mugs of hot coffee sloshing
and dripping on my hands and the floor. Bev Clifford followed me.

Those in the living room were posed as though they were
on a stage set.

Blaze Buchanan had stopped screaming and was now sobbing in Thomas's arms. Skye was sitting near the bookcase, her knuckles white as she held on to the chair arms. Patrick stood behind the chair, his hand on her shoulder. Marv Mason and Marie O'Dell were sitting on the couch.

They all looked in shock.

"What's happened?" Bev whispered behind me.

I put the mugs of coffee on a glass table near the detectives and gestured to Bev that we should go back into the hallway.

"I found a body in the back field," I told her quietly. "You saw the police there. Patrick thought it was Paul Carmichael. We told Ethan and Pete. Looks like they've told Paul's friends."

"Poor young man," said Bev. "Such a future ahead of him. I was going to ask him for his autograph before he left. Going to frame it for the Wild Rose Inn."

A little late for that.

I went back into the living room. Pete and Ethan were glancing at each other. "To confirm that the man we found is Paul Carmichael, we'd appreciate one of you who knew him coming outside to the ambulance and identifying him," Ethan said, quietly but firmly.

"I knew him better than anyone," Blaze said, raising her head from Thomas's chest. "We were going to be married!"

Thomas and Marie exchanged surprised looks.

Blaze wasn't wearing a ring. Not every engaged woman wore one, but I suspected Blaze would have.

"But I can't do it! I can't see him . . . like that!" she sobbed.

"I'll come with you," Thomas said. He left Blaze and walked toward Ethan. "We all knew him. Do you have any idea what happened?"

"Not yet," Ethan said. "Thank you. This won't take long."

He and Thomas left. Pete stayed and picked up one of the cups of coffee. No doubt he wanted to hear anything the others said.

"Understand you folks had a long flight today," he said.

"We flew in from Edinburgh," Skye said quietly. "The flight was about six hours, but we were delayed taking off because of heavy fog in Scotland."

"Not many overseas flights to Portland. Fly into Logan and connect there?"

Pete's questions were more than casual interest. I'd heard him investigate suspects before. He was filling out a time line.

"The studio provided a private plane. We flew into Brunswick," said Skye. "Why?"

"Just wondering how long you folks had been here," answered Pete.

"We arrived in Haven Harbor at about four," said Skye. "We've all been in this house since then."

I was sure she believed that. But if the body outside was Paul Carmichael's, at least one of them had left the house between four and six o'clock. Patrick had told me they'd planned to go to their rooms, unpack, rest, and make phone calls. Had Paul told anyone else he was going outside? Had he been admiring the view, as Patrick and I had been? Was he meeting someone?

Possibilities whirred through my head.

Ethan and Thomas came back in, shaking newly fallen snow off their shoulders and feet.

Everyone stared at them, waiting to hear.

"It's Paul," said Thomas. He sat heavily on the couch next to his wife. "No doubt."

Blaze started sobbing again. Or at least her shoulders were heaving as she hid her face in her hands.

"How could this happen?" asked Skye. "What happened to him?"

"We won't know until the medical examiner takes a look at him," said Ethan. "In the meantime, I'm going to ask you all a few questions. You were the last people to see him alive."

And the only people in town who knew him, I thought.

"They got in from the Brunswick airport at about four," Pete said.

"And then what did you all do?" asked Ethan. His notebook was already in his hand. He sometimes used a tape recorder, but this was early in the case. If it was a case. I kept hoping they'd find that somehow, despite all that blood I'd seen, Paul Carmichael had died of natural causes.

Skye spoke for all of them. "We took our bags to our rooms. Mrs. Clifford had a pot of chowder and platters of sandwiches prepared, so then we came back downstairs and ate." She looked around. "We scattered. I went to my room to unpack and lay down and fell asleep. I came back downstairs at about six-fifteen." She looked at Ethan, explaining. "We'd said we'd meet downstairs for drinks at six thirty, before dinner. I wanted to check with Mrs. Clifford to make sure everything was set for the evening."

"Was anyone else downstairs when you got here?"

Skye shook her head. "Just Mrs. Clifford."

Ethan nodded. He'd want to talk with Bev later. But she'd disappeared . . . no doubt back to the kitchen.

"And the rest of you? Ms. Buchanan, do you feel up to talking now?"

Blaze shook her head, but turned around. "Paul and I went upstairs first, like Skye said." She glanced at her hostess. "We looked at the fantastic views from both our rooms."

"You and Mr. Carmichael had separate rooms?" Ethan asked.

Blaze managed to giggle through her tears. "Officially, sure. We hadn't announced our engagement."

Thomas and Marie exchanged looks again. I suspected this was the first time they'd heard of any engagement.

"We talked and then came downstairs and had lunch, like Skye said. Paul had a cup of chowder, I had a peanut butter sandwich, and Paul had two of the roast beef ones. And a couple of beers."

Skye looked surprised. "Mrs. Clifford didn't serve beer with lunch."

"No," Blaze confirmed. "He went into the kitchen and asked for it."

"And then what did you do?" asked Ethan.

"I went back upstairs to unpack. Some of my clothes crush easily, and Mrs. Clifford told me she didn't do ironing."

I glanced at Patrick, who was swallowing hard. He'd hired Bev to live in and cook, and she'd volunteered to help with getting the house ready for his mother's guests. He hadn't hired her to be a maid or valet.

"When you went upstairs, what did Mr. Carmichael do?"

"He was sitting there." Blaze pointed to where Thomas and Marie were sitting. "Finishing his beer. I didn't see him after that. I went upstairs and called my agent and my sister, straightened up everything I brought with me, and took a little beauty nap. I didn't sleep much on the plane."

"Did you hear or see anything before you came downstairs again?"

She shook her head. "I'm sensitive to noise. I always sleep with earplugs and a mask. I didn't hear a thing."

"And when did you come downstairs?"

"At six-thirty, when Skye said we should be here," she answered, almost demurely.

"Okay—how about you?" Ethan turned to Marv Mason, who'd gotten up from the couch and was standing by one of the bookcases.

"I was upstairs the whole time. I skipped lunch." He patted his stomach. "Been eating too much on the set. I went over some notes about the script I wanted to discuss with Thomas and Marie after dinner, called some people, and checked my computer for messages. The usual. I didn't come down until a little after six-thirty."

"Did you have any contact with Paul Carmichael after you went upstairs to your room at about four?"

"None. I had no reason to talk to him."

Thomas and Marie were next. "We were together the whole time," said Marie. "Ate lunch, unpacked, talked about the script in our room, and I downloaded a mystery set in Maine—one of Kate Flora's—and started to read it. Thomas outlined some ideas to talk to Marv about after dinner." She turned to her husband. "I don't know what will happen to the script now, with Paul gone."

Thomas patted her hand. "We'll talk about that with Marv and Skye later, dear."

I noticed he didn't mention discussing the script with Blaze.

"And, Patrick?"

"I helped Mom and the others in with their bags and then went to my place." He looked at the group. "I live in the carriage house, down the drive from here. I called Angie and asked her to join us for dinner tonight. When she got to my place we decided to take a walk before dinner. I was due back here at the house by six to set up the bar because I was going to act as bartender for the evening."

"And that's what you did?"

"Exactly."

"When did you and Angie go out for your walk?"

He glanced at me. "About five-thirty."

"And where did you go?"

"Left my place, walked here to Aurora, followed what is usually a path around the house, and went into the field."

"Did you take a flashlight? It was dark by then."

"No flashlight. The moon's full, and it was bright enough for us to see. We weren't far away from the house."

"Did you see any other footprints besides yours and Angie's?"

"Not human. A couple of deer had walked across the field, and some birds. And squirrels?" He shrugged. "I don't know how to recognize wildlife footprints in the snow. Not yet, anyway." He smiled at me. "Angie and I talked about how light it was, and the Harbor lights, and . . . other things."

"And when did you find Paul?"

"I didn't. Angie did. We were going to turn back when she saw something. She went on ahead."

"And what did you see, Angie?" Ethan turned to me.

"A depression in the snow. A shadow. I thought someone had shot a deer and left it there." I hesitated. "Instead, I found a man lying facedown in the snow."

Blaze gasped, and Skye paled. I decided not to mention the blood.

"I checked his pulse. He didn't have one."

"Patrick wasn't near you?"

"I told him not to come near. I didn't want to mess up the snow." Or the crime scene, I thought to myself. "But I took a picture of the body with my phone to show him."

"And?"

"And he said the man was wearing the sweater he'd seen Paul Carmichael wearing earlier in the afternoon. Then I called nine-one-one. You know what happened after that."

Ethan closed his notebook. "I have a lot more questions. But until the medical examiner rules on cause of death, there's nothing else to do. I assume you folks are all here for the holidays?"

"We are," said Skye.

"We'll be talking again. Soon. In the meantime, if any of you think of something else I should know, please call me." Ethan handed his business cards to each of us. "This isn't Los Angeles or New York. We don't take kindly to dead folks being found in Haven Harbor. Let's all hope Mr. Carmichael died of natural causes. If he didn't, you'll be seeing a lot of me in the next few days."

Pete had been pretty sure Paul had been shot. But until the medical examiner ruled, that question was officially open.

No one said anything for a few minutes after Pete and Ethan left. Bev Clifford came into the room. "Chowder's hot and pizza makings are ready in the dining room. Come and get it."

Chapter 17

"When doing very delicate work, use an ivory thimble, and if you find the warmth of your hands is running the colors of the wool or silk, wash them in hot water and bran, drying very thoroughly before again touching the work."

—From *The Ladies' Guide to Needle Work, Embroidery, etc.*, by S. Annie Frost. New York: Adams & Bishop, Publishers, 1877.

Bev Clifford's chowder was as good as it had smelled in the kitchen, thick with chunks of haddock and potato and pieces of bacon, in a rich, creamy broth she'd flavored with sherry. I had a large bowl while the others, who'd already had chowder for lunch, were choosing toppings for their mini pizzas. Patrick made one with cheese, mushrooms, and sausage, and one with cheese, sausage, and bacon. "We can share if you want more than chowder," he explained.

I took one piece and left the rest for him. The chowder was wicked good.

Even Blaze, who'd repeated several times that she'd never be able to eat a thing, managed to finish a pizza piled high with peppers and onions and a cup of the chowder she'd declared she couldn't eat at lunchtime. Had she reconsidered being a vegetarian? I didn't ask.

After Marv's toast to Paul, no one said much.

After we finished we carried our cups of coffee or tea into the living room, where Bev had put dishes of home-made fudge and penuche on the tables.

I planned to finish my coffee and go home. I'd never met Paul, and these people were mourning his loss. It wasn't my place to stay.

Marv was all business. "Okay, before we hear any more bad news, let's admit we have two problems. First: yes, it's sad Paul's no longer with us."

Blaze sniffed loudly.

"But we need to decide what to do about the film. Write Paul's part out? That would mean rewriting the whole script, or reshooting his scenes with a new actor. I convinced the producers this film wasn't in the toilet and we could fix it. That's why we're here, and not with our families this week. What am I going to tell them now? If they withdraw support they'll have to absorb a major loss. And I don't want them to hear about Paul's death from the press, which will have the news soon enough. Before I call our press rep and tell him to release the information, I want to know how Paul died—and have a plan for the future of the film."

"If we don't say anything, no one will know about his death," said Marie. "Luckily for us, he doesn't have any immediate family who have to be notified."

"He has an agent," Blaze reminded them.

"True enough. And she'll be pushing for us to keep the footage we have of him. Make the film a memorial to him. His last film, and so forth," said Marv.

"I don't see how we can rewrite the film and leave him in," said Thomas. "He is—was—the male lead. He was working with Skye's character to solve the mystery. We could kill him off, I suppose—get a stunt double to play the death scene— but what happens to the rest of the plot?"

I pointed to the door. Patrick got up to follow me. No one seemed to notice, or care. We weren't—or at least I wasn't— part of their world.

"I'm going home," I said. "I shouldn't be listening to this, and I have other things to do." Like, finish the needlepoint pillow for Patrick's Christmas present. I was the one who'd promised to make a pillow for Paul. Now I wouldn't need to finish it.

"Let's get our coats," Patrick agreed. "I don't need to be here, either. I'll tell Mom we're leaving. We can see every- one tomorrow. I'll call you when I know what our plans are."

Tomorrow? I'd planned to bake bread and cookies for Christmas tomorrow. These people weren't my friends or family. I didn't need to be with them. But I'd deal with that later. For now, I wanted to get out of here and go home and feed Trixi and watch one of the sentimental Christmas movies networks ran every night during the week before Christmas.

While Patrick talked with his mother and got our coats, I looked up at their enormous Christmas tree.

One Christmas bulb had burned out. Years ago that would have meant a whole string went dark, but today lights glowed separately. The dark bulb was hardly noticeable.

A knock on the front door startled me. Who would be calling at this time of night? I glanced at my watch. Almost ten o'clock. Late for Maine, but not for most of the world.

Should I answer the door? It wasn't my house.

Patrick came out of the living room, shrugged at me as if to say, "Who would it be?" and threw open the door.

He was met by blinding spotlights, cameras, and a microphone stuck in his face. A crowd of reporters, sound equipment, and cameras filled the drive. Several people spoke at once. "Well-known actor Paul Carmichael died here this afternoon. Can you tell us any details about the tragic death of this young star?"

Those in the living room listened. No one moved.

Luckily, Patrick was the son of a famous actress. "We have no comments at this time," he said calmly. Somehow he managed to shut the door.

I heard cell phones ringing in the living room. So much for Marv's plan to keep Paul's death quiet.

Word was already out.

At least no one had used the words *killed* or *murdered*. I hoped they would remain unnecessary. How long would the medical examiner take to determine how Paul died?

Chapter 18

"The rising morning can't assure
That we shall end the day!
For death stands ready at the door,
To take our lives away."

—Poem embroidered below three
   alphabets and surrounded by a wide
   border of yellow tulips and white
   flowers by Ann E. England in 1820.
   Ann lived in Pennsylvania.

"Who told the press?" Gram asked. "Do you know?"

"I don't," I said into my phone from the warmth and
comfort of the blankets and quilts on my bed.

Patrick and I'd managed to escape from Aurora through
a small back door that wasn't lit, and struggled through deep
drifts to walk around the driveway, not on it, to get to his carriage house. Luckily, I'd parked facing the road. I hadn't

turned on my headlights until I was out on the street, away from the media trucks, and headed home.

"The only people who knew were Pete and Ethan, and they wouldn't say anything, and the people at Aurora."

"And the crime scene folks, and those at the morgue," Gram pointed out. "Paul Carmichael was famous. Word was going to get out sometime."

"I know. But my feet and legs are still frozen from pushing through those drifts in the dark tonight. Why couldn't those people from the media leave everyone at Aurora alone?"

"Did you make yourself a mug of hot cocoa?" Gram asked. Cocoa was her winter cure-all. (Lemonade was her answer to summertime woes.)

"No," I admitted. I wished she'd been here to make it for me. Sometimes being grown up was no fun. "I fed Trixi and got out of my wet clothes and into my flannel nightgown and under the covers." When I was a little girl and couldn't sleep, or had nightmares, Gram would bring me a mug of cocoa and tuck me in and sit on my bed and talk with me until I fell asleep. Tonight I felt myself relax as I curled up under the covers and listened to Gram's soothing voice.

I might be an independent woman who knew how to use the Glock I'd hidden in the front hall bureau downstairs, but I still needed my grandmother.

"You'll be fine. What do you think happened to Paul?" she asked. "Tom had a late meeting about the Sunday school pageant. He's taking a shower, so I'm in bed, reading. Go ahead and talk. You're not keeping me up."

"I don't know what happened to him, Gram," I said. "I don't think he had an accident. Unless you're walking downstairs, you don't fall forward. And if you slip, you brace yourself. He was lying on his face. But I didn't see any other footprints in the snow near his. And who would have wanted to kill him? The only people who even knew he was there were in the house. And Patrick and me, of course."

"Your friend Clem could have told someone at her station that he was coming. She was at your party when Patrick told us who his mother was bringing home for Christmas. Or someone saw the plane arrive in Brunswick and asked questions."

"You're right. More people knew he was here than I thought. But how would they have found out he was dead?"

"I have no idea, Angel."

"And, if I'm right and someone killed him, why? Blaze, the young actress, said they were engaged. And his death is creating major problems for the director and screenwriters—and they were already worried about the producers pulling the plug on the whole film." I paused and thought back. "Someone said he didn't have any close family. That's sad. But it means his relatives don't have to be investigated."

"He was famous. He'd made a lot of movies recently. He was rich, right?"

Skye was rich. But she'd been a famous actress "of stage and screen" for decades. How much did a handsome young actor make? "Probably he had money. More than Mainely Needlepoint makes, or your Tom earns as a minister."

I could hear the smile in Gram's voice. "Ministers and needlepointers aren't the same as people whose lives are followed by *Show Business Daily*."

That program my needlepoint customer—Carly?—had said she watched. Sometime I should pay more attention to what is going on in the rest of the world. I hadn't even heard of that program until this week, and now I knew even Gram watched it sometimes.

I heard Reverend Tom's voice in the background. I didn't

want to keep the newlyweds apart. "You go to sleep now, Gram. I'm okay. But thanks for listening."

"Call me when you hear something new," she said. I pushed the off button and plugged my phone in for the night.

Patrick had said he'd call in the morning. I hoped he wouldn't need me for anything tomorrow. I didn't want to go back to Aurora, especially if the media was staking out the house. I wanted to stay home and make cookies.

And eat them, too. Comfort food sounded good.

I fell asleep dreaming of gingerbread children dancing on top of walls of snow, daring me to catch them.

Chapter 19

"*Dear Mother I am young and cannot show*
Such work as I unto your goodness owe
Be pleased to smile on this my small endeavour
And I'll strive to learn and be obedient ever.
If all mankind would live in mutual love
This world would much resemble that above."

—Verse stitched by nine-year-old Mary Ann Brody
    in 1789.

I wanted to sleep in. It was a dark day, the blue-gray sea reflecting the gray sky. Night winds had cleaned most of the snow that had sparkled yesterday off roofs and tree branches. Early-morning plows had, as always, cleared the streets, but left piles of snow near street corners and on the edges of parking lots. By February it would be hard to park anywhere.

Five days until Christmas.

I wasn't even looking forward to the twenty-fifth.

I buried my head under my covers.

Trixi didn't approve. She crawled under the quilts with me, gently patting my cheek with her little black paw. When I pretended to be asleep she reached out and pulled my hair.

"Ouch, cat!" I said, sitting up quickly. "What are you trying to do?"

"Squeak," she answered, racing to the end of the bed.

She wanted breakfast. She might not be able to tell me in words, but I got the message.

"All right, all right," I said, getting out of bed. I looked longingly at the warm blankets. I headed to the bathroom to take a fast shower. Trixi followed me. I didn't know what she did when I was away from home—probably she slept—but when I was home she was a Velcro cat, or, more correctly, kitten. She was now about six months old. Old enough to know what she wanted, and whom she could get it from.

She watched while I pulled on jeans, a flannel shirt, and a sweatshirt. I pinned up my damp hair—it was finally long enough for an imperfect ponytail—and we headed for the kitchen.

I'd filled her bowl and put the coffeepot on when I heard someone on my front porch.

I wasn't expecting anyone.

I peeked out the glass panel on the side of the door.

Carly Tremont waved back at me. She was wearing warmer clothes than the last time I'd seen her, but she still looked cold. I hadn't done anything about her needlepoint order. I hoped she wasn't there to cancel it.

I opened the door.

"Angie! I thought you'd be at home this early in the morning."

I glanced at the clock in the hall. Eight-thirty. Despite my wanting to stay in bed this morning, most days people in town would not only be up and awake at eight-thirty, but at their schools or places of work. Those still lobstering in December had probably been out on the water two or three hours by now.

It was December 21. The shortest day of the year. Only a little over seven hours of sunlight.

I was sure Carly wasn't at my front door to discuss the winter solstice.

"I need to talk with you. Now!" She barged in. "I smell coffee!"

"Would you like a cup?"

"I'd die for a cup. Thank you!"

I winced at her choice of words, but I got the message. "Hang up your coat"—I pointed to the coat rack in the hall—"and come out to the kitchen."

A few minutes later we were sitting at my kitchen table, drinking coffee together like old friends. I didn't have any hot food to offer this potentially lucrative customer, but I made a plate of Gram's maple raisin oatmeal cookies left from Friday night's party and put it on the table between us. Oatmeal was breakfast food, right?

Carly seemed to think so. She didn't hesitate to take several.

"With the holidays, I haven't had a chance to work on the designs for your cushions," I said.

She shook her head. "I didn't expect you would have. I came to ask what happened at Skye West's home yesterday. Is her son all right?"

"Patrick's fine," I said. "Why do you ask?"

"The Portland news this morning reported that Paul Carmichael, that handsome young actor, had died at Skye's house. I hoped her son hadn't been hurt either."

I frowned. "Why would you think that?"

She sat back and gulped more of the hot coffee than I could have swallowed at one time. "I was just worried."

"You don't have to worry. Patrick's fine." Fans could be a little strange.

"But Paul Carmichael's dead?"

"I can't talk about him," I said. "Maybe the entertainment news will have more about him in a day or two."

"But he was staying with the Wests?"

I sighed. Probably everyone in the western hemisphere knew by now. "He flew into Maine with Skye and some other friends yesterday."

"Who else was with them?"

I stood. "The Wests want their private lives kept . . . private. I've already said more than I should have."

"They live in that big Victorian house in back of the stone wall right outside downtown, am I right?"

Anyone in town could have told her that.

"Yes, and there's a gate in the wall. For privacy."

Although everyone in town also knew it wasn't always closed. It hadn't been last night, which was how the media people got to Skye's front door. I suspected it would be closed and locked today.

"I really hope that story about Paul Carmichael isn't true. It *is* a rumor, right? Unless he was drinking and using drugs again. We've lost so many of our talented young actors that way."

"Paul Carmichael used drugs?" I knew he drank—sometimes more than he should. Drugs were a new thought. But I wasn't going to confirm anything.

"I'm sure. They all do," Carly said, brushing off her remark. "I'll be going now. I just wanted to make sure Skye and her son were all right. It's so awful for someone to die at this time of year, isn't it?"

At any time of year, when someone was that young. Paul was only a few years older than I was. I shivered, despite the hot coffee.

"I'll be in touch," she said as she headed for the door. She hesitated in front of it. "You know, I'd do anything. *Anything*. To meet Skye West."

"I'm sorry. But she's busy right now, with the holidays, and her guests." Not to mention a death.

"Well, if you think of any way it could be arranged, you let me know." Carly put on her jacket. "I could make it worth your while. I'm staying at Betty Chase's bed-and-breakfast. She's letting me use her kitchen, because I'm her only guest, so I'm there evenings."

Was she bribing me for an introduction?

"I hope you have a lovely holiday," I said as I opened my door. "Haven Harbor sponsors many special events this time of year."

"I have the local paper," she said. "Not to worry about me! I have my days all planned."

I shut my door as she disappeared down the walk to the street.

A strange conversation. But she'd already given me a thousand dollars, with the promise of more to come. I could afford to put up with an unusual customer for commissions like that.

My cell rang. The day was beginning. It had to be better than yesterday.

Chapter 20

*"To Colleges and Schools ye Youths repair
Improve each precious Moment while you're there."*

—Embroidered by Nabby Martin in 1786
Rhode Island, above her depiction of the State
House in Providence and University Hall at
Brown University.

"Angie! Hope you slept better than I did last night."

It was Patrick. Patrick was usually calm, even in the face of problems, but he didn't sound calm this morning.

"Can you come over this morning? Mom's off the wall. Everything's a jumble at Aurora. Thomas and Marv sat up last night drinking and are hung over, and Blaze has been tweeting for hours about her lost love. The only ones who seem calm are Mrs. Clifford, who made blueberry pancakes this morning that almost no one ate, and Marie, who's been sitting in front of the television, channel-surfing to see what's been covered about Paul's death. And on top of everything, Ethan called. He and Pete are coming over to talk about the medical examiner's report."

"Take a deep breath, Patrick. Are the media people still there?"

"Only one truck, last time I checked. But there are paparazzi everywhere. A man with a camera peeked in my studio windows this morning. He must have climbed over the wall. I locked the gate after you left last night."

I sighed. I had a brief vision of the Christmas cookies I'd planned to bake flying out the window.

"I don't know how I can help."

"Mom is sure you can. You helped last June when the police kept showing up. You know Pete and Ethan—hell, I know them by their first names now. And Mom's comfortable with you. She keeps saying, 'Angie's grounded.' I'm her son, but she still thinks of me as a little boy. She wants someone here to handle the media. And you're it. She trusts you."

"I don't even know those Hollywood friends of hers. And, yes, I know our local detectives. They're the ones who should handle the media. I'm not going to chase men with cameras."

"Please, Angie. I told Mom all that, but she wants you."

I heard a note of desperation in Patrick's voice. And frustration. Skye had always hired people to take care of whatever needed to be done, from finding a private boarding school for Patrick when he was young, to paying building contractors and decorators, to hiring Sarah and I to clean out Aurora before the construction began. She'd been thrown into caretaker mode last summer when Patrick was badly burned in the carriage-house fire. But he was better now. Not painting, true; his hands still couldn't hold a brush well. But he was living on his own, and now he owned a gallery.

On short notice he'd even gotten Aurora set up the way she wanted it for the holidays.

Although he'd done it with help from me, and my Mainely Needlepoint friends. Patrick, too, I had to admit, was most comfortable handing over messy or challenging situations to other people.

"Are you still there, Angie?"

"I am. And, yes, I'll come. But I want you with me. Your mom needs to know you can handle situations, too." And you need to be more confident, I added to myself. A thirty-two-year-old man shouldn't be calling his girlfriend to handle deaths, paparazzi, and the media. "Is the back gate open so I can come directly to the carriage house?"

"I'll unlock it. And I had Jed clear the path from the carriage house to Aurora with his snow blower after he plowed the drive this morning. We won't have to walk through drifts today. I hadn't thought to have the path cleared before. I always walked down the drive to get to the big house. But with all those cameras behind the fences now, I want us to have a more private walkway."

"Give me half an hour."

"Thank you, Angie. I'll tell Mom."

Another Christmas preparation day lost to Patrick and Skye. I liked them both. And they were dealing with a sticky situation.

But I'd had other plans.

I looked in the mirror. I should put on some makeup and a turtleneck and one of Mama's good wool sweaters Gram had saved all these years. I wouldn't be wearing cashmere from Scotland or high heels, but I would be me. A more dressed-up me than usual, but still me.

I was the only one who cared—Patrick and Skye had both seen me in torn jeans with dirt on my face—but I didn't want to let anyone down, including myself.

Chapter 21

*"Lord thou were pleased to bestow on me a Mother
    truly kind,
Whose constant care was to instill good precepts
    in my mind:
And plant the seeds of virtue in my young and
    tender breast,
Ere thou didst snatch her from my sight with thee
    to be at rest,
Grant me, O Lord, thy constant aid to do thy holy
    will,
That a tender Mother's pious wish may be in me
    fulfilled."*

—Ten-year-old Eliza Richardson worked her 1837
mourning sampler in colored silks. She chose to
include birds and flowers instead of the weeping
willow usual in a mourning picture.

Patrick was waiting for me at his door. I glanced around, but didn't see anyone with cameras.

"You were right," he said after we'd hugged as tightly as two people wearing down jackets could. "I called the police station this morning after I talked with you and told them the media people were here, and some were trespassing. I heard Sergeant Pete yelling at someone to get over here. Our privacy is now being protected by the Haven Harbor police."

Our police force was tiny—four officers when no one was sick or on vacation.

With their regular beats, extra people in town to visit friends or families for the holidays, and day-trippers who'd come to see the annual lobster boat parade and arrival of Santa by sea, I wondered how they'd provide the security Patrick had asked for.

"I said we'd pay overtime if necessary, and Pete said he knew a couple of retired cops who could fill in. He was really angry when I told him where the photographers had been wandering. Some of them were back in the field, near where you found Paul's body."

Messing up what I was sure hadn't been ruled out as a crime scene. No wonder Pete had found a couple of people to provide private security for the Wests.

Whatever worked to get the interlopers away from people dealing with a tragedy. Famous or not, they deserved privacy.

Patrick and I closed the small back gate I'd driven through, and headed over to Aurora on the now-cleared path. It wasn't snowing today. I missed it. After ten years in Phoenix, I was enjoying Maine's winter.

The main gate to Aurora was closed, I noted, and a police car was parked outside on the street. The Channel 7 van was still there. The police couldn't do anything about that; the street was public.

As we got to Aurora's door another state police car pulled up. "Ethan's here," I said to Patrick, pointing. "Probably Pete's with him."

Patrick and I went inside, where he pushed a button I hadn't noticed, near the door.

"It opens the gate," he explained. "That way every time someone we know wants to come in we don't have to go out and open it manually."

Made sense.

The house was silent. The only noise I heard was the crackling of the fire in the living room fireplace and rattling of dishes in the kitchen. Bev was cleaning up after the breakfast Patrick had said few guests had eaten.

He answered Ethan's knock. "Good morning. Or is it?" he asked calmly. This was the man who'd called Pete earlier today about police protection; not the man who'd almost begged me to come and help him handle whatever was going to happen in his mother's house today.

"Morning," said Ethan, entering the room and nodding at me. "Morning, Angie. Suspected I'd see you here."

Pete followed him in.

"Is everyone here?" Ethan asked. "Everyone who was here last night?"

"So far as I know. We just arrived," said Patrick, removing his jacket and taking mine. "Who are you looking for?"

Ethan and Pete exchanged glances. "We'd like to talk with everyone right now."

"I'll find them for you." Patrick threw our jackets on a chair in the hallway and headed up the stairs. "Go on into the living room. Angie, see if they want coffee. I'm sure Bev has some brewed."

"Bev?" said Pete. "Who's she? I don't remember a Bev from last night."

"Bev Clifford," I explained. "I told you yesterday. Skye hired her to live in for the next week and do the cooking. She was here last night, but in the kitchen."

Pete nodded. "Good woman who's had to cope with hard times."

"We need to see everyone who was in the house yesterday afternoon or evening," said Ethan. "Whether they were in the living room or the kitchen."

"I'll get her," I said.

"What are you doing here, Angie?" Ethan asked. "I know you got to know the Wests last summer, but I didn't expect you to be here during the holidays."

"Or be the one to find Paul's body?" I said. "I've been seeing Patrick West for the past couple of months. His mother asked me to be here this morning." I headed for the kitchen before Ethan could say anything else.

Some people in town thought Patrick and I were a strange couple, and I didn't know what our future would be, individually or together. But it wasn't any of Ethan's business. Sure, I'd had a crush on him in high school. But now he was married.

Although maybe he was just curious. Or checking alibis. With Ethan it was hard to tell.

Bev Clifford was at one of the sinks, slicing apples. Meals had to be made. "Bev?" I said. "The police are here—Pete Lambert and Ethan Trask. They want to talk to everyone who was here yesterday afternoon and evening."

"Me too? All I've been doing is cooking and cleaning up. Angie, what do you think of an idea I had? I'll ask Ms. West first, of course, but looks like we'll have a lot of food left over. These Hollywood types don't eat like my guests at the inn. Or like most folks I know. One of them is lactose intolerant, and that skinny young woman won't hardly eat more than a lettuce leaf. Glad you're here now. I know you eat!"

"I do," I agreed.

"So would Ms. West mind if I took some of the food folks here don't choose to eat over to the Baptist Church? Three nights a week they serve a free supper there for those who need it."

"I don't think she'd mind at all," I said. "That's a great idea. But you'll have to check with her yourself."

"I'll do that," said Bev, taking off her apron. "So I'm supposed to come with you now?"

"Please. Patrick went to get the others."

People were beginning to gather in the living room. Ethan and Pete were standing by the fireplace. I had the feeling they were taking mental notes about everyone as they came in.

Skye was sitting on the couch, looking like a mother hen surveying her chicks. Thomas and Marie were sitting in matching armchairs. Patrick hadn't returned. I assumed he was getting Blaze and Marv. Checking three stories of rooms would take a few minutes.

Bev and I settled in straight chairs by the doorway to the hall. We were the only two with no relation to Paul, so I figured we were the least important.

Clattering steps on the stairs preceded Marv Mason's arrival. For a guy in his fifties with a hangover, he was moving pretty fast. "Sorry to hold everyone up. I was calling the coast."

"You haven't held anyone up, Marv. We're still waiting for Patrick to find Blaze."

Marv joined Skye on the couch, adjusting a couple of

needlepoint cushions so he could sit farther back. "Last I saw her she was muttering about a headache."

Thomas and Marie exchanged glances.

"Can you start without them?" Skye asked Ethan.

He shook his head. "We'll wait."

We sat in silence. I'd heard Ethan talk to groups before. It was never good news. He must have the results from the medical examiner, and since he was here and not on the telephone, I assumed they'd ruled Paul's death a homicide. Did anyone else in the room understand what Ethan's presence meant?

Skye might. She'd met both Pete and Ethan before. But she looked relaxed. Although, I couldn't forget, she was an actress.

Voices penetrated the room. "I can't believe you're making me come downstairs to see people when my hair is still wet. I look atrocious. The world won't end if I dry my hair first." Definitely Blaze. And her room must be on the third floor. They weren't here yet.

Patrick's soft reply was blurred.

"I don't care if the governor is here! They're cops. We already know Paul's dead. It's horrible. We're sorry. His agent should arrange his funeral. Give one of the networks exclusive rights to cover it. I wouldn't mind speaking. Now we need to get on with life. His death should give a real boost to the film. Last days and so forth!"

Those words brought her to the living room door. She flounced into the center of the room wearing her usual heels, skin-tight jeans, a lavender sweatshirt imprinted with the Scottish coat of arms, and a white towel tied around her head.

"Thank you for joining us," Ethan said drily. "Please find a chair and sit down."

Blaze gave him a dirty sideways look, then reversed and turned on the charm. "I'm so sorry to have delayed the meeting. But in this dry air I needed desperately to condition my hair." She sat on an armchair near a window overlooking the field where I'd found Paul's body.

Patrick sat near Bev and I. The line of outsiders, I thought.

Ethan began. "All right. You all know Paul Carmichael died yesterday. I'm aware that you've been bothered by media people. I want to apologize for that. We in Haven Harbor value our guests, and we'll do our best to make sure you have privacy. I want to assure you, however, that no one connected to Maine law enforcement told anyone about Mr. Carmichael's death. I don't know how members of the public and the media found out, but it concerns me as much as it does you. I have to ask you all to keep the details of what happened yesterday within this house and with Sergeant Lambert and me."

"What's the big deal?" asked Blaze. "Paul died. I tweeted about it this morning. His fans want to know all the details."

Ethan walked toward her. "I'm asking—no, telling—you not to tweet, or Facebook, or use any social media. Beginning right now."

"What?" said Blaze. "But my fans . . ."

He handed Skye a piece of paper. "We have a search warrant for this house and the carriage house, and we'll be taking your phones and any computers or tablets you have with you. Your fans will have to wait. Right now putting information online is interfering with the police investigation."

"Police investigation?" repeated Skye. "Then you're telling us . . ."

"The medical examiner ruled Mr. Carmichael's death a homicide," said Ethan.

Blaze gasped and tears rolled down her cheeks. Could

she cry on cue? If I'd heard my fiancé had been killed, I wouldn't be posting on social media.

Did actors act all the time? Skye had always seemed normal. But, as Gram would have said, Blaze wasn't my cup of tea.

Marie and Thomas reached out their hands to each other. Marv was gritting his teeth. No one said anything.

Skye was the one who asked, "How? How did he die?"

"Right now we're not releasing that information."

"We'll do whatever we can to help you, of course," Skye assured Ethan.

"I'd like you all to stay on the first floor of the house while our investigators search the upstairs. Sergeant Lambert and I will also interview each of you, separately. Ms. West, is there a private room we could use?"

"A small sitting room behind the kitchen," she acknowledged. "It's a solarium that used to be a dining room for the staff. I had it fixed up as a retreat."

"The retreat sounds perfect," said Ethan. "Thank you. The crime scene investigators should be here anytime now. They'll be checking your back field, tracing Mr. Carmichael's steps yesterday, and then working on the second and third floors."

"It's getting late in the morning. Perhaps Mrs. Clifford could get a simple lunch together for everyone, including both of you," Skye said, standing up. "It sounds as though you'll be here for a while."

"Thank you, Ms. West. You all go ahead and eat." Ethan looked at his phone. "But no one leave the first floor. Our colleagues from Augusta are outside. I'll be working with them and begin talking with each of you. You've been chatting since yesterday; some of you may even have been in Mr. Carmichael's room. As of now, that ends."

Bev Clifford stood and started toward the kitchen.

"How soon can you serve lunch?" Skye called to her across the room.

"Half an hour. Maybe sooner," she answered.

I stood, too. "I'll help."

"Thank you, dear," Bev answered. We both left the room as Ethan opened the front door to three crime scene technicians and their equipment.

The silence from Paul Carmichael's dear friends was deafening.

They'd just realized they were all suspects in his death.

Chapter 22

"Let my few remaining days
Be devoted to thy praise
So the last, the closing scene
Shall be tranquil and serene."

—Verse stitched by Eliza Benneson in 1835 in
   either Baltimore or Delaware. Above and below
   her verse are alphabets and a small landscape.

"Good of you to volunteer to help," said Bev. "Those Hollywood folks think I'm here to wait on 'em. Not a one has volunteered to as much as carry a platter from the kitchen to the dining room. Had to tell that Paul they're all lamenting that I didn't do room service. He wanted me to bring a plate of sandwiches to his room."

I shook my head. "When did he do that?"

"Oh, not long after they arrived. Said he had calls to make and couldn't take the time to sit with the others and eat." Bev tied her apron on again. "He found time when I told him I didn't deliver. Guess he has plenty of time to himself now."

"What had you planned for lunch today?"

"Figured this crew should choose their own. I'm not exactly a full restaurant. Yesterday I made a salmon mousse, and this morning I fixed some deviled eggs and a platter of rolled-up pieces of ham, salami, turkey breast, and some raw veggies. Got croissants and sandwich bread from the bakery, and thought I'd make up a macaroni salad with tuna and olives and such and steam some mussels."

"Sounds delicious." I'd skipped breakfast. "And more than enough. What can I help with?"

She pointed at a large pan. "Fill that with water so we can get the pasta cooking. The mussels can steam in wine and herbs while I chop the mixings for the salad. If you could get out a clean tablecloth and plates and silverware, that would save time." She pointed at one cabinet. "Tablecloths and napkins are in there. Plates are in the cabinet next to the dining room door."

She pulled out olives and celery and red onions and several cans of tuna while I filled the designated pan.

"Skye is so lucky you were free to help her out with all these guests," I said.

"Your grandmother is a dear to have thought of me. I was going to have a quiet Christmas, and then join your gram and the reverend and you for dinner. Would have left me too much time to think, to tell the truth. Now I've got no time to sit and stew. That's a blessing."

"I'm glad it worked out for everyone. It's no fun to be alone on Christmas."

She stopped chopping and looked at me. "It's not. Especially when memories are bitter. I hope you never have to live with a past that's never over. You're young. Enjoy life for all it's worth. Today may be all you've got. Hope things work out for you and that Patrick. Seems like a nice fellow, for all he's from away."

"He is," I agreed.

"You make sure he's the right one, and if he is, you grab him. Never know how long you've got."

I reminded myself to ask Gram about Bev's story. I'd been out of town for ten years, and out of touch. Gram knew everything that had happened in town for the past fifty years. Or more.

I remembered a boy named Luke Clifford a few years behind me in school. What had happened to him? And were he and Bev related? I sensed this wasn't the time to ask.

I found a white linen tablecloth for the large dining room table and a smaller one for the sideboard, and put out stacks of plates and silverware. As I passed the windows I saw crime scene investigators photographing and measuring barely visible footprints in the snow, some of them mine and Patrick's from yesterday afternoon.

Yesterday seemed a long time ago.

Other investigators had gone upstairs to look for . . . what, exactly? And why hadn't Ethan told us how Paul Carmichael had died?

The whole situation seemed strange. If any of these people had wanted to kill their colleague, why hadn't they done it on a movie set in Scotland, where I assumed there'd be dozens of people around to be suspects and provide alibis?

The newspaper article I'd seen online said Paul had gotten into a brawl of some sort at a pub in Scotland. He'd been taken to the hospital there. Had someone tried to kill him and failed the first time?

I shook my head. My imagination was going crazy.

There had to be a simple reason for what happened yesterday. Motive, opportunity, means. But how to figure it out without any pieces of the puzzle?

"Angie, get those platters I made up earlier out of the walk-in fridge while I mix up the salad."

Bev had already drained the pasta and was adding it to the ingredients she'd mixed in a large salad bowl. Mussels were simmering in her wine and herb sauce on the stove. Bev had estimated thirty minutes. In fifteen she was able to stand in the door of the living room and announce formally, "Luncheon is served."

Patrick had opened the bar again, but was suggesting tea or coffee or soda instead of anything heavier. Marv insisted on a martini, although Patrick talked him into trying the local cranberry gin. Blaze cut herself a sliver of salmon mousse and selected one deviled egg, two mussels, and several carrot sticks. I didn't watch what anyone else ate. I was too busy filling my own plate.

"Thank you for helping Mrs. Clifford," Skye said to me quietly. "I suspect she feels she's being neglected. But there's been so much going on."

"I understand," I said. "She's happy to be here. It's a good fit for both of you."

"She's done a lovely job. Lovely. Oh—and by the way, I got distracted by the food. Ethan Trask wants to talk with you in a few minutes. He's talking with Patrick now."

Patrick and I were the first to be interviewed?

We were the two most unlikely suspects. I'd never met Paul, and Patrick hadn't met him until he'd arrived in Maine.

At least that was what he'd told me.

But, on the other hand, we'd been the ones who'd found the body.

I took another deviled egg. At least I could eat before I was grilled.

Chapter 23

"No surplice white the priest could wear
Bandless the bishop must appear
The King without a shirt would be
Did not the needle help all three."

—Stitched by Mary Miller on her sampler
in 1735 England.

I was nervous. I'd been consulted about murders before. I'd never been officially interviewed.

I went into the kitchen. When I was with Bev I could see the door to the little room Skye had called her retreat. Gram, who'd visited this home decades ago, had always referred to it as the solarium, where the cook in those years grew herbs for the kitchen and protected plants from winter's cold, and the staff ate their meals.

No plants bloomed there today.

My mind raced. I had to focus on something other than what Ethan and Pete were going to ask me.

I hoped the Needlepointers were almost finished with the pillows Skye wanted as gifts.

With all that was happening, needlepoint seemed the least of anyone's problems, but I couldn't forget I'd promised she'd have the pillows before Christmas Eve.

I went over the list in my mind. Sarah was stitching one pillow. I hadn't talked to her or seen her since I'd visited her shop and bought a gift for Gram. Dave was doing one. And Captain Ob and his wife, Anna, who lived across the street from Aurora, were each stitching one.

Had Ob and Anna noticed the media vans here? The police cars? They had to have.

Ethan had said not to talk with anyone about what had happened, but I was strongly tempted to call them. Or at least text. Let them know what was happening in their neighborhood. Anna had birding binoculars. She'd be watching, and wondering.

"If you're going to stand there, you could check the dining room for empty platters and dirty dishes," said Bev. She'd already started loading the dishwasher.

"I'm waiting to be called in to talk with Ethan and Pete," I said. I hoped to have a moment to talk with Patrick after he came out of the room. "Can I help with anything in here?"

"No, I've got it under control. You look as though you need a purpose. You've been pacing for the past five minutes."

"I have?" I hadn't noticed.

"They're not such bad guys, those police. They have a job to do. Just tell them the truth, whatever they ask you. Don't try to fool them about anything, or hold anything back."

I turned and looked at Bev. She had brown hair streaked with gray and was a widow in her fifties. What would she know about police investigations?

"I'll be fine. I'm not worried," I lied.

"Then stop wearing out the floor and get me the bowl the mussels were in," she said. "Be careful not to spill any broth that's left."

I managed to get the bowl to the kitchen without spilling a drop.

"I have to wash that bowl separately," said Bev, taking it from me. "It's Waterford. Probably worth a fortune." She shook her head. "That Ms. West, she seems all right. Wonder what it's like to be able to buy whatever you want, and do whatever you want?"

"She works," I pointed out, although I'd sometimes had the same thoughts. "She was working in Scotland. The only reason she's here and having a break for the holidays is there were problems on the set."

Bev raised her eyebrows. "Problems on the set? Sounds dreadful. She may have been doing what she calls work, but I'm pretty sure it didn't have anything to do with scrubbing dishes or toilets."

"Running the Wild Rose Inn must be hard," I said. "But last summer Skye told me about where she came from. Neglectful mother, not always enough to eat. Lived on the Lower East Side of New York in a rough neighborhood. She was lucky to get a scholarship to a private high school. She worked hard to get ahead."

"Not saying she didn't. If she had the intelligence and courage to take advantage of opportunities, good for her. Not everyone has those opportunities."

Bev was right, of course.

But I liked Skye, and I liked her son, whose biggest problem growing up was not having a father, and living in boarding schools when his mother had to work. I'd scrubbed a few toilets myself, and steamed a few lobsters, and waitressed.

"Angie! There you are. I thought you'd be in the living room with the others." It was Pete. "Hi, Bev. We'll need to talk with you later. Ms. West said you're living in?"

"Not going anywhere."

"Good. We'll try to get to you before you're working on dinner. Com'on Angie. Let's get started."

I'd been talking with Bev and hadn't even seen Patrick leaving the solarium. What questions had they asked him?

Whatever they were, we hadn't had a chance to compare notes.

Which was exactly what Ethan and Pete wanted.

In any case, I didn't know anything I hadn't already told them. "No problem, Pete. I'm coming."

"You'll be fine, dear," Bev whispered. "You didn't kill that man, did you?"

Chapter 24

"For embroidery designs, we suggest natural forms such as strawberries and their leaves. This delicate needlework in pure white forms a graceful design. But when embroidered in the natural colors of the leaves and fruits on a boy's or girl's jacket, stand cloth, or ottoman cover, on cloth of scarlet or gray, it is pretty enough for the most fastidious. Moreover, this leads you to observe and study nature, which from your life-long intimacy with it, may have failed to specially interest you."

—From *The Farm and Household Cyclopedia: A Complete Reference Library for Farmers, Gardeners, Fruit Growers, Stockmen and Housekeepers,* Published by F.M. Lupton, 1885.

Cooks had picked fresh herbs in this solarium; housekeepers and owners had enjoyed fresh blooms throughout the year. They'd looked down at Haven Harbor, or watched lightening cross the sky, or, as today, seen the white field and the dark blue North Atlantic beyond.

Today there were no flowers or herbs in the small room. Ethan and Pete sat on one side of a glass-topped table which might once have been used to pot plants. Today it was the center of an interrogation.

The chair they set for me faced them and the clapboard wall which once had been the outside of the house. Snow covered the slanted glass roof.

"I've already told you all I know about Paul Carmichael," I said.

"But you may know information you may not realize is important. We want to go over everything again."

I nodded.

"Please say yes, to indicate you understand," said Ethan. "We're recording the interviews."

"I'm a suspect?" I asked, incredulously, looking from one of the men to the other. I knew them both. We'd worked together before. Today neither would look me in the eye.

This wasn't good. What did they know . . . or imagine?

"You've known the Wests—Ms. West and her son, Patrick—since they first came to Haven Harbor last June."

"Yes."

"Do either of them, to your knowledge, own a gun?"

A gun! They must have confirmed that Paul Carmichael had been shot, as Pete had assumed when he first saw the body. I couldn't imagine either Skye or Patrick with a gun, but I answered carefully. "I've never seen either of them with a gun, and neither has ever mentioned having one."

"You own a gun."

"Yes, I brought my Glock with me from Arizona."

"Do Patrick or Ms. West know you have a handgun?"

I thought back. "Patrick does. I don't think Skye does, unless Patrick mentioned it to her."

"Have you ever seen any guns in this house?"

"No."

"How well do you know the Wests?"

"I know Patrick. We're friends. We've been . . . dating . . . for a couple of months. I've met his mother several times, and done some work for her. But I'm not a close friend of hers."

"Have either of the Wests ever mentioned having a problem with Paul Carmichael?"

"No." I thought carefully. "Patrick told me there were issues on the set in Scotland, but he never said exactly what they were. Just that the film was going over budget, and they'd have to rewrite the end of the script."

"You didn't hear anything specific about Paul Carmichael?"

"Several people who learned he'd be visiting Haven Harbor mentioned how good looking he was."

"I meant, any reason someone would have to resent him, or want him dead."

"No, nothing."

"When did you first meet Mr. Carmichael?"

"I never did. Patrick met his mother and her guests at the airport. I was expecting to meet them all yesterday evening."

"Did he ask you to accompany him to the airport?"

Where were these questions going?

"He did. I told him I had other things to do. It's almost Christmas, after all."

"When did you arrive at Patrick's home yesterday afternoon?"

"About five-thirty."

"And whose idea was it that you and Patrick take a walk in the cold and snow before you went to Aurora?"

"It was Patrick's idea." I thought back. "Yes."

"During your walk, did you see any footprints?"

"We walked on the drive until we were close to the big house. There were footprints in front of the house. I didn't pay attention. People had been coming and going." I thought carefully. "As I told you yesterday, we decided to walk around the house and over the top of the field."

"Why?"

"Because the view is better from there. We could see the lights at the center of the village. The sky was clear, and the moon was full, so we had no trouble walking."

"How long were you walking?

"About half an hour. It was cold, and Patrick suggested we go back, into Aurora. He had to set up the bar for his mom's cocktail hour."

"But yesterday you told us you continued, by yourself."

"For a short distance, yes. I thought I saw something in the snow, and I was curious."

"You were alone when you found Paul Carmichael's body."

"I was. I checked his pulse and took a picture with my cell phone. I wanted to know whether Patrick recognized him. I didn't."

"Patrick West never came near the body?"

"No, I told him to stay away. In case it was a murder, I knew we shouldn't mess up the scene with more footprints."

"Did you see any footprints in the field that were not yours or Patrick's?"

"I saw indentations near Paul's body that I assumed were his footprints. The snow had almost covered them. They appeared to lead to the other side of the house, the side near the woods."

"And what did Patrick West say when you showed him the picture you'd taken."

"He said the sweater the man was wearing looked like the one Paul Carmichael had been wearing that afternoon. You know what happened then. I called nine-one-one and we waited for you, Pete."

"Did you see anyone besides you and Patrick outside the house either before or after you found the body?"

"No, Skye and Blaze came to the front door, but we called to them to stay inside. We were waiting for you."

"And had you seen Blaze Buchanan before that?'"

"No! I told you, I hadn't met any of Skye's friends. Patrick told me the woman with Skye at the door was Blaze."

Ethan turned to Pete. "Can you think of any other questions to ask Angie?"

He shook his head. "No, not now."

"Angie, is there anything else we should be questioning you about?"

"No, I had nothing to do with Paul Carmichael's death. I just found his body!"

"Then that's it for now. If we need to clarify anything, we'll get back to you."

I got up from the table feeling drained.

Why had they been questioning me so closely? Sure, I'd found Paul's body. But they knew me. I wouldn't hide anything from them.

And what was all that about Skye and Patrick having guns?

I needed to talk with Patrick.

Chapter 25

"My dear Rose," said Miss Tremaine, smiling, "I think you are working quite too steadily upon that embroidery of yours. If Doctor Summerville were here, he would lecture you for working and me for letting you work so steadily. I think I must send for him, to come and impress some sanitary restrictions upon your use of your needle."

—From "Mademoiselle," a short story by
   D.R. Castleton, published in *Harper's Magazine*
   in 1862.

I felt like taking a hot shower after getting out of the solarium.

I'd questioned people myself. After all, I'd worked for a private investigator, and often that involved asking questions. But I'd never been "in the hot seat" myself.

Bev was no longer in the kitchen. I heard movement from upstairs. I glanced out the window; the crime scene investigators' truck was still here. They must be checking the bedrooms.

I headed for the living room.

Skye and her guests seemed more relaxed than I'd assumed. The television in the corner was turned on, and everyone except Marv was watching a soccer game. The afternoon after a murder, and they were watching sports. Marv was reading a book. Patrick wasn't there.

"Ms. West, we'd like to talk with you now," Ethan said, following me into the living room. She got up and followed him to the solarium.

I sat next to Blaze, who was yawning. I suspected soccer wasn't her choice of entertainment. But where was there to go when investigators were everywhere?

"Do you know where Patrick is?" I asked her softly.

"Carriage house. The police wanted to search it, too."

Why would they want to search the carriage house? But why had they asked me whether Patrick or his mother had guns?

I doubted Patrick could shoot easily with his burned hands. I should have mentioned that in the solarium. The question had never come up before.

"How are you coping?" I asked Blaze. "It must be painful to lose the man you loved." I'd be distraught if anything happened to Patrick, and we'd never used the word *love*.

"Paul and I were engaged," she said, without blinking. "Not married. And I'm sorry he's dead. I'm worried about who they'll get to take his place in the film. I finally get a big break and work with a box office star and he goes and gets himself killed." She shook her head. "But I may get some sympathetic publicity from it."

"You didn't love him?"

"Don't be naïve. I loved the attention we'd get from fans and producers who saw our pictures together. It's business. I mean, the guy was okay most of the time. But did we have happily-ever-after romantic love?" She looked amazed that I'd ask. "No way!"

"Did he have a gun?"

That startled her. "What? You think he shot himself? He had a gun on the set; a prop. That's the only gun I ever saw him with. He wouldn't hurt himself. He loved himself too much."

"You knew him well."

She thought back. "He once told me he'd hunted when he was a kid. The prop guy didn't have to show him how to handle the gun. But a real gun? Paul was too wimpy. Besides, guns are hard to get in the UK. I never saw anyone with one in Scotland. Not even our security guys."

"How about you? Can you shoot?"

"What's with the gun questions? No, I don't shoot. I also don't swordfight or box or"—she gestured at the flat screen in the corner—"play soccer. I can sing a little and dance a little and I work out a lot. And I act. I mean, really—do you have a gun?"

"Actually, yes, I do."

She hadn't expected that. "For protection? Because you're a woman alone?"

"I used to work for a private investigator. I needed a gun for my work."

"A private investigator! Awesome. Is that why you've been asking me all these questions? Are you investigating Paul's death?"

A good question.

I answered it with a smile and a touch on her shoulder as I left the room. Pete and Ethan couldn't have meant me when they told people to stay in the house. I was going to find Patrick.

Chapter 26

I was halfway down the drive to the carriage house when I felt my phone vibrate. Had Ethan or Pete discovered I'd left Aurora and wanted me back? They'd told us not to talk to each other, but I assumed that meant it was forbidden before they interviewed us.

Patrick and I had both survived that.

I pulled out my phone, to check.

A text from Carly Tremont, the woman from Texas. She'd stopped to see me and I hadn't answered my door. Had I heard anything more about Paul Carmichael? How was Skye coping? Was she still at her house? Was Patrick there? Where was I?

Sorry, Carly. I don't wait around for Skye's fans to drop in so I can divulge her location.

Carly was harmless enough, but she seemed obsessed. If there wasn't so much drama at Aurora, I might have tried to figure out a way for her to (briefly) meet Skye. After all, she was going to pay Mainely Needlepoint thousands of dollars.

I'd answer her text later. I had more important situations on my mind right now.

Blaze had been right. One of the crime scene vans was at Patrick's house. Under the circumstances, I walked in.

He was making coffee in his kitchen.

"Enough for two?"

"Definitely. Good to see a friendly face. I figured someone would tell you where I'd gone."

"Blaze did." I looked around. "Where's Bette?" Bette was Trixi's sister. Dave and Patrick and I had adopted kittens from the same feral litter.

"She's in her carrier, in the studio. I didn't want her to get in the way of the investigators." Patrick lowered his voice. "Those crime scene guys are looking through the bedrooms and studio. Since the guest bedroom isn't finished—it only has cartons of art books in it—and I haven't been using the studio much, they shouldn't take much longer. They took my computer and phone, though. You won't be able to call me tonight."

They hadn't taken my phone. But I probably hadn't been at Aurora when Paul was killed. Had they estimated his time of death? If so, they hadn't shared it. But there was a short interval between when he was eating lunch at Aurora at about 4:30 and I found his body at 6:00.

I kept my voice low. "They asked me whether you or Skye had guns."

He turned away to pour our two mugs of coffee.

"I assume Paul was shot," I added.

"They asked me about guns, too," he said, handing me a mug.

I started toward his living room.

"Why don't we stay here in the kitchen? I don't think they can hear us from here."

We sat at the small table near his kitchen window. "I told them you and Skye didn't have guns. I was right, wasn't I?"

"Of course. I don't have a gun. Never did. Mom's had to shoot in a couple of her films, but she's never owned a gun. At least not that I've ever seen or heard about."

I relaxed. "Good. Because Ethan was insistent when he was questioning me. And if Paul *was* shot . . . it might make a difference."

"But all guns are different, right? You know more than I do about them. The police could tell what gun killed Paul. Just because someone had a gun doesn't mean they killed him."

"Of course not. I'm no forensics expert, but I know if they recover the bullet they can tell the make and model of the gun it was shot from. To tie the bullet to a specific weapon, they would have to have the gun."

"A lot of people here in Maine have guns, right?"

"Sure. Most for hunting, but people have them for protection, too. It's easy to get a gun in Maine. No background checks unless you buy one at the local branch of a national retailer. They have to meet federal standards. Why all the questions? Thinking of getting one?"

"Paul was killed in my backyard. That's scary. And even my girlfriend has a gun."

"Your girlfriend's pretty tough," I smiled. "You don't need a gun."

"Mr. West?" A man in a crime scene jumpsuit stood in the doorway between the kitchen and main room. "We're finished here. Sorry about the mess we made. Comes with the territory, I'm afraid."

"Are you taking anything other than my computer and phone? And when can I get those back?"

"We removed the trash in your wastebaskets. Assuming there aren't problems, we should have your computer and phone back to you in a few days."

"Thank you."

Patrick's voice sounded different, somehow. I glanced at him. He looked pale.

"Are you all right?" I asked.

"Fine," he said, gulping his coffee. "Never had my house searched by the police before."

"Why don't I help you clean up?" I suggested. "If he said they'd made a mess, I suspect they did."

"It's okay," he said. "I'm tired. I'll rest for a while. You go on home. I know I interrupted your plans for Christmas, and you don't have anything to do with this."

"I found the body."

"Thank goodness. Or we would have been calling the police looking for a missing person when Paul didn't show up for dinner. But, I'm serious. Please, go home. I need some time to think about all this."

Something was wrong, but I had no idea what it was. Maybe Patrick was spooked. A man had been killed near his home. That was scary, especially since we had no idea why.

I started to drive home, then made a slight detour and drove to Gram's house.

When I had a problem, she was my rock.

I wasn't sure I had a problem now. But I needed to talk with someone. Someone who hadn't been at Aurora yesterday and wasn't a murder suspect.

Chapter 27

"The earliest sampler known is dated 1643, unfinished, and worked by Elizabeth Hinde. It is only six inches by six and a half inches, and is entirely lacework . . . a lady in Court dress holds a rose to shield herself from Cupid, a dear little fellow with wings, who is shooting his dart at her heart. Perhaps poor Elizabeth Hinde died of it."

—From *Mrs. Lowes' Chats on Old Lace and Needlework.* London: T. Fisher Unwin, Ltd., 1908.

"Angel! I didn't expect to see you today." Gram's cheek was smudged with flour and her home smelled of ginger and vanilla and pine. Christmas carols were playing softly in the background.

Here was the Christmas I'd missed during my years in Arizona.

No one here was talking about guns, or wearing three-inch heels. No bodies were in the backyard.

"Come, help me decorate the gingerbread people," she

said, pointing me to the kitchen. "My back is driving me crazy, sitting here and putting candies in the dough."

"Sounds like fun." I hadn't decorated gingerbread people since I was twelve or thirteen.

"I was crazy to volunteer to bring four dozen to the Christmas Eve pageant reception," said Gram. "I'd forgotten how much work they were."

I'd be at Skye's party Christmas Eve. I'd miss the children's pageant. I'd been an angel in the cast one year when I was about seven. I touched the gold angel on my necklace and smiled, remembering. I'd been so proud of my wings.

"How's Patrick? And Skye? I assume you've been out at Aurora the past couple of days."

"They're fine," I said, sitting at the kitchen table and starting to sort raisins and candies for the gingerbread people's faces and buttons. "You haven't heard what's happened there?"

"I saw your friend Clem on television the other day, talking about all the celebrities converging on Haven Harbor. Nothing since then."

I'd always been blunt with Gram. "One of those celebrities is dead. Murdered. I found the body."

Gram put her floury hand on mine. "Oh, Angel. How awful. And at Christmastime!"

"They questioned me, Gram. I can't be a suspect. But Patrick's been acting strange, and I don't know what to do."

"Talk to me," she commanded. "And keep putting eyes on the gingerbread people. I'll do the buttons."

I told her about finding Paul ("That poor man! Handsome is as handsome does, of course, but he sure was a looker.") and calling the police, and today, hearing he'd been killed. "It didn't surprise me, Gram. But it was still awful. They're treating everyone in the house as a suspect. They questioned me, and Patrick. Even Bev Clifford is on their list."

"Poor Bev. This is an awful time of year for her, anyway." Gram shook her head.

"She asked me to thank you for recommending her. She complains sometimes. But she's glad to have the job."

"No doubt. She doesn't earn a lot running that inn. I'm glad the job worked out."

"Why is this a hard time of year for her?"

"Her husband died on Christmas Eve, a few years back."

"That's awful!"

"It was. And being questioned about another death won't be easy for her, even though I'm sure she had nothing to do with this young man."

"I want to help Patrick. He's more upset than I would have thought."

"We never know exactly how we'll react to tragedies—our own, or even others'. All you can do is be there for him, Angel. He's had a hard year. Is he painting yet?"

"I don't think so. He's getting better at holding things, but slowly. I don't mention it."

"Wise woman. He moved to a new place, and then spent two months in a hospital or rehab center, knowing his hands, the hands he depended on to paint, would never be the same. His life was his art."

"Now he has the gallery. I hoped that would help."

"I'm sure it does. But it's also a reminder he may never be able to paint the way others do. Every day he works with those paintings must remind him of what he's lost."

"You're right. I don't notice his hands anymore. I'm taking it for granted that he'll be fine. He has money. He lives in a beautiful place and has a business."

"And he has you." She put up her hand. "Maybe not forever. I'm not pushing anything, Angel. I don't know what will happen between the two of you. But for now, he isn't alone. And that's important. Remember, he may be more concerned about how he looks than you know. After all, he grew up in a world focused on looks as well as talent."

"I hadn't thought about it that way. He's a good man, Gram. But I think he knows something about Paul's death that he isn't telling anyone—or at least not telling me. That means it isn't anything good."

"Angel, there's nothing good about a young man dying too soon. And being murdered? It's horrible. I hope they find out who did it so everyone else at Aurora can relax, and you can enjoy the holidays."

"I do, too, Gram. Although I know that's selfish. At first I resented everything Patrick wanted me to do to prepare for his mom's coming home and bringing guests. I'd planned Christmas this year, and I didn't want to change any of those plans. It's been a long time since I was home in Haven Harbor for Christmas."

"Ten years. I know. But Patrick didn't create this situation. He didn't ask his mother to come home, and I suspect part of him resents all he's having to do—not for her—but for her colleagues. The best thing you can do—besides taking that tray of gingerbread people out of the oven right now!—is be there for him, relax, and help him enjoy his first Haven Harbor Christmas."

I pulled the tray of cookies out of the oven.

"I will. And to start—could I have two of the gingerbread children to take to him?"

"You can. One boy and one girl. Choose your favorites. And try to get him to come to the Christmas Cheer festival tomorrow. Who can resist seeing Santa and his moose arrive by lobster boat?"

"No one," I agreed. "Ethan and Pete should have finished talking with everyone by then. Patrick should be able to get away for a little while."

Without the others, I added to myself.

Chapter 28

"*The most famous of all English queens is Katherine of Aragon, who came from a land [Spain] celebrated for its Embroideries and Lace, and who enlivened the many sad hours of her life by instructing her maids of honour and the poor people living near her palace in the art of making Lace and Embroidery.*"

—*Dictionary of Needlework: An Encyclopaedia of Artistic, Plain, and Fancy Needlework* by Sophia Frances Anne Caulfeild and Blanche C. Saward, London: L. Upcott Gill, 1882.

I helped Gram with the rest of the gingerbread people. We talked about her plans for the holiday and what she was cooking for Christmas dinner, and sat near her Christmas tree, drank tea, and watched Juno, her coon cat, batting a low-hanging light.

Juno was an old, sedate cat. Gram didn't worry about broken Christmas balls the way I did with Trixi.

By the time I left for my house I felt much better.

I checked Trixi's food and made sure all Christmas balls were in place as I turned on my tree lights and candles. I planned to wrap a few presents, indulge in a simple dinner of cheese and crackers, and not think about what was happening at Aurora.

I started to call Patrick, then remembered the police had his phone.

Instead, I called Sarah.

"I'm closing the store up for the night," she said. "I didn't expect to hear from you, with all the doings up at Aurora."

"Tonight they'll be doing without me," I declared. "I plan to stay home and wrap presents and listen to Christmas music and take it easy."

"Any chance you'd like to join me for dinner first? I have nothing in my apartment but cookies, and I'm sick of cookies. I put a plate out for my customers and I've been nibbling them myself all day. I'd like to go to the Harbor Haunts for an early dinner and then finish up the needlepoint pillow I'm working on for Skye."

I had a fleeting vision of stilton and brie, the cheeses I'd planned to eat. Then I thought about a warm dinner with Sarah. "Meet you there in half an hour?" I suggested.

To get to that warm dinner, I had to put on boots and a scarf and heavy jacket and walk downtown. Parking was limited there to begin with. Taking my car that short a distance would be a hassle.

In the summer and fall I'd loved walking downtown, especially in the early morning, watching the lobstermen taking their boats out while the sun rose over the Three Sisters, the three islands that protected Haven Harbor's port from the North Atlantic. Now days were short. Dawn was at about seven in the morning.

Tonight the streets that had been filled with vacationers and locals earlier in the year were empty, but the moon was full, and the silent storefronts, many of which would close after the holidays, were lit with colored or white lights that were reflected in the snow.

It was peaceful. My nose crinkled with cold, but my feet were cozy in wool socks inside my boots, as I inhaled the frosty sea air blowing inland from the ocean.

Christmas would come, even after the worst of times.

Whatever was bothering Patrick couldn't be horrible. I was sure he hadn't killed anyone. He was probably just tired after everything that had happened in the past few days. Tonight he'd rest and clean his house, and tomorrow I'd convince him to come downtown for Haven Harbor's Christmas Cheer festival.

The Harbor Haunts was only half full. I wasn't surprised. This wasn't July. This was an early evening a few days before Christmas.

Sarah waved from a table near the fireplace. The fire made the room feel welcoming.

On my way to her table I nodded to several people I knew. Not everyone in town was Christmas shopping at the Maine Mall in Portland, or at home baking cookies and breads or decorating trees.

"So glad you called," said Sarah as I slipped into the chair opposite her. "I love it when the fire is burning. I sometimes come here alone, but it's more fun with two of us."

"Agreed," I said.

A waitress appeared behind me. "Drinks, ladies?"

"A glass of pinot noir?"

"Make that two," said Sarah. "I wanted to tell you—I'm glad you came into the shop when you did to pick out a gift for your Gram. Those needleworking tools are selling even better than I expected. I'm glad I got them in time for Christmas. I keep wrapping them up for people and thinking . . . in a way, I'll be under their Christmas trees this year."

"I like that thought," I agreed. "You're coming to Skye's Christmas Eve party, and to Gram's for dinner on Christmas Day, right?"

"Looking forward to both. How does Aurora look? I can hardly wait to see it. I haven't been inside since we ran that enormous yard sale for Skye last June, when the wallpaper was torn and plaster was falling off most of the ceilings."

"You won't believe what it looks like now," I assured her. "Spectacular. And yet comfortable. She decorated the way I would, if I had her money."

"And how's Patrick?"

"Tired, but okay. I suspect he would have liked more notice before his mom flew in with guests. But so far so good." I lowered my voice and glanced around to make sure no one else was in hearing distance. "Except for the murder."

Sarah stared at me. "What? What murder?"

"I'm glad you haven't heard. Gram hadn't, either. That means neither the ladies of the church nor the businesses downtown have gotten the word. The media people know someone died, but not that it was murder. The police are trying to keep it quiet as long as they can."

"Who died? Where? Anyone we know?"

"One of Skye's guests. Paul Carmichael."

"Have you ladies decided what you'd like to eat?" The waitress put our glasses of wine on the table and looked at us expectantly. Tonight she was wearing a reindeer sweater and tiny red Christmas balls as earrings. 'Twas the season.

Sarah and I knew the menu well. "A cup of onion soup and the fried oysters sandwich," I decided.

"A cup of haddock chowder and the broiled scallops with sweet potato fries," Sarah ordered.

"We're not going to be hungry for a while," I commented.

Sarah leaned toward me. "So—details! What happened to Paul Carmichael? After I left your tree-trimming party the other day I Googled everyone Patrick said would be at Skye's party Christmas Eve. Paul was the good-looking actor, right? The one with a drinking problem?"

"He's the one," I agreed. "You must have seen the same sites I did. Ethan and Pete haven't officially said he was shot, but they're asking a lot of questions about guns, so I'm assuming that's what happened. He was in the field in back of Aurora, only a few hours after he'd arrived. Patrick and I found his body."

"No! Too many people have been killed around here in the past six months. Does Ethan have any idea who did it?"

"I don't think so. He and Pete have been questioning everyone at Aurora, including Patrick and me. They asked whether Patrick or Skye had guns."

Sarah turned her head. "Speaking of whom . . . guess who just walked in?"

Ethan and Pete were taking seats at the far end of the bar, where they could see the entrance. Automatic seating decision for cops.

"Guess they've finished interviewing everyone at Aurora. I hope they found out something. I get along with them pretty well, but this morning I felt as though I was a suspect, or at least they thought I knew something that would lead to the killer."

"You have a gun," Sarah pointed out.

"True. And it's hidden at home, where it is most of the time. I didn't take it to Aurora the day Paul was killed." I sipped my wine. "And as far as I know, neither Patrick nor Skye have guns."

"Everyone else at Aurora flew in from Edinburgh at the same time, right? On the same plane?"

"And as far as I know went straight to Aurora."

"It's pretty unlikely anyone would have brought a gun from Scotland. I've been in the UK. Their gun laws are incredibly strict compared to those here."

"In Maine you can buy a gun from a local dealer or pawn shop or friend and not even go through a background check," I agreed. "Hard to be more open about guns than that."

"So who managed to get one?"

"I can't imagine. You're the one who Googled everyone. Any ideas?"

"Let's see. We'll pretend it's a game. Blaze Buchanan, the pretty actress?"

"She announced to everyone yesterday that she and Paul were engaged. Then this morning she told me their relationship was all for the publicity. She didn't seem horribly disturbed by Paul's death, despite her histrionics when she first heard about it. She also told me she didn't know how to shoot."

"What about the director, Marv Mason? Maybe he was jealous of Blaze and Paul. He had a reputation of liking to work with the young and the beautiful."

"Paul's death could be the end of the film they're making. He'd lose a lot of money, I suspect. Doesn't make sense."

"The screenwriters? Maybe the guy, Thomas, is secretly bisexual and was having an affair with Paul he didn't want his wife to know about. Paul threatened to tell everyone, so—bang!"

I started to giggle. "Not a chance. Thomas and Marie go around holding hands."

Sarah threw up her hands dramatically, almost overturning her wineglass. "I'm out of ideas. Guess you and Ethan and Pete will have to solve the case yourselves. Does Paul's death mean the party Christmas Eve is off?"

"As far as I know, everything is still on."

The waitress delivered our soups, and neither of us said anything for a few minutes.

"Will you be coming to the Christmas Cheer festival tomorrow? I'm hoping the day inspires last-minute Christmas shoppers. The parade goes right by my shop, so I won't miss it."

"I'm hoping to get Patrick to come. He seemed troubled this afternoon—especially after those crime scene folks left his house in a mess."

"You didn't mention that. What were they looking for?"

I shrugged as the waitress removed our empty bowls and put our main courses on the table. "A gun that wasn't there, I guess. They took his computer and telephone, too, along with all the laptops and telephones from Aurora. So I can't call him to see what's happening tomorrow."

"Guess you'll have to go out there and see."

"That's what I'll do. In the morning."

Chapter 29

"There was an Earthquake on the 8 of September 1692 in the city of London but no hurt tho it caused most part of England to tremble."

—Sampler inscription signed by Martha Wright, 26 March 1693. She embroidered her memory of an unusual event below two alphabets.

Sarah's and my conversation turned to more important topics, like what we were planning to wear Christmas Eve, as the waitress brought us maple bread pudding for dessert. Christmas wasn't a time to diet, I told myself, thinking of all the cookies I'd consumed in the past week.

"I'm sure Skye's planning an elegant evening. I've collected a few vintage cocktail dresses at antiques shows and auctions. I'm planning to wear one of those. I even have a mink coat."

"A mink coat?" I looked at her. Sarah? My friend who lived on tomato soup and tuna sandwiches? "I've never seen you wearing anything like that!"

"A present to myself. I bought it at an auction last summer. It's really old—the lining's ripped a little, and it hasn't been cared for well. But it's mink, and warm."

"How much, may I ask, did you pay for it?"

"You won't tell anyone, will you? Jewelry and furs and personal items can go really low at auctions. Not for pennies, but below appraised value. Some people aren't into secondhand."

"You mean, vintage?" I'd hung around Sarah long enough to pick up some of the lingo.

"Exactly." She leaned toward me and whispered, "My mink cost a hundred dollars."

"Wow! I should start going to auctions!"

"Let me know if you're serious about that. After the holidays, I'll be going to a lot of them, collecting inventory for next summer. I'll only open the store Tuesdays through Thursdays in January and February. Most of the good auctions are Friday, Saturday, or Sunday. I'd love your company. What are you going to wear to Skye's Christmas Eve party?"

"A red sweater and black pants. That should be seasonal."

She looked doubtful. "You should ask Patrick how dressy it will be. If we each wear what we've planned, one of us will be underdressed, or one of us overdressed."

"You're right. I should ask Patrick." If the evening called for a dressy outfit, I was in trouble. I didn't own anything dressier than a decent sweater.

"I'd love to sit and talk, but I have a needlepoint pillow to finish," Sarah said. "'We talked as Girls do— Fond, and late— We speculated fair, on every subject . . .'"

"Emily?"

"Of course. She always had the right words. And you said you have Christmas gifts to wrap," Sarah reminded me.

"True enough." I raised my hand to get the waitress's

attention. As I looked around the room I caught Pete's eye. He was alone. Ethan had vanished.

"You take care of the check," I said to Sarah, handing her my credit card. "Tell her to divide the bill, as usual. Let me talk to Pete for a moment."

Sergeant Pete Lambert, as the local Haven Harbor detective, couldn't officially work homicides—that was up to the Maine State Police, the law enforcement agency Ethan Trask worked for. But Ethan knew Pete longed to someday be a state trooper, so he let Pete help him out when there was a local homicide.

Ethan would never tell me any details about his cases, but sometimes Pete gave me hints. It was worth a try, anyway. I perched on the high bar stool Ethan had vacated.

"Saw you with Ethan. He's left?"

"Went home to put his little girl to bed." Pete looked at the beer in front of him. "I decided to have one more before I head out."

"Doesn't your wife have a list of Christmas tasks for you?" I teased.

Pete didn't smile. "I haven't told a lot of people, but the wife and I are separated. She went home to her family in Bangor."

"Ouch. Sorry. I didn't know, Pete."

"She couldn't deal with being married to a cop, and I wouldn't change professions. It happens, I hear from other cops."

"How're you doing?"

"As well as can be expected. Don't mind working over the holidays this year, for sure."

"How did it go this afternoon at Aurora?"

"About as Ethan figured. No one knew anything; no one saw anything. Everyone loved Paul Carmichael."

"Based on the questions you asked me this morning, I assume he was shot."

"Sure was. Don't know why he was wandering around in the snow wearing those expensive cowboy boots, or why anyone would have shot him. Ethan's beginning to think a hunter was trying to get a deer and missed, and the bullet hit Carmichael. There were footprints in the woods on the far side of the field."

"It's not hunting season. And the Wests' land was posted."

"That wouldn't stop someone desperate for venison. And you and Patrick saw deer prints in the snow."

True enough. When I was a child a hunter shot and killed a young mother hanging clothes to dry in her backyard. He said he didn't see her; he was aiming at a deer.

I wasn't the only Mainer who wore blaze orange during deer hunting season, even when I was in town, and especially at dawn and dusk, when deer were most likely to be spotted.

The sun went down about four on December afternoons. Paul Carmichael was shot at dusk, or a little after.

"What's going to happen now?"

Sarah slipped my credit card into my purse and waved as she headed home.

"It's a celebrity case, so Ethan's dotting every i and crossing every t. He doesn't want questions from any of those media folks when he doesn't have good answers. It'll take a day or two to get the results from what the crime scene folks took today. Until then, looks like life will go on as usual."

"You'll be at the parade tomorrow?"

"Expecting most of the town, and some from out of the area. Haven Harbor's getting known for its Christmas Cheer festival. All members of the force will be around, in case anything happens."

"Like, Santa gets kidnapped?"

"More likely a lost kid or a shoplifter. Or someone looking for a place to park who blocks traffic." Pete paused. "My wife always liked Christmas Cheer."

I put my hand on his shoulder. "Maybe she'll change her mind and come home."

"Not likely. She's wicked set on starting over."

I got up. "Good to see you. And thanks for the update about Carmichael. Horrible though it is, I hope all the evidence points to a hunter. See you tomorrow at Christmas Cheer!"

"Merry Christmas, Angie." Pete took another deep swallow of his beer.

I headed for the door. I had Christmas gifts to wrap, and I was looking forward to a good night's sleep.

If Paul Carmichael had been accidentally shot by a hunter, everyone at Aurora could relax. They'd still have to deal with the media, and with what they were going to do with the end of their film, but at least none of them would be arrested.

I hoped they'd examine the evidence quickly. It was darn inconvenient not to be able to call Patrick.

Chapter 30

"Seek first the Lord be timely wise
Truth Virtue and religion Prize
For these extend beyond the tomb
And will through endless ages bloom."

—In 1822, Eliza Ann Wallingford
(1809–1838) of Dublin, New Hampshire,
stitched this sentiment, along with several
alphabets, a house, and a frame of flowers,
in silk threads on linen. She died,
unmarried, at the age of twenty-nine.

Snow had moved in last night, covered Haven Harbor with a
fresh coat of white, and then moved out to sea. The morning
sun was making the snow sparkle.

A perfect day for the Christmas Cheer festival.

I checked in with Captain Ob and Anna and Dave. They
all promised to have the needlepointed pillows they were
doing for Skye finished by December 23. I'd pick them up,

along with Sarah's, and deliver them to Aurora the day
before the party, in plenty of time for Skye to wrap them,
hide them . . . or whatever she planned to do.

While I was checking times for the Christmas Cheer
events, Trixi became fascinated by the cardinals and blue
jays and chickadees dodging in and out of the holly bush
by our front porch, competing for the seeds in the feeders.
As I watched, a downy woodpecker landed on the cake of
suet and blueberries and started his breakfast, and a pair of
juncos arrived.

I left Trixi at the window, staring out at the excitement
she couldn't reach, and headed for the carriage house at
Aurora. By the time I got there it would be late morning.

I used the back entrance, in case the media was still in
front of Aurora.

I hesitated, then knocked on Patrick's door.

After the third time I gave up, headed up the drive to
Aurora, and knocked on the door there.

Patrick opened it. "So glad you came! I wanted to call
you, but no one has their phones back yet. We're hoping
they'll be returned by tonight."

He pulled me into the front hall, where I noticed Christmas packages had appeared under the tree.

The kissing ball we'd bought from Arvin and Alice
worked just fine.

"Good morning, Angie!" Skye walked down the stairs,
carrying a jacket. "Isn't it a beautiful day? I'm so glad you're
here. The wagon should arrive soon."

"The wagon?"

"Remember, Mom wanted a sleigh ride? And Captain Ob
said no one around here used sleighs anymore?" Patrick
reminded me.

"Snow mobiles, more likely."

"Ob called a cousin of his who has a farm outside of town. He's going to hook up a couple of his horses, fill a wagon with hay, and come by. He says he's ours for the day, to go anywhere we'd like."

"Exactly. And we've all been cooped up here since we arrived, and haven't shown our guests how beautiful the State of Maine is, so we're excited!" Skye took my jacket and hung it in the closet near the door to the kitchen.

"I was hoping you and I could go to the Christmas Cheer festival together this afternoon," I said quietly to Patrick.

"We'll all be going," he said. "Mrs. Clifford had a copy of the local paper, so everyone's been handing it around. Apparently the police blotter is the funniest thing anyone's ever read."

Didn't sound as though Patrick and I would be enjoying the celebration on our own.

Skye peeked out the front window. "I suspect rumors about Paul's death have made their way to the Internet. We don't have computers or phones, of course, thanks to that state trooper and his friends, but the media's back."

I looked. Clem's Channel 7 friends were there, and several other vans and cars I didn't recognize. "They might know about Paul. Or they might want to cover your visit to Maine," I pointed out. "But you won't be invisible if you're all in a horse-drawn wagon."

Patrick tried to hide a smile. "Mom knows that, Angie. It was Marv's idea. He figured pictures of his cast celebrating Christmas in Maine would be good publicity for the movie."

Did they want publicity or privacy? I didn't fully understand.

"I have a proposition for you, Angie. You grew up here. You know Haven Harbor better than anyone else. We'd love for you to join us in the wagon and be our tour guide. Pick out the most interesting places to see, direct the driver where to go, and tell us all about what we see," said Skye.

That wasn't what I'd hoped for today. But how could I say no?

"Haven Harbor's a pretty small place. There's the lighthouse and Pocket Cove Beach and the Green and the downtown area, the four blocks of stores, and the wharves. That's about it."

"We'll go slowly, to absorb the atmosphere. Then we'll park the wagon and check out the stores, and be there when Santa arrives on his lobster boat and leads the parade. It sounds perfect!" Skye had it all planned.

"Christmas Cheer is fun," I agreed. "But it's not fancy." Haven Harbor's parade wasn't like Macy's. And where could we "park" a horse and wagon?

"That guy we bought the wreaths from said there was a lobster boat parade," Patrick pointed out.

"There is. Right before Santa arrives. And later there'll be fireworks over the harbor. Although you can see those from your back field, too."

Oops. From where I'd found Paul's body.

"Fireworks. Like the old days," Skye said.

I'd forgotten for the moment that she'd been a guest in this house forty plus years ago. A guest when, during end of summer fireworks, her best friend had died.

"Just a few fireworks," I explained. "The Chamber of Commerce sponsors them. They're set off from Second Sister Island."

"They sound lovely," Skye said. "Mrs. Clifford is going to put out some lunch for us in a few minutes, and by the time we've eaten, the wagon should be here and we'll be off."

How many photographers would be here by then? Would they follow us around town? I shuddered. Most of the people in Haven Harbor knew me. Many of them knew Patrick and I were together. But what would they think seeing me in a crazy horse-drawn hay wagon with these Hollywood people?

Skye was fine. She'd met a lot of people in town, and, at least on the surface, they'd accepted her for what she was: a famous actress who wanted a private retreat.

But this was different. Even Skye seemed different when she was with her friends. Maybe it was Paul's death.

Patrick had warned me at the tree-trimming party that this group could be . . . interesting. Reverend Tom had suggested they keep whatever excitement they provided at Aurora.

Now it seemed they were not going to stay at Aurora, and they were incorporating me in their plans.

Patrick had gone to the kitchen; I assumed to talk with Mrs. Clifford about lunch.

I wished I could escape. Run to where my car was parked and drive off.

But this was part of Patrick's life. It wasn't a part I'd seen before. But if we were a couple, it was a part of my life, too.

I straightened my shoulders. I could do it. Haven Harbor gossip be darned.

Chapter 31

"So false religion shall decay
And darkness fly before bright day
So man shall God in Christ adore
And worship idols vain no more.
So Asia and Africa
Europa with America
All four in concert join shall sing
New songs of praise to Christ our king."

—Sampler in silk thread on linen made by
   Ann Isabella Littlefield in Wells, Maine.
   Ann was eleven years old, and the year
   was 1835. A few years later Ann married
   lawyer Nahum Morrill and they moved to
   Auburn, Maine, where they had three
   sons. One died at the age of six months;
   the other two grew to adulthood and also
   became lawyers. Ann died in 1906 and
   Nahum in 1917.

Skye's schedule held up. After a leisurely lunch, during which most of her guests indulged in wine or beer to accompany their salmon, bacon, lettuce and tomato salad, and blueberry muffins, Ob's cousin, Seth Harlow, pulled his hay wagon up in front of Aurora's gate alongside the media trucks. Didn't those guys ever take breaks? Seth was wearing a Santa hat. As though on cue, one cloud paused overhead and it started snowing. The sun was still shining, so the snow looked like a glittery curtain.

It all fit Skye's script perfectly.

Seth had clearly heard the message that Skye West had requested a sleigh. I'd seen a fair number of hay wagons, although none recently, and certainly none in the residential sections of Haven Harbor. Most were pretty grungy. This one had been spruced up, benches added to the sides, and the hay that filled it wouldn't have kept one horse alive for more than a day or two.

Seth's two horses had been brushed until they shone, and he'd braided red ribbons in their manes and hung large wreaths (also with red ribbons) on the sides of the wagon. Several of the paparazzi left their warm cars to take pictures even before the celebrities left Aurora. As Seth stepped off his seat at the front of the wagon, he waved a cow bell at everyone. I suspected he'd take a few pictures of his own before the day was out.

"Not bad," I said to Patrick. "I'm impressed. That's the closest I've ever seen to a horse-drawn sleigh in Haven Harbor."

"Thanks to Ob Winslow. His cousin Seth acts in the local theater group—I didn't know Haven Harbor had one of those!—and he took the job as a challenge." Patrick bent over, touched my shoulder, and whispered, "Plus, he's starstruck."

"He does look as though he's having fun," I agreed.

Patrick had arranged the day, but Skye was staging it. "We'll all put on our coats and gloves and walk to the wagon, and then get on, allowing time for the media people to snap a few pictures. Some of the photographers will probably follow us for the afternoon, but I'm hoping this scene will be perfect enough that at least some of them will leave us alone after the photo op."

I suspected she was being optimistic.

Everyone in town would gawk at this setup and who was in the wagon. Santa Claus was going to have competition for attention this afternoon, at least among the adults in town.

Patrick and I hung back as Skye and her guests walked casually toward the street and the wagon. After all, the photographers weren't interested in us.

Blaze posed next to one of the horses, her short black leather skirt and high leather boots (not waterproof) competing with the horse for attention. Weren't her legs cold? Then Skye joined her, wearing a white jacket and red scarf over her slacks, ready for a holiday picture. The photographers weren't as interested in Thomas and Marie, who were the first to climb onto the wagon. They weren't holding hands today, and sat on benches on opposite sides of the wagon. Patrick and I joined them without anyone paying attention. I sat near Seth, so I could tell him our route, and Patrick sat close beside me. We weren't exactly snuggling, but feeling his body next to mine was almost as good.

Marv was posing with the horses and actresses. He had his arm around Skye, who was not only older than he was by about ten years, but several inches taller.

When they all finally decided to end the photo session, Marv helped Blaze negotiate climbing into the wagon. Several photographers took advantage of the display her tight skirt and high heels gave them. Marv's hand on her rear gave her a final push to get in.

Who'd given her the idea that a tight leather skirt would be appropriate for this occasion? She'd be freezing that tight ass of hers off before we got far.

Everyone settled in. Blaze cuddled next to Thomas, and Marv squeezed in between Skye and Marie.

"Seth, let's go slowly, and head to the Haven Harbor Lighthouse."

"No problem about going slow. My old girls here aren't ready for the Derby." He called out, "Happy holidays! Ho, ho, ho!" to the delight of the photographers and Blaze's giggles, and we headed out.

Captain Ob and Anna waved from their barn across the street. We waved back, like tourists waved to passengers on other boats.

As long as I didn't worry about what people in town would think, it was fun. I'd been on hayrides when I was a kid, but that was a fall activity. Despite the new layer of snow gathering on the road, the sound of the horses' hooves was loud enough so Skye had to raise her voice when she called out, "Angie, tell us about Haven Harbor's history."

Two cars of paparazzi were still following us.

Thomas and Marie turned toward me. Blaze made a point of shifting in her seat so her back was to me. History must not be her favorite subject.

It hadn't been my favorite, either. But I knew the basics about my town.

"Haven Harbor's a typical Maine coast community," I

said, stretching my voice so if Blaze wanted to hear me, she could. "We have a safe harbor protected by three small islands—the Three Sisters—so fishermen from northern Europe made it a camp and trading center in the early 1600s. By 1646 a few families had settled here, in what was called the wilderness of Massachusetts. We were primarily a fishing community then."

"What about lobsters?" Marv called out.

"Early settlers only ate lobsters when waters were too rough to fish and they didn't have any dried fish left. Lobsters were thought of as bottom-scavenging bugs. The lobstering industry didn't take hold until the nineteenth century. Fishermen still call lobsters 'bugs.'"

Blaze shuddered. "Didn't they farm? Didn't they have vegetables?"

"Some," I admitted. "But the rocky coast of Maine wasn't good for farming. Inland, in later years, yes. But at the coast people ate seafood, and traded fish and lumber from the trees they cut down with people who farmed, or who lived in cities and had access to imported goods. They had animals, though. Cows and chickens and pigs and goats. Most communities, like Haven Harbor, kept their animals on islands near the mainland, so they didn't have to use wood for fencing that was needed for building houses, heating them, and trading. That practice became a major problem during the American Revolution. British war ships sailed along the coast from Canada and stole the animals off the islands to use as food for their sailors. Along the way they destroyed any boats they found, cutting people in towns like Haven Harbor off from the rest of the world. Without boats they couldn't fish, they couldn't trade for food, and, remember, their land was too rocky for farming."

"Couldn't they ride their horses to other towns, inland, where there were farms?" asked Marie.

"Haven Harbor, like many towns on the end of peninsulas, was isolated. Boats were their transportation; rivers and sea their highways. No roads led here. The few roads there were—abandoned Indian trails—were rough. No horses were north of Brunswick until after the Revolution. Oxen were used for hauling lumber, but they were either stolen by the British or eaten early on. People living on the coast of Maine were close to starvation during the American Revolution."

"I didn't know that," said Patrick.

Blaze took a mirror out of her bag and refreshed her lipstick.

"The first place we're going to see is Haven Harbor Lighthouse," I continued. "It was built about the time of the War of 1812 to warn vessels away from the cliffs you'll see, and to watch for British ships that might attack the harbor."

"Did any attack?"

"No," I admitted. "But other towns along the coast were attacked. People here felt the Light had protected them."

"What about shipwrecks?" asked Thomas.

"There were several in the couple of hundred years before the Lighthouse was built," I said. "One ship full of coal from England hit the ledges in fog and sank. All winter local residents carried baskets down to Pocket Cove Beach—we'll go past there today—to collect coal to use for heat that winter."

Seth turned around. "I don't want to take the horses up the hill to the Light—the parking lot at the foot of the Light is plowed, but the trail won't be."

I relayed his message. "We can't get close to the Light with the horses. Even in the summer, people have to park at the bottom of the ledges and climb to the Light itself. Today the path won't be shoveled."

"Does anyone want to hike up the trail? Or shall we just look at the Light from the base?" asked Skye.

The overwhelming vote was to stay in the wagon.

We rounded the corner to the Light's parking lot. "You can see the Light from here. A lighthouse keeper and his family used to live there, but today all the lights on the Maine coast are automated. The small building at the base of the Light is the cottage for the lighthouse keeper. Some lighthouse stations were considered hardship posts—they could only be reached by sea, and keepers had to keep the oil lamps burning even in winter nor'easters. Today some, like the Haven Harbor light, are open to the public in the summer months. But this time of year it's a dangerous climb over the snow and rocks and ice, so lighthouse tours end on Columbus Day."

As we sat for a few minutes at the base of the ledges leading up to the Light, Thomas pulled a silver flask out of his jacket and handed it to Blaze, who accepted it gratefully and drank.

"Thomas!" Marie said. "Put that away!"

"It's a cold day, and I'm not driving? Why not?" Blaze handed the flask back and he took a good swig himself. "Anyone else?"

Marie frowned and shook her head, but Marv reached across the wagon to take the flask. "Good stuff," he said, offering it to Marie and Skye, who both shook their heads. "Thanks, Thomas."

"Haven Harbor isn't a large town. You can see how the land curves around the three small islands." I pointed. "They're called the Three Sisters. No one lives there."

"Why not?" asked Marie.

"No fresh water or electricity. They're basically pines and underbrush on top of rocks. The town owns them and doesn't plan to develop them. Kids camp over there sometimes."

"How about grown-ups?" Patrick elbowed me.

"Not often," I answered. "We're going to drive past Pocket Cove Beach, a small, stony beach open to the public, and then we'll pass the town wharf and several private wharves, ending up on the other side of the harbor with the yacht club. It's closed this time of year. Recreational sailors put their boats in dry dock for the winter, but a few fishermen work all year-round. You'll see Christmas trees and lights on some today. At dusk this afternoon the lobstermen and fishermen will circle the harbor in their boats, in a parade to welcome Santa Claus, whose boat will come from the other side of Second Sister Island and take him to the town dock. He'll have several elves with him, and a moose."

"A real moose?" Blaze asked, finally showing some interest.

"No, someone dressed up as a moose. Sometimes Frosty the Snowman and Rudolph and Jack Frost are also with him." I smiled. "Santa will walk up to the Town Hall, on the Green, accompanied by the Haven Harbor High School band and representatives of local groups—Scouts, 4-H, the YMCA, and so forth. There'll be a Carol Sing on the Green, and children can have their pictures taken with Santa."

We were already down the hill, passing Pocket Cove Beach, and were beginning to see groups of people walking through the streets. Most smiled, and some waved. Seth waved his Santa hat at them, and Skye and Blaze waved back.

The car of photographers following us hadn't disappeared.

"Seth, after we go around the harbor, why don't you cut

up to go around the Green and then head back to Main Street. I'm not sure where you can park downtown."

"What about in the parking lot behind my gallery?" suggested Patrick. "It's sheltered."

"Don't want to leave the horses alone," Seth pointed out.

"Maybe Patrick can open the gallery so you can stay warm inside there and watch them?" I suggested.

"Sure. Can do," said Patrick.

Thomas took another swig from his flask and passed it around. This time Marie sipped from it, too, despite her clear disapproval.

"It's a charming little town," said Marie as we passed the wharves, where several fishermen were decorating their boats. "You've been telling us the official history. But what about the stories? Mrs. Clifford told me there might even be a ghost at Aurora."

Skye didn't answer immediately, so I did. "No ghosts. Although a young woman was murdered there in 1970. Any town this old has seen a lot."

"What a terrific set this would make for a movie," Marv said as we left the Harbor waterfront and headed for the town Green, ringed with Christmas trees and old houses wreathed and lit for the holidays. The Congregational Church, where Reverend Tom ministered, was a classic New England design with a center aisle, clear glass windows, and a steeple at the end of the Green farthest from the Harbor.

"That's my house," I volunteered, pointing it out as we passed.

"Who's that on your porch?" Patrick asked.

"Darn. That's Carly Tremont," I said. "She's in town for the holidays. She's a major fan of your mother's—has seen every movie she's been in, she says—and she commissioned a large order from Mainely Needlepoint. She's stopped to see me a couple of times."

What did Carly want now?

"Seth, stop! I want to meet her," Skye said, to my surprise. "It will make a great picture for the media. Famous actress meets fan." Seth pulled up the horses just past my house and Skye climbed out of the wagon and headed for my porch, waving to the photographers following us.

Chapter 32

*"May I govern my passions with absolute sway
And grow wiser and better as life wears away."*

—Eliza Ann Cummings of Plymouth,
New Hampshire, stitched this verse on her
sampler when she was fifteen. She
surrounded her words and alphabets with
embroidered wildflowers. Eliza married,
moved to Vermont, had one child, and lived
to be eighty-three.

I climbed down after Skye, considerably less gracefully than
she had. Carly might be a pain, but she was a good customer,
and I didn't want her to be a nuisance to Skye.

Carly watched in amazement as Skye headed for my
house.

So did the photographers who'd stopped their cars and
followed Skye.

"Hello," said Skye, putting out her hand. "I'm Skye West. Angie tells me you enjoy my movies."

Carly looked as though she'd faint at any moment. "I *love* your movies. I don't believe I'm actually talking to you! This is a dream come true!"

"I was passing by with some friends, and Angie mentioned you were a big fan, and I was inspired to jump off and meet you."

"I can't believe this. I don't." Carly dug out her phone. "Please, Angie, would you take a picture of Ms. West and I? My hands are shaking too much right now. I'm so excited!"

I snapped a couple of pictures of them together.

Skye was doing a great job of being utterly charming. "I understand you're from Texas, Carly. I have good memories of Texas. One of my earliest movies was filmed in Houston. What brings you to Maine this Christmas season?"

"I wanted to see a white Christmas, and then I read that you owned a home here, and I decided Haven Harbor was the place to come. It must be meant! I never dreamed we'd meet!"

"You're in town by yourself, Carly?"

"I am. Staying in one of the B and Bs in the harbor."

"No one should be alone for the holidays. I'm having a little dinner for a few friends Christmas Eve at six at my home. I'd love for you to join us if you're free."

"Me? To your house? Christmas Eve?" Carly started to cry. "I'd be thrilled!"

"Then I'll count on seeing you there," said Skye, turning toward the wagon. "Angie can give you directions."

Carly looked as though she was in shock. "This is the best Christmas present ever. And you don't have to give me directions, Angie. I know where Ms. West lives."

"See you in a couple of days, then," I told her. "Were you looking for me?"

"It was nothing important. I hardly remember why I came here. I can't believe it!"

I handed her phone back to her.

"I can't wait to look at those pictures and post one on Facebook! My friends in Texas will never believe this!"

"I'm glad," I said, heading back to the wagon and waving. "See you Christmas Eve!"

"Look at all these old houses," Thomas was saying as Patrick helped me back into the wagon. "I'll bet they've been here a hundred years."

"Some more than that," I said. "My house was built in 1809."

"When did you buy it?"

I tried not to laugh. "I was born in Haven Harbor. My house hasn't been out of my family since it was built." I gestured toward the other houses around the Green. "A lot of these homes are owned by the original families."

"They must all have stories connected with them," put in Marie. "Secrets."

"I suppose so," I agreed. "Everyone has secrets. Every town is full of them. And, you're right. These houses have seen a lot over the years."

Marv and Thomas had pulled out cameras and started taking pictures.

Why not? Haven Harbor was a scenic village.

"Seth's going to take the wagon downtown. We'll have an hour or so before dusk so you can check out Main Street. There's a great bookstore there, and a patisserie. I'd especially recommend From Here and There, an antique shop owned by my friend Sarah. Several stores sell souvenirs of

Maine, or heavy sweatshirts or sweaters." I glanced at Blaze. "Hubbel Clothing has warm clothes and boots, too."

"This would be a perfect location for a film," Marv interrupted me as he snapped away. "Maine. Dark secrets behind wreathed doors."

"What do you think, Marie?" Tom asked.

"I love it! Remember how successful all the Stephen King movies are. People love Maine! And wasn't *Peyton Place* set here?"

"It was filmed in Camden," I said. Were they kidding? Was this serious?

"A remake!" said Marv. "Bring the story up to date. More sex, more violence, and a more diverse cast." He looked at me. "How diverse is Maine?"

"More diverse than it used to be," I said honestly. "We've welcomed refugees from all over the world, and people have moved to Maine from other parts of the United States. It's always been a place that respected individuals. People who lived life a little differently."

"Perfect!" said Thomas. "As usual, a brilliant idea, Marv. I'm going to start taking notes and pictures as we walk around town. We wouldn't have to bring a lot of cast members. Just the crew and major actors. We could hire local people as extras."

"I'm not sure that's a good idea," Skye put in, as the wagon circled the Green and headed for Main Street. "It would interrupt the town. Besides—we still need to figure out a new ending for the film we're working on now."

"We will, Skye, don't worry. But you told us what a perfect place this was. I'll admit I doubted it. But now I'm sure—it's a perfect place for a movie!" Thomas pulled out a small notebook and a pencil.

Were they serious? The Chamber of Commerce would no doubt be delighted. Filming here would bring money and fame to our little town.

Money and jobs, even temporary ones, would be important. But fame?

I had a feeling Haven Harbor would be divided about that prospect.

All afternoon, no one had mentioned Paul Carmichael's death.

If he'd been a friend or colleague of mine, I wouldn't have been able to forget what happened so easily.

Were these people acting? Or didn't they care?

I sighed as the wagon negotiated narrow Main Street, where sidewalks were filled with holiday shoppers carrying bags, taking pictures, and waiting for Santa to arrive.

Patrick squeezed my hand. "One day at a time, Angie. Don't worry. Just take one day at a time."

A minute later Sergeant Pete Lambert stood in the middle of the street and stopped our wagon from continuing down Main Street.

Chapter 33

*"Joy and gladness banish sighs
Perfect love dispel our fears
And forever from our eyes
God shall wipe away our tears."*

—Mary McClave completed her sampler on
  Christmas Eve of 1835. She was fifteen.
  Her work was surrounded on three sides with a
  framework of vines and flowers, and, at the
  bottom, a rural scene with houses near a river
  and tall trees. She used very long satin stitches,
  adding luminescence to her work.

"Stop right there!" Sergeant Pete Lambert called as Seth
tried more or less successfully to slow his horses. Pete
walked over to us, shaking his head. "This is no place for a
hay wagon and horses, Seth. Too many people are on the
sidewalks and in the streets for the celebration. Not to

mention that the parade'll be coming along here soon, and we don't need horse shit on the road."

"Sorry, Pete. I didn't think."

"I guess not. When I saw you I thought the parade had started early."

"Where should I go, then?"

Pete scratched his head. "There may be space on Water Street, by the town wharf. A few of the groups in the parade are already gathering there."

I stood up. "Who's in charge of the parade this year, Pete?"

"Hi, Angie. Didn't expect to see you up there," he called back. "Chamber of Commerce puts on the whole shebang. This year Ed Campbell's organized it."

Two children, a boy and a girl, ran out into the street and started petting the stopped horses.

"Hey, kids, this is no place to be. Main Street's no petting zoo." Pete tried to shoo them away, but they didn't pay attention to anything but the horses.

"Do you know where Ed is now?" I asked.

"Last time I saw him he was down by the town wharf with a clipboard."

I nodded. "Okay. Let's head for Water Street."

"Slow the whole way," he cautioned. "Kids, get back to the sidewalk!" He waved the children away from the horses. "Just get off Main Street, Seth!"

"Will do," said Seth, winking at me.

The horses were glad to be on the move again. Seth guided them through a narrow side street from Main Street down to the harbor.

Shoppers moved to the side of the street as we went by.

Some smiled and waved when they saw the wreaths and red bows.

"See what a friendly place this is?" Marv said. "It would be perfect as a movie set."

"But . . . *Peyton Place*? Isn't that old-fashioned?" Blaze asked.

"Didn't someone say there was a murder at Aurora back in 1970?" said Thomas. "Maybe we could use that as a basis for a movie. "Dead teenager, townspeople divided . . ."

"Don't even think about it," said Skye. "Nothing related to Aurora. That's definite."

Seth pulled the wagon into a line of spaces reserved for yacht club members. Marie and Patrick stood, looking over the dark blue harbor at the fishing boats with white twinkling lights in their rigging. It would be dark enough for the parade of boats in about an hour. Then Santa would arrive and the parade through the town would begin.

Blaze started to get off the wagon.

"Hold it, everyone!" I instructed.

"You said we could go shopping," said Blaze.

"You can. But first let me check with the head of the local Chamber of Commerce to make sure we can leave the horse and wagon here." It was a little fib. I didn't know if my idea would work. But I'd seen Ed Campbell, Chairman of the Haven Harbor Chamber of Commerce, and, according to his television ads, king of the local used car dealerships, talking to someone near the town wharf.

That's where I was headed.

"Ed!" I said when I got close enough. "Guess what Skye West brought to add to the parade!"

He looked up from the clipboard he was holding. "What?

Oh, it's you, Angie." He looked beyond me. "And what is *that*?"

"That's Seth Harlow's hay wagon, decorated for the holidays. Skye West asked him to do it to entertain some of the Hollywood celebrities she's hosting this Christmas. Maybe you could use it in the parade."

"Celebrities?" he asked.

I'd dealt with Ed Campbell before. He was in favor of any publicity for Haven Harbor, good or bad. And, of course, the best publicity was for Ed Campbell himself.

"Heard you were all palsy with Skye West and her son. Patrick, that's his name. Owns the old Ted Lawrence art gallery now. Made a point of meeting him when he opened up a couple of months ago. Seemed a reasonable enough fellow." Ed was now being his most charming.

"He is. And so is his mother. Skye's here. And Marv Mason, the famous Oscar-winning director, and screenwriters Thomas and Marie O'Day. And you've heard of Blaze Buchanan?"

"Can't say as I have," he said. I'd turned and was heading back to the wagon. Ed came with me.

"I'm sure you'll recognize her," I said. "She's been in a lot of big films recently."

Maybe she had been. I wasn't sure. But I figured Ed would believe that when he saw her. "I was wondering whether you'd like the wagon to take Santa and his elves and the moose from the dock up to the Town Hall? There'd be room for Cub Scouts and Brownies, too." I'd seen several children wearing uniforms under their warm jackets.

"Great idea," he said. "Hi, Seth!"

Seth nodded down at him.

"Seth, you know Ed Campbell. He's an important person around here." I could feel Ed puffing up next to me. "Head of the Chamber of Commerce. He was wondering whether you and the horses would mind being a part of the parade? Maybe take Santa from the wharf to the Town Hall. Everyone lining the streets could see Santa and his friends better if they were on your wagon."

"High school band going to play, Ed?" asked Seth.

"Sure is."

"My horses aren't fond of music."

"What if the band was a couple of blocks ahead of the wagon?" Ed looked at his clipboard again. "We could put the fire department and the cheerleaders and the Lions Club between you and the band. Maybe even the YMCA—they have a float."

"That would work," Seth agreed. "Wicked smart idea, having the wagon in the parade. Never been in a parade myself."

I gestured that everyone should get off the wagon. "You two can work that out, Seth. We'll meet you and the wagon at the Town Hall after the parade so you can take us back to Aurora."

"Sure thing, Angie!"

"Ed, I'd like you to meet Skye West. You know she bought the old Gardener place."

"Aurora. Of course. Pleased to meet you," said Ed. "I've had the pleasure of welcoming your son to town already. Merry Christmas, Patrick."

"And these are their guests for the holidays," I said, introducing Blaze, Marv, Thomas, and Marie. "I'm afraid some photographers have been following us all day. I hope you won't mind if they take your picture."

Two of the photographers who'd been following us in their car had parked and were stealthily approaching us from the other side of the street. I waved at them, and they came over at once. "You might want a picture of Skye and her friends here at the harbor, talking to the head of the Chamber of Commerce."

They were more excited about taking pictures of Skye and Blaze than of Ed, but they took advantage of the invitation.

"You know, Ed, I'm glad we got a chance to meet," I heard Marv saying as the photographers snapped their pictures. "Just now we were all talking about the possibility of making a film here in Haven Harbor."

"Here? A movie?" said Ed. "Seriously?"

"Such handsome old homes and a beautiful harbor. Of course, we'd need your permission, and we'd want to hire a few local people as extras." Marv put his arm around Ed and they headed back to the town wharf. Marv was a politician, too.

"Everyone? The parade of lights on the harbor will start in a little under an hour, and then Santa will arrive. Make yourselves at home in town. We'll meet Seth at the Town Hall after the parade. You can't miss it. Everyone in town will be walking there for the Carol Sing and pictures with Santa." I grabbed Patrick's hand and pulled him away from the others. "Let's get out of here. The Harbor Haunts will be packed, but if her store isn't busy Sarah could make us some instant cocoa. I'm frozen. And tired of talking!"

"Lead on," Patrick agreed. "This crew can find their way around town. As you pointed out on your tour, it's a small town."

We headed back toward Main Street, leaving the others taking pictures at the harbor.

"Are they serious about making a movie in Haven Harbor?" I asked.

Patrick shrugged. "No way to know. Lots of ideas for

movies die early. They'd have to have at least a storyboard, if not a full script, and then find backers. It's nothing to be worried about now."

But what if they were serious? When would it be time to get worried?

Paul was killed in Haven Harbor two days ago. How could his friends already be excited about a new movie?

Chapter 34

Sarah had large urns of coffee and hot water plugged in and
ready to serve customers (or friends, in our case) with
coffee, tea, or cocoa if they wanted a break from Christmas
shopping. Or, better still, to sip while shopping in her shop.

She looked surprised when Patrick and I walked in.
"What's the latest on the murder?" she whispered to me.

"No updates. Last I heard the police thought the shooter could have been an out-of-season hunter with a bad aim."

She shook her head. "'In this short life That only lasts an hour, How much—how little—is Within our power.'"

"Emily?"

She nodded.

"If Paul was killed by a hunter, that would mean no one at Aurora would be arrested for murder," I pointed out.

"You're right. That would be good. By the way, last night I finished needlepointing the pillow."

Patrick and I helped ourselves to cups of cocoa (me) and coffee (Patrick).

"I can't take it now," I said. "Everyone from Aurora is downtown for the parade, and we have to meet to go back to Aurora together. I'm going to collect the other pillows tomorrow morning. I'll stop for yours then."

"It'll be right here, behind the counter," Sarah said.

"How're sales?" Patrick said softly, so the couple checking out Sarah's selection of antique iron banks wouldn't hear him.

"I'm not making enough to take a buying trip to Paris," she answered, "but not bad. I was smart to buy that collection of needleworking tools. They're walking out of the store for holiday gifts. And I sold my whole Schoenhut Circus yesterday."

Patrick and I exchanged glances. "What's a Schoenhut Circus?" he asked.

"An elaborate set of wooden animals, clowns, and other figures, all hand-colored, with movable limbs. They look like folk art, but they were toys manufactured at the beginning of the twentieth century. I had several dozen figures in inventory, but kept hoping to find more pieces, or an authentic tent, so I didn't have them displayed. But a collector stopped in and asked if I had any, and I was happy to unpack mine. He bought every piece I had, including wooden stands for the animals and the dumbbells for the clowns. It was a good sale. This time of year sales are especially important so I have cash to buy more inventory for next summer. And speaking of the end of the year . . . did Angie ask you about what to wear Christmas Eve?"

"She didn't," Patrick answered, nudging me.

I threw up my hands. "Sorry, Sarah. I forgot."

"So I'll ask. How dressy will the party be?"

"Mom likes to celebrate. The men will be wearing dark suits, I assume, probably with red ties. Men are predictable. Mom'll wear something fancy—but not an Oscar dress. Short cocktail should do it."

I groaned.

"Is that a problem?" Patrick asked.

"It's fine," I said. "No problem." Except that I had absolutely nothing in my closet that remotely said "cocktail dress."

One more challenge to be figured out in the next forty-eight hours. Thank goodness Sarah had asked, or I would have shown up woefully underdressed.

I made a mental note to warn Dave and Ruth about the dress code. Dave probably had a suit. But did Ruth have something dressy? I hoped so.

We dropped our empty paper cups in Sarah's waste-basket. "Now we're going to the harbor to see the parade of lights," I explained.

"Enjoy! I've seen it several years, so I'll be hanging here," said Sarah. "Who knows? Other people might want to get warm and come in and find their dream Christmas gift!"

"It's Patrick's first Christmas in town, so we're doing the

whole festival. I doubt if they have lobster boat parades in Los Angeles," I said, taking his arm.

"Good guess. I'm looking forward to this," said Patrick.

"And it's my first Christmas back home. From what I've heard, the Christmas Cheer festival is more elaborate now than it used to be."

Sarah laughed. "The world is, Angie. You guys have fun! And I'll see you tomorrow morning, Angie—and you on Christmas Eve, Patrick!"

Patrick and I followed the crowd down to the Harbor. Several people waved at us and we waved back. Everyone in town seemed to be there, smiling with holiday spirit. Boats lining up across the harbor for the parade appeared and disappeared in lightly falling snow.

"It's magical," said Patrick. "Like a movie."

I grimaced, and then smiled and took his arm, just in time for the official celebration to begin.

The Haven Harbor High School band played "Jingle Bells" and "White Christmas" while the high school chorus sang until the crowd joined in. A dozen fishing and lobster boats circled the harbor. The Christmas lights on their decks and rigging, and Christmas trees on their decks sparkled. I spotted Alice and Arvin in their *Little Lady* and pointed them out to Patrick.

As the parade of seasonally lit boats passed the town wharf, those on board waved at their friends and other on-lookers snuggled in warm hats, boots, scarves, gloves, and fleece or down jackets along the waterfront.

A cheer went up when the band switched to "Santa Claus Is Coming to Town" and the *Emma Marie,* which in summer months took tourists on day trips, appeared from where it had been hiding, behind Second Sister Island. Santa Claus waved from the deck as the boat approached the town dock.

Next to us, a little girl in braids and a red stocking hat jumped up and down, chanting "Santa! Santa!" as the vessel docked, and Santa and his costumed friends (elves, Frosty, the usual Moose, and, new to me, Santa Claws, a large lobster) disembarked and made their way up the ramp to where Seth's wagon was waiting.

Patrick squeezed my hand in delight. "Does Santa Claus always arrive by boat on the coast of Maine?"

"In a lot of towns," I agreed. "But he arrives by train in some towns—and by helicopter at several lighthouses."

"Helicopter?"

"Years ago, when lighthouse families were isolated in winter, their lights were navigation points for small planes, and pilots and lighthouse keepers became friends. In 1929 a pilot from Rockland decided to drop gifts and candies for the children in the lighthouses he passed. After that he made it a yearly event, visiting more lighthouses. People called him the 'flying Santa.'"

"Didn't you say on our tour that no one lived in the light-houses now? That they were all automated?"

"True. But the tradition continues in some places. The man who began it all died years ago, but other pilots continue the tradition. Santa's helicopter lands near a lighthouse, and he gives candy and sometimes small toys to local children on the peninsulas or islands. The tradition's even spread to other states. Flying Santas deliver candy to lighthouses as far south as Long Island in New York."

Patrick grinned. "So many things to learn about Maine."

Santa and his friends climbed onto Seth's wagon, along with the thrilled children Ed had recruited to accompany them. The band led the way, followed by what seemed like half the residents of Haven Harbor, from the high school and middle school cheerleaders to the library staff to representatives of various service clubs. The other half of Haven Harbor's population stood on the sidewalks and clapped or waved.

I should pull a float together next year for the Mainely Needlepointers, I thought, as Patrick and I stomped our feet in the cold and cheered for all the participants, from the Pumpkin Patch Day Care Center to the Haven Harbor Hospital Auxiliary to the float of senior citizens from the local assisted living center.

I waved at Gram and Reverend Tom, who were walking with the Congregational Church Choir that would lead the Carol Sing at the Town Hall.

We stayed until the end of the parade. A couple of times I looked around for the others from Aurora, but didn't see them. When all the floats and marchers had passed, Patrick and I joined the crowd heading up the hill to where a large tree-shaped stack of lobster traps lit with white lights was in the center of the Haven Harbor Town Hall lawn.

When I was a child the tree had been made of wooden traps. Now wooden traps were "vintage," as Sarah would put it. Summer visitors bought them, covered them with glass tops, and used them as coffee tables in summer cottages. Traps used by lobstermen today—and the tree in front of the Town Hall—were made of stainless steel. They were lighter to haul and lasted longer than the traditional wooden ones.

The trap tree had been a part of Haven Harbor's Christmas for as long as I remembered.

Ahead of us the choir and the high school chorus were singing "We Wish You a Merry Christmas."

I reached up to kiss Patrick's cheek.

Haven Harbor was a wonderful place to live. How could I ever have left?

And despite a few issues, it was December 22, and everything would work out perfectly.

How could it not? Patrick was right. It was magic.

Chapter 35

"A garland of flowrets so gay
The works of the God of all truth
I have wrought with attempt to display
While in the blest sunshine of youth."

—Words stitched in the center of a wreath
 of flowers by Ann Ward of "Washington
 City," in 1826, in silk on linen. Ann
 was the daughter of Irish immigrants
 who operated a dry goods store on
 Pennsylvania Avenue. She married
 Joseph Little Peabody, another dry goods
 store owner, in 1834.

Patrick began scanning the crowd for his mother and her
guests as we waited for Santa to address his followers and
the community Carol Sing to begin.

 "Over there," he said, pointing toward a group of people

standing slightly apart from the rest of the crowd. "Let's join them."

I followed, reluctantly. I'd hoped to spend a little more time with Patrick.

But as we approached the group, I realized the men and women surrounding Skye and Blaze weren't waiting for the town sing to begin. They were asking for autographs and posing for selfies with the actresses. Carly Tremont was one of those in the crowd. That woman seemed to be everywhere! But where else would she be but at the festival? And now that Skye had invited her to the Christmas Eve party at Aurora, we'd be seeing her again at least once more this week.

Skye'd often said she was a private person, but she'd been the one who'd decided to come to a public event where she was sure to be recognized. I remembered dreaming of Kate Winslet and Leonardo DiCaprio after Gram bought me the VHS tape of *Titanic*. I watched it a dozen times when I was a young teenager. It was the most romantic and tragic story I'd ever seen. If Kate or Leonardo had come to Haven Harbor, I would have the first in line to meet them. A rolled-up *Titanic* poster was still in the back of my bedroom closet.

On the other hand, most of those talking to Skye and Blaze weren't teenagers.

The photographers who'd been following the Hollywood group had withdrawn to the other side of the street. They'd taken dozens—maybe hundreds—of photos today, and Haven Harbor autograph-seekers weren't subjects that would interest editors.

Luckily, Skye and Blaze didn't seem to be objecting.

The fans were ignoring Thomas and Marie. . . . Who would recognize a screenwriter? They were standing to the side, conspicuously bored with the scene.

Another group of Haven Harbor residents was surrounding Marv Mason, some of them pushing their children or teenagers forward. I recognized some of the families from church and others from around town, although none were close friends. Ed Campbell was with Marv, taking notes, as the director spoke with individuals and photographed some of them.

I had a sinking feeling. "What's that all about?" I asked Patrick.

He shrugged. "I'm guessing Marv's collecting names of potential extras for the movie he's dreaming of setting here. That'll start people buzzing. He likes buzz. And so do the producers he'll be looking for to fund the production."

"Can't you stop them?"

"Me?" asked Patrick. "No way. You're the one who introduced Marv to that Chamber of Commerce guy."

I had nothing to do with Marv's screenplay fantasies—or Ed's dreams of bringing the world to Haven Harbor and (maybe) selling them all cars. They were both taking advantage of each other and of people in town. Why get people excited about something that would never happen?

Luckily, at the moment I was about to interrupt the fan group to talk with Skye, the chorus and choir began to sing "We Wish You a Merry Christmas." Skye took Blaze's arm and they headed toward Seth's hay wagon behind the Town Hall. Marv and the other Aurora guests followed her, and so did Patrick and I.

It was cold, it was snowing, and Skye and her guests had gotten a peek at Haven Harbor.

If my car hadn't been at Aurora, I would have gone home now. Only one more day before Christmas Eve. I still had Christmas elf chores to do.

Plus, Trixi would be missing me.

I snuggled next to Patrick as we sat in the corner of the wagon and headed back to Aurora. Haven Harbor was at its Christmas best. Lights were bright, candles and wreaths shone from windows, and snow was gently falling in the glow of street lamps designed to look like gaslights.

No one said much, although Skye mentioned they could watch the town fireworks from Aurora later. Everyone except Blaze was smiling and relaxed as we headed out of town. Blaze was shivering. I hoped she'd bought herself some warmer clothes; she'd retrieved three shopping bags that she or Seth had put in the wagon.

Paul's death hadn't been mentioned all afternoon, and I wouldn't bc the one to bring it up.

As the snowflakes swirled, I leaned on Patrick's shoulder and wished I didn't have to go home alone.

No one should be alone on Christmas. But I wouldn't be. Tomorrow was the twenty-third, and the twenty-fourth was Skye's dinner party, and I still planned to spend Christmas Day with Gram and Reverend Tom.

When I'd returned to Haven Harbor in May I promised Gram I'd stay for six months. It had already been seven.

For better or worse, Haven Harbor, Maine, was again my home.

At least for any future I could imagine tonight.

Chapter 36

"In the bloom of youth no ornament is so lovely as that of virtue, nor any employment equal to those of which we partake in fully resigning ourselves to the divine will."

—In about 1820 Sidney Fitz Randolphs (a twelve-year-old boy in Virginia) made this sampler that included five alphabets. In small schools and orphan asylums, boys as well as girls were taught needlework.

I left Thomas O'Day adding wood to Aurora's living room fireplace and Marie and Marv asking Skye questions about the history of her home. She'd said she didn't want them writing about the death of her friend. But she was answering questions.

Sarah had texted me; she'd found a dress she hoped would be perfect for me to wear Christmas Eve. Plus, she had cookies ready to taste. (When had she found the time to bake those?)

I texted back that I was on my way.

Patrick's hug and whispered, "I'll miss you," made me hesitate. But I was going to see him the next day. I wanted to make sure I was ready for both Christmas Eve and Christmas Day.

My phone buzzed twice on my way to Sarah's apartment. Whoever was trying to reach me could wait. I was tired and cold and the roads were slippery. Ahead of me, a car with a North Carolina license plate skidded across two lanes. Someone visiting for the holidays wasn't used to driving in vintery weather. Luckily, I was able to steer around them.

I parked behind the building that held Sarah's shop and apartment, and knocked on her door.

Inside, smells of pine, from her Christmas tree, and cinnamon and vanilla, from her kitchen, greeted me as warmly as Sarah's smile.

"Glad you could come so quickly," she said, handing me a glass of bright red Danish cherry wine.

I dropped my coat on a chair near her door. "Brr! That wine looks delicious!"

"It's sweeter than the wines we usually drink," she admitted, "but it looked so much like Christmas I couldn't resist it."

"Your apartment smells amazing."

"Cookies," she nodded.

"But I saw you two hours ago in your shop!"

"Mixed them up this morning and put the dough in the refrigerator. All I had to do was preheat the oven and put the cookies on a cookie sheet. Presto!" She pointed at two cooling racks, one covered with oatmeal cookies and one with sugar cookies decorated with red sprinkles. "But if you're like me, you're ready for some real food first. I sliced some pepperoni and mozzarella for sandwiches. Okay?"

"Yum," I answered. "How do you make those?"

"Easy. Sip and watch," she instructed. She turned her oven to broil, split two baguettes ("from the patisserie"), and put them under the broiler to toast. After they were slightly browned, she spread a thin layer of tomato sauce on each one, covered them with layers of thinly sliced onions, pepperoni, and mozzarella, and put everything back under the broiler for a few minutes. What emerged were two deliciously spicy sandwiches.

"Wow," I said, taking a second bite of mine. "You've added a recipe to my limited list of easy dinners."

"Glad you like it. Fast, easy, and filling."

I nodded, taking another bite. "Delicious," I managed to say.

"Save a little room," Sarah counseled. "With only two days until Christmas, we should have a few cookies. Just to make sure they're edible." She winked.

"I agree. A cookie tasting seems in order."

My phone hummed again. I dug the phone out of my pocketbook. "Excuse me—I got a couple of texts on my way here and forgot to check them." I sighed as I saw the first message. "Remember Carly Tremont?"

"The woman who wanted needlepointed chair seats?"

"Right. Today I introduced her to Skye West, to her great delight. And, believe it or not, Skye invited her to the Christmas Eve dinner. Carly's sent me two texts," I said, looking at my phone. "First, thanking me for the introduction, and then wanting to know what she should wear. I haven't even figured that out."

"Tell her short cocktail attire," Sarah advised. "Wait until you see what I've come up with for us to wear!"

I dutifully texted Carly back. "She's been a pain," I added to Sarah.

"'Fame is the one that does not stay,'" said Sarah. "Skye's being kind to her to help protect her fan base."

"Maybe," I agreed. "And it will be a big order if she likes the designs I come up with. I wouldn't be as bothered if it weren't Christmas week—or she didn't keep asking me about Skye."

"She'll love your designs," Sarah assured me. "Let me make a plate of cookies while you take care of your messages."

The next text was from Pete: ME says Carmichael shot with handgun.

"Darn," I said out loud, answering him with an OK.

"What?" Sarah asked, putting a generous plate of cookies on the coffee table between us.

"Pete Lambert says Paul Carmichael was shot with a handgun."

She looked at me. "And that means?"

"It means he wasn't shot accidentally by a hunter. It means he was murdered."

The cookies were delicious, but after that news I couldn't focus on eating. After a few minutes Sarah pulled out the dresses she'd found for us in the wardrobe she kept of vintage clothing.

The long-sleeved, V-necked silver sheath from the sixties she'd chosen for herself was extra short ("it's a mini," she explained) and sparkly. It fit her as though it had been designed for her. Like me, Sarah usually wore jeans. I'd never noticed her legs were spectacular. They were, and the dress she'd chosen showed them off.

"Wow!" I said. "You'll outshine the Christmas tree. In a positive way! And that silver makes your hair shine!"

Sarah was the only one in Haven Harbor who had white hair highlighted with pink and blue streaks.

"I wish I had silver heels," she said, turning around so I could see the back of the dress. Her exit would be as form-fitting as her entrance. "But I have a pair of black high-heeled sandals I can get away with."

"Which you'll carry. You're wearing boots to Aurora, right?"

"Of course! In this snow? Bean boots, a silver cocktail dress, and a vintage mink coat. I'm a Mainer now!" she assured me.

Mainers would agree about the boots, but I doubted many had dresses like the one Sarah had found. Or minks of any vintage. "And you said you had something I could wear?"

"I hope so," she said, reaching into the wardrobe. "If you like this, try it on and we'll see."

Sarah held up a sleeveless red velvet dress with a fitted top and flirty skirt that would fall below my knees. I touched it gently. "So soft," I said. "It's a perfect Christmas dress. And so different from yours!"

"We don't want to look like twins. This one is from the nineteen fifties. You like it?"

"Love it," I said, removing my boots and peeling off my jeans to try it on. "I hope it fits."

I liked that it was longer than Sarah's; my legs weren't as thin as hers. And I loved how it showed off my shoulders.

Sarah had guessed my size perfectly.

"The darts could come in a little at the bust and waist," she said critically. "Shall I stitch them for you?"

"You do dressmaking as well as needlepoint?" I asked, surprised.

"Not really. But I've done some adjusting over the years, and I have a sewing machine."

"Then I trust you," I agreed. "I'll be wearing black shoes, too. But mine will be flats. It's been years since I wore heels."

"We'll both look terrific," Sarah said, looking at both of us in the full-length mirror in her bedroom. "That young actress—Blaze? She'll have nothing on us."

Blaze. What would she wear? And how would she and everyone else at Aurora be feeling after they officially found out Paul had been murdered? Would Skye cancel the dinner?

I twirled in the mirror.

I hoped not. Selfishly, I wanted Patrick to see me in this dress.

Although I felt guilty, thinking about dresses when I should be thinking about who murdered Paul.

I twirled again. "Can I pick the dress up from you when I stop for your needlepoint pillow tomorrow?"

"Absolutely. My sewing machine is downstairs in the shop, behind the counter, so I can use it while I'm waiting for customers. I'll have the dress ready for you by noon or before. What are your plans for tomorrow?"

I thought of Pete's message. "I have to pick up all the pillows," I said, "and deliver them to Aurora." And check on what was happening there.

Chapter 37

"Let spotless Innocence and Truth
My every Action Guide
My Unexperienced Youth
From Vanity and Pride."

—Ruth Smith of Bristol, Rhode Island,
    made this sampler in 1799. She
    included a large house with five dogs
    playing outside and a floral border.

Trixi didn't come running when I opened my door. I turned
on the Christmas tree lights and candles in the windows, assuming she was asleep somewhere. Then I heard a loud
squeak coming from the Christmas tree.

"Trixi?" I asked. I didn't see her, but that squeak was
definitely from my cat. "Trixi? Where are you?"

"Squeak!" was the slightly louder response. Why didn't
Trixi meow, like other cats? The sound had come from the
tree. I turned on all the lights in the room and searched

the branches. Trixi had knocked several balls off the tree. Luckily, they hadn't broken.

"Squeak!" This time it was more demanding. I went through the branches again, one at a time. And . . . there she was. Next to the trunk, near the top of the tree, beneath my foil star.

I reached in through the branches and picked her up. She was shaking a little, and immediately cuddled into my hands. How long had she been up in that tree? Hadn't she known how to climb down? I felt guilty as I stroked her. How scared had she been? Had she nibbled pine needles or anything else she shouldn't have? Should I call the vet?

Trixi picked herself up, jumped off my lap, and headed for her (empty) food dish in the kitchen.

The speed at which she gobbled her dinner assured me that whatever her trauma, she'd survived it.

How did people manage to be responsible for children? I felt guilty trying to take care of a cat.

I thought of baking tonight. Sarah's cookies had been inspiring. Gram's had been delicious. No doubt Bev Clifford was baking up a storm at Aurora. I was probably the only person in Haven Harbor not making cookies.

But I was exhausted. This wasn't my year to make Christmas goodies.

I wrapped the last of my gifts—Patrick's pillow and a bottle of cognac I'd bought for Reverend Tom.

The house was chilly. Winters weren't easy for houses built in the early nineteenth century, before insulated walls. (Adding insulation to the attic and basement helped, but didn't solve the problem.) Luckily, Skye's home was warmer. I'd be able to manage a sleeveless dress there Christmas Eve.

In the meantime I turned my furnace up a little, pulled on

my comfiest flannel nightgown, and crawled under my quilts. It had been a long day. The town festival had been fun, dinner with Sarah was delicious, and she'd solved one of my problems—she'd found a great dress I could wear Christmas Eve.

Now I needed sleep.

I woke up when Trixi sat on my shoulder and repeatedly stroked my cheek with her paw. It was time for her breakfast. Groggily I got up, pulled on my bathrobe, and headed for the kitchen.

Fifteen minutes later her dish was empty again, coffee was brewing, and I was scrambling myself a couple of eggs.

I turned on the small television set in the kitchen. The Portland meteorologist was reminding his listeners (Reminding? Did I know to begin with?) that the winter storm making its way up the coast would be hitting Maine sometime in late afternoon. "Our first real nor'easter of the season," he happily informed his viewers. "Do your last-minute Christmas shopping early today, because hazardous road conditions and gusting winds will be the rule by sunset. Local electrical outages may result from falling branches, so check that your supplies of firewood and water are accessible. Keep tuned to Channel 7 for weather updates throughout the day."

Goodie. Gram and Reverend Tom had a generator in case of outages. I didn't have one, but I could bring in extra wood for the living room fireplace (the only one in the house that was lined and therefore safe to use), and if an outage lasted any length of time I could sleep on the couch at the rectory.

When I was fourteen we'd had an ice storm that knocked out power in Haven Harbor for almost two weeks and closed many of the roads. I shivered, remembering it. Gram and I had bundled up in practically everything we'd owned, piled on all our quilts and comforters, and both slept in her bed. We'd read books during the day (of course, without power or heat school was closed), and at night she'd told me stories about when she'd been young, living in a house across town, and then, as a newlywed, living in our house, before she and Grandpa had saved enough money for a furnace. They'd only had fireplaces and a space heater. I'd suspected that on winter days they'd done a lot of cuddling in their high double bed.

"Trixi, you and I may be cuddling up tonight," I informed her.

She didn't look impressed.

Dressed in my warmest lined jeans, plaid flannel shirt, wool sweater, and barn coat, I brought several armloads of wood in from the wood pile, leaving a trail of snow from the back door to the living room.

Trixi jumped at each bit she could see and shook herself when the pretty white flakes turned into water.

"Lucky for you you're an indoor cat," I reminded her.

She squeaked in answer and jumped up to her window perch to watch me fill the bird feeders and put out fresh suet. Nor'easters weren't fun for any creature.

Chores needed to be done. But I had to pick up the needlepointed pillows for Skye and then get to Aurora and find out what was happening there.

I hesitated, then filled an extra cereal bowl with dry food for Trixi and a second dish of water. "In case I'm delayed," I explained to her. She purred in understanding. Or maybe just in thanks.

It was later than I'd thought: after ten-thirty.

First, I called Ruth to tell her the dinner Christmas Eve

called for cocktail attire. She wasn't thrilled and muttered something about fitting into dresses at the back of her closet.

Then I called Dave and Ob. Their pillows were finished, and they were waiting for me. Then I checked with Sarah. The red dress was ready! (And her pillow, of course.)

What was happening at Aurora? I started for my car and then turned around. Someone at Skye's house had a handgun. Someone was a murderer. Based on what Patrick had said, I was sure he and his mother didn't have weapons.

Maybe I'm paranoid, I told myself. Or maybe just careful.

I got the Glock I kept in a drawer in my front hall. It was loaded. (Why have a gun that isn't loaded unless you have children around?)

I slipped it into my pocketbook, along with the foil-wrapped gingerbread people Gram had given me for Patrick. I'd forgotten to give them to him the day before.

It was Christmas. Time of joy, and peace, and happiness.

But it hadn't been for Paul Carmichael, and I didn't want anyone else to suffer the same fate.

I headed for Sarah's shop, and Dave's and Ob's homes, hoping Pete and Ethan had solved Paul's murder before I got to Aurora.

That would be a really Merry Christmas.

Chapter 38

"Large bags to place slippers in for parties, or to carry rubbers or waterproofed shoes to opera or theatre, are made of gray, brown or stone color, with a monogram embroidered, braided, or outlined in the center."

—From *The Hearthstone; or, Life At Home: A Household Manual* by Laura C. Holloway, Philadelphia: L.P. Miller & Co., 1888.

"A suit?" Dave sighed. "Sure. I've got one of those in the back of my closet. Had to get one a few years back when one of my students got married. I hope it still fits."

I suspected Dave's trim ex-Navy physique wouldn't present any wardrobe problems.

"Sarah's found the most wonderful vintage dresses for she and I to wear," I confided. "Wait until you see!"

"I'll look forward to being overcome with your elegance," said Dave. "But are you sure this gala is still on? The postmaster told me one of Skye West's guests died suddenly."

Not everyone in town followed entertainment news. But clearly word was getting around in Haven Harbor. I hesitated, and nodded. "True. But she hasn't said anything about canceling the dinner. Yesterday she even invited someone else to join us." I didn't mention that Paul hadn't just died; he'd been murdered. Why bother Dave with details? A close friend of his had been killed earlier this fall. Murder wasn't a topic he was comfortable with.

"Dinner may fall into the category of 'the show must go on,'" Dave said drily. "In any case, I postponed my plans in Boston, and here's the pillow she wanted. Although it's so small it's really more of a sachet." He handed me a paper grocery bag and I peeked inside.

"Looks perfect," I pronounced. "I'm going to deliver the pillows to Skye this morning so she has them to wrap before tomorrow. She already has a few packages under her tree." I glanced around. "Speaking of which—where's your tree?"

Dave shook his head. "No tree this year. It's me here, alone—and with a new kitten? Since I was going away for part of the holiday, I didn't want the hassle."

"Where *is* Trixi's brother?" I asked, realizing I hadn't seen him.

"Probably under a chair or behind the couch," Dave said. "He's not a very brave cat. Friendly enough to feel comfortable tangling the threads in my needlework stash, but not used to company. I don't have many guests. My neighbor's agreed to stop in and feed him and change the litter while I'm away. I suspect he'll never even see Snowy, although I'm sure the cat food will disappear."

"What will you do in Boston?" I asked.

"I planned to spend Christmas with an old Navy buddy and his family," said Dave. "I don't see him often. I don't like to leave my poison garden unless it's covered with snow.

Plus, between my teaching and his job, we're both tied up. Because of Skye's dinner I called and told him I'm staying here Christmas Eve. He was impressed that I was going to have dinner with such a famous actress. It'll take less than four hours to drive to his place Christmas Day. I should arrive in time for their dinner, which is fine. We'll spend a couple of days checking out the sights in Boston. I got us all tickets for a Celtics game, and we'll probably go to the aquarium. His daughter loves that place. I'll be back by the twenty-ninth . . . rotten fish and guests, right?"

"Right," I said, recognizing what was probably a quote, but not able to identify it. Skipping college meant I'd missed out on a few things. Usually nothing major. I picked up the bag. "I'd better get going. I still have to stop at Sarah's and then see Ob and Anna. See you tomorrow night!"

"Looking forward to ogling those dresses!" Dave winked and followed me to the door. "Make sure you get your errands done before the middle of the afternoon today. Storm that's coming in's supposed to be a doozy."

"I'll be careful!" I called back as I walked toward my car. "You, too!"

Sarah was busy showing a customer a Winslow Homer wood engraving of a woman (who wasn't even wearing a coat), her husband, and their son digging a path from their home in snow up to their shoulders. "It's called 'A Winter Morning—Shoveling Out,'" Sarah was explaining. "You can see the date—January of 1871. It was a newspaper illustration; this is the archivally matted and framed page from that newspaper. Homer's work from 1858 until 1874 was only published as newspaper illustrations, and this one is hard to find because it was published in *Every Saturday*, a newspaper with a small circulation."

"I love that the woman is throwing seeds or crumbs onto

the snow for the birds," her customer noted. "That's what I do when the snow is too deep to get to my feeders."

When Sarah saw me she nodded toward the back of her counter. I found the pillow she'd stitched, plus the red velvet dress, newly taken in and hung in a garment bag. I took both, gave her a thumbs-up, and left her to her customer.

I hung the dress in my car, resisting the temptation to touch the deep, soft fabric. It wasn't snowing yet, but clouds now covered the southern sky, and the scent of new snow was in the air. I needed to get to Captain's Ob's home and pick up the two pillows he and his wife had stitched.

His wife, Anna, answered the door. She was wearing an apron, and her hands and one spot on her face were white with flour. "Angie! Come on in."

"Baking, I see," I said, walking into her kitchen, warm from both her electric stove and her woodstove.

"It's that time of year. Without Josh the holidays won't be the same, so Ob and I decided we'd volunteer to help serve Christmas dinner at the Baptist Church. It'll get us out of the house, and not think about the past. Chicken soup's about finished." She gestured toward the woodstove, where a large pot was steaming. "Would you like a cup? You must be cold, and the soup's good and warm."

I was tempted. "No, thank you. I should get over to Aurora. I came to pick up the pillows."

"Right," she nodded. "Have to admit Ob helped me a little so we could make your deadline. My needlepointing's still on a learning curve. Let me get them."

She looked through several bags near their Christmas tree. No wrapped packages were under it.

"Your tree is lovely," I said. It was covered with ornaments like the ones on my tree—the kind made by a child. Josh, I assumed, years ago.

"We couldn't be without a tree," Anna said, returning and handing me a bag. "Josh loved Christmas so much." Her eyes filled and she looked away.

"Thank you for helping Patrick find a Christmas tree for Aurora, and for talking Seth into taking everyone on a wagon ride yesterday," I added. "I'll admit I was doubtful, but it turned out to be fun."

"I'm glad. I'll tell Ob. He's not in right now. He had errands to run," she said. "He said he'd get extra batteries and water before the storm. But we have plenty of batteries and water. I suspect he has some Christmas secrets. Although I can't imagine what they are, since we don't exchange gifts."

"Maybe he'll surprise you this year," I suggested.

She shrugged. "I've been watching all the doings across the street. Heard that actor, Paul Carmichael, died the other night. Sad thing to happen at Christmas."

Anna and Ob must not have heard he'd been murdered. "It's an awful thing to have hanging over the holidays."

"It is," she agreed. "And let's hope all those photographers and media trucks will disappear and leave Skye and her friends in peace." She bent toward me. "Do you know, two of those people came here and asked to use our bathroom? I told them to find facilities somewhere else. Skye and Patrick are good, quiet people, even if they are famous. I told those people they were wicked rude to stay outside Aurora, just watching. Then those men started asking questions about the Wests. Thank goodness Ob was here. He told them both exactly where they could go." Anna leaned toward me. "Let me tell you, he wasn't telling them to go back to their truck."

"I can imagine," I said, grinning at the thought of Captain Ob telling off the media folks.

"One question, though. That young actor who died—that was a couple of days ago, right?"

"Right," I agreed, heading for the back door.

"Then what was that ambulance doing over there about an hour ago?"

"What?" I asked, turning back to Anna. "What ambulance?"

"So you don't know, either. Hope no one's sick, or had an accident. That house's had more than its share of problems over the years."

"It has indeed," I agreed. "Thank you for the pillows! I really appreciate you and Ob taking the time to make them."

"Not a problem, dear," said Anna. "But you check on what's happening across the street. I hope nothing bad's happened to Skye or Patrick. Their year has been trouble enough."

Chapter 39

"One will find more pleasure in lunching out-of-doors if sandwiches, cream and sugar are covered. We suggest covers of rose-colored cotton with white beads suspended from each corner to prevent any chance breeze from playing pranks with them. Embroidered pink and blue flowers should be in the center of the cloth, and edges finished with white picot."

—From *The Modern Priscilla; Home Needlework and Everyday Housekeeping*, a monthly magazine, May 1918.

I pulled into the driveway at Aurora, grabbed the bags holding the pillows and the two gingerbread cookies, and rang the doorbell.

Thomas O'Day opened the door. "Angie! Glad you're here. Come on in."

I didn't waste any time asking my question. "I was across

the street," I said, "talking to one of the neighbors. She said an ambulance was here."

"Afraid so," he said. "May I take your coat? Or maybe you'll want to go on to the hospital. The medic or EMT or whoever was in the ambulance didn't seem to think it was serious, but Skye insisted."

"What wasn't serious? Insisted what?" I asked, glancing around as though whatever the answer was it would be right in front of me. I kept my coat on.

"Her son, Patrick. He ate some cookies and got dizzy and started throwing up." Thomas wrinkled his nose. "Probably overindulged, with the holidays and all. Or he's caught the flu. But he was having a lot of stomach pain, and Skye got worried." Thomas didn't look concerned. "You know how mothers are."

Actually, I didn't. My mother had disappeared when I was ten. "Is anyone else sick?" I asked.

"No, we're all fine," said Thomas. "The rest of us have been working on the screenplays. Marie came up with a great idea for the end of the script. All we'll have to do is write the new ending and hire a stunt driver to play Paul in one scene. We got so excited about solving that problem, and we all loved seeing Haven Harbor so much yesterday, that we've been outlining another script to be set here. Skye explained about her friend's death, and we promised not to use that, but Patrick told us about a local author and we've been checking her work. So many ideas!"

"So no one else is sick," I said, trying to get back to what I was most interested in.

"No one. Skye went with Patrick in the ambulance, but everyone else is in there." He pointed toward the living room. "We're finally getting some work done."

"What cookies did Patrick eat?" I asked. I saw Bev

coming into the hall from the kitchen. "What kind of cookies did you make, Bev?"

"The ones made that man sick weren't none of my baking," Bev answered. "No one's gotten sick from *my* cooking. Only cookies he ate so far as I know were the ones you made for him."

"What? The cookies for my tree-trimming party were gone days ago. I haven't baked any cookies since then." The gingerbread cookies Gram had given me for Patrick were in my pocket. All I'd done was decorate those.

"Patrick found a tin box of cookies outside his door this morning," said Bev. "Told me they must be from you. Had a note on them from his 'secret admirer.' He thought that was sweet. Wouldn't let any of the rest of us eat a one. Just as well, considering."

"Are the cookies still here?" I asked.

"Those EMT fellows took the ones left," said Bev. "What did you put into those cookies? Maybe you added something you didn't know the poor man was allergic to."

I headed for the door. Then I remembered when Dave had suddenly become ill, back in October.

"Where did Patrick throw up?" I asked.

"Right on my clean kitchen floor," said Bev.

"Did you clean up the vomit?"

"Certainly did." She hesitated. "Funny thing. The EMT guy asked the same question. Can't imagine why his mess wouldn't have been cleaned up."

I knew, but I didn't stop to explain.

I was still holding the bag of needlepointed pillows as I jumped into my car and headed for the Haven Harbor Hospital emergency room.

Testing a sample of Patrick's vomit could reveal what caused him to throw up.

But that was for the medics and doctors to figure out.

If I could figure out what "secret admirer" would have left cookies for Patrick, then maybe I could guess what was in them.

But I had no clue where to begin.

Chapter 40

*"Then I will not be proud of my youth or my beauty,
Since both of them wither and fade.
But gain a good name by well doing my duty
That will scent like a rose when I am dead."*

—Worked by Betsey S. Nichols in Searsport, Maine,
in 1830. Betsey was the youngest of ten siblings,
all born in Searsport. Betsey was born in 1818.
Her father was a shipbuilder. Betsey herself
married three times and had five children.

The drive to the hospital took forever. I drove too fast on roads beginning to ice over, despite the sand and salt dumped on them in anticipation of the storm to come. When I almost didn't make a curve, and envisioned my little red Honda in a ditch or wrapped around a snow-covered tree, I slowed down.

Last June I'd followed an ambulance from Aurora to Haven Harbor Hospital's emergency room. That ambulance had also held both an injured Patrick and his concerned mother. That time he'd been sent by helicopter to Boston's best burn unit. I hadn't seen him again until August.

Where had those cookies come from? Not from me, for sure. From whom, then?

Sarah'd been interested in Patrick when he'd first arrived in Haven Harbor, but I'd eaten Sarah's cookies, and they'd been fine. Plus, I couldn't imagine Sarah leaving a box of cookies in the snow (they must have been in the snow) with a cryptic note.

Bev Clifford had seemed certain the cookies weren't hers, and she would have known if anyone else at Aurora had been baking.

She'd mentioned allergies. Was Patrick allergic to anything?

He'd never told me he was, or refused to eat anything for medical reasons. I smiled to myself, despite my fears, as I remembered he'd once said he liked Maine oysters, but prairie oysters weren't for him.

I hadn't thought much about that until I'd Googled prairie oysters—and fought not to gag.

That was the only time I remembered him mentioning something he didn't like to eat.

The hospital emergency department parking lot was full. Pete had once said holidays were the worst days of the year for crimes and accidents. People were excited, overeating, climbing ladders, lighting candles and fireplaces and fireworks, and worst of all, drinking too much and partying (and arguing) with friends and relatives they managed to avoid the rest of the year.

Not to mention driving on icy roads.

I found a place to park in the back of the lot and walked toward the emergency room entrance, doing my best to avoid snow-covered patches of ice, black ice, and any other treacherously dangerous spots. I didn't need to become a patient.

Neither Patrick nor Skye were in the waiting room. Good. That meant Patrick was being cared for.

I waited my turn at the desk, after a mother with a six-year-old who'd been sledding and banged her head against a tree and an elderly woman whose hand was bleeding. "We have a bread slicer, but she insisted on using the knife. I should've told her I'd sharpened it," explained her husband.

By the time I got to the front of the line I almost felt foolish. "I'm here to see Patrick West. He was brought in by ambulance."

"Your name?" the clerk asked.

After I'd practically given her my entire life's history, she handed a note to another clerk. "Have a seat in the waiting area," she said. "We'll let Mr. West know you're here."

I watched as three other patients told their stories, showed their insurance cards, and were admitted to the back. After a few minutes I couldn't sit any longer. I got up and paced.

A television in the waiting room was tuned to CNN, with broadcast breaks every few minutes warning of a severe winter storm approaching the northeast. One shivering newswoman was reporting from the Boston Common in pelting snow falling heavily enough to blur the camera image. As I watched, her hat blew off.

I was more worried about Patrick than a storm. The Haven Harbor emergency room allowed each patient two visitors. Why hadn't anyone come to get me? How seriously was he sick? Did he have food poisoning? An allergy I didn't know about?

And who'd left cookies for him? Maybe he did have a secret admirer I didn't know about.

My thoughts whirled, like the snow on the television screen.

"Miss Curtis?" A nurse's aide stood in the doorway. "You may go in now. Mr. West is in room 7A."

"Thank you." Finally! I walked past her and into the busy room filled with doctors, nurses, and patients.

It was a busy afternoon. Two patients were lying on overflow stretchers in the hallway. Small rooms for patients surrounded the desk, where nurses hovered, calling specialists, scheduling laboratory tests, and entering patient information in their computers.

Room 7A was at the far end of the large room.

Patrick was asleep, lying on a bed, hooked up to an IV drip. His skin was pale, almost a pale blue.

"Angie!" Skye rose from her chair in the corner. "When the nurse said you were here, at first I didn't believe it. How dare you come here? I never want you to see me or my son again. I don't know what you put in those damned cookies, but they almost killed my son. One of the doctors said it might be arsenic. Arsenic! Thank goodness she recognized the smell of almonds and had the antidote in stock. I thought we were friends. That you and Patrick cared about each other. Thank goodness it looks as though he'll be all right, no thanks to you."

"I didn't . . . ." I began.

"Don't lie to me. Patrick told me you'd left those cookies for him. 'Sweet gesture,' indeed. Cookies laced with poison! And, by the way, the doctors reported it to the police. Any poisoning must be reported. So don't think you can get away with this."

"But I didn't leave him any cookies," I managed to say, before someone grabbed my arm. I turned slightly. "Pete!"

"Sorry, Angie. We need to talk." He looked over at Skye. "Thanks for letting the medical staff know what happened.

I hope your son will be all right. If you or Mr. West think of anything else that would help us, please call me." He handed Skye his card. She must have a collection of them by now. "Now, Angie, let's leave the Wests in peace. They've had an extremely difficult week."

"But . . ." I tried to explain as he guided me past the doctors and nurses (all of whom were, of course, watching) and headed me out of the emergency room.

We stopped outside the hospital entrance. "I didn't do anything, Pete! You know me; you know Patrick. I wouldn't hurt him!"

He looked at me. "Skye West's convinced you tried to kill her son. The hospital would have notified me when they knew for sure Patrick had been poisoned, but she called me as soon as that possibility was mentioned. I had to respond. Skye's influential. I'm surprised the press isn't here already. Even before I got to the hospital she'd called again. Now she's decided you also killed Paul Carmichael."

"What?" I couldn't believe what Pete was saying.

"I'll admit, that caught me by surprise. But you have a Glock. Paul Carmichael was killed with a Glock, which I hadn't even told her. And you were the one who found his body."

"But Patrick and I were just taking a walk!"

"And then her son ate cookies you left for him, suddenly became very ill, and his doctor suspects he was poisoned."

I took a deep breath. This situation was incredible. But Pete was serious. I needed to stay calm.

"I didn't kill Paul Carmichael. I didn't even know him. And Patrick and I are friends. Hell, Pete, we're more than friends. I rushed to the hospital the minute I heard he was sick."

"Maybe that was to cover your story," said Pete. "I'll admit, I can't imagine a motive for you. Did you and Patrick have an argument? Were you upset with the Wests? Jealous of what they have that the rest of us don't?"

I didn't feel the cold or the wind. All I could think was that Skye, and maybe Patrick, believed I was a murderer.

I shook my head and tried to focus on the facts. "Patrick and I are fine. When he can talk, he'll tell you that himself. I haven't baked any cookies for anyone in the past few days, and I didn't leave any for Patrick. If I *had* baked cookies for him, I would have given them to him, not left them in the snow outside his door."

"They were in one of those tin boxes women put Christmas cookies in," Pete said.

"Whoever put those cookies in the box probably also left their fingerprints," I pointed out.

"The box was in the snow, maybe for hours. We won't be able to find fingerprints on the outside of the box." Pete hesitated. "Could be some on the inside, I suppose."

"Where's the box now?" I asked.

"Here at the hospital, I guess. Skye said the EMTs who responded to her call took it for testing."

"Which means the EMTs, and people at the hospital, touched it. I hope no one ate any cookies left in it. You need to find that box, Pete."

"You're right. I do. I'm going to do that right now." He turned to go back into the hospital and then turned again. "Do you have your gun with you?"

I reached into my bag and handed it to him. "It hasn't been fired in months."

He took it carefully. "We'll check it. If it wasn't the gun used in Paul Carmichael's murder, we'll get it back to you. But you're now a person of interest in two investigations, Angie. I shouldn't be saying this, but be careful who you talk to and what you say."

The snow was beginning to pile up. I walked slowly back to my car, got in, turned on the heater, and started to cry. How could this happen? How could Skye believe I would hurt Patrick—or Paul Carmichael, a man I'd never met?

Paul's murderer and Patrick's poisoner were still out in the world. Probably somewhere in Haven Harbor. And although I hadn't used my gun in months, I felt naked—unprotected—without it.

Cookies! I picked up the gingerbread people I'd planned to give to Patrick, broke the head off the boy, and then crumbled both cookies and threw them out the car window onto the snow. Maybe the birds would like them. They wouldn't think they were poisoned.

I sat, crying, until the tears were gone, and I felt empty and numb.

I had to prove I was innocent.

I had to find out who'd poisoned Patrick—if he had been poisoned—and who'd shot Paul Carmichael.

And I needed to get the damned needlepoint pillows to Aurora, so when Skye thought about them, they'd be there.

That was the easiest task. Skye would be at the hospital for a while.

I headed back to Aurora. I'd give the pillows to Bev. She'd deliver them for me.

She wasn't a murder suspect.

Chapter 41

"Mr. Buriat, just arrived from Cape Francaise, has the honour to inform the public that he embroiders on and with all kinds of materials, such as gold, silver, silk, cotton, twill, thread, on all sorts of woolen, silk, lawn, cambric, linen, cotton, etc. He embroiders coats of arms in the most delicate stile. He lives in New-street, No. 65, between Second and Third Streets."

—Advertisement in the *Federal Gazette*, Philadelphia, June 1794.

As I'd anticipated, no one stopped or questioned me when I walked in the back door at Aurora, the door to the small solarium where Pete and Ethan had questioned me two days before.

Bev was in the kitchen. Ironically, she was rolling out dough for Christmas cookies. Two cooling racks of decorated stars and angels were already on one counter. She looked up when she heard me. "Angie! You startled me. You've never come in that door before." She dusted her floury hands on her apron. "Did you see Patrick? How is he?"

"I saw him. He was sleeping, but his mom said he'd be all right." I paused. "The doctors are saying there was poison in the cookies he ate. Maybe arsenic."

Bev clapped her hand to her mouth, leaving a dusting of flour on her cheek. "No! Who would do such an awful thing? And at Christmastime."

Poisoning at any time of year sounded awful to me, but I knew what she meant. Christmas was supposed to be the time of year for peace and joy, when families and friends joined together and celebrated. Poisoned Christmas cookies definitely were not in the spirit of the season.

I hesitated a moment, but decided she'd find out soon enough. "Skye says I did it."

Bev took two steps backward, hitting the counter and knocking two angels off the cooling racks. They lay, broken, on the floor. "No! How could she believe that, Angie! After all you've done for that woman, and what you've meant to her son. I don't believe it. She must be out of her mind."

I almost smiled. "Maybe so. But she called Pete Lambert at the police department. I don't think he believes I did it, but he doesn't have any other suspects. You're the only one who's baked cookies here, right?"

"That's for sure," Bev sniffed. "Only time those folks come to the kitchen is when they want a cold beer or a late-night snack. Most helpless folks I've seen in a while. That Blaze Buchanan complains about something at every meal, and never volunteers to even bring her dirty plate to the kitchen to be washed." She paused. "Although someone must have been in the kitchen late last night. Everything was spick 'n' span this morning, but the oven was on. I've never left an oven on overnight in my life."

I believed her. "I'd like to ask a favor, Bev."

"Whatever I can do, dear. What you need to do is find out who made those cookies. Arsenic! I remember when I used it for rat poison, back when that was still allowed. Looks like sugar, it does. Maybe someone got it mixed up."

"You were here. What kind of cookies were in the box? What did Patrick eat? Did he say how they tasted?"

"Cinnamon and sugar, they were. All of them. Those snickerdoodles children like. My son was always asking me to make them."

"Then they weren't special Christmas cookies." Even I'd made snickerdoodles. They were addictive. But they were a far cry from the shortbreads and shaped and filled cookies most people baked for the holidays.

"He thought they were from you, so they were special to him. Found them in a tin outside his door this morning, on his way here, so he brought them along and opened them right here." Bev pointed to the largest pine table in the kitchen. "Saw him myself. He smiled when he saw your note, Angie, and then he ate one or two of them. He collapsed before he could eat more. Made a mess on the floor, I'll tell you. He didn't look so good, so I ran into the front hall and yelled for his mother. She was talking in the living room—those folks have been plotting and planning since they got back from that wagon ride yesterday afternoon. She closed the box of cookies and called nine-one-one."

"Did you see the note?"

"Wasn't much to it. Typed, it was, like on a computer. I'm pretty sure Patrick put it in his pocket before he bit into that cookie."

"Thanks, Bev. That's a help. But now I have to ask another

favor. Skye's furious with me right now, so for the time being I'm going to stay out of her way. But she commissioned the Mainely Needlepointers to make gifts for her guests. I was bringing them to her this morning, when I heard about Patrick." I handed her the bag of needlepointed balsam fir pillows. "Would you give her this when she gets home from the hospital?"

"Of course, I will. Don't you worry about that," said Bev, taking the bag and tucking it in a corner of the kitchen.

I turned to leave. "You said her guests were plotting. A new end for their movie?"

"I heard Mr. O'Day say they'd have no problem finding a stunt actor to take the place of that Paul. His wife even said a stunt actor might be easier to work with." Bev shook her head. "Not a lot of mourning's been going on in this house. The only one who seems distressed is Blaze. I caught her yesterday morning, using my phone. She was telling someone she was heartbroken about the death of her fiancé. That sounded sad, so I stayed outside the door to give her some privacy."

"Of course," I said. The police must not have taken Bev's phone.

"But then she asked this person if he could get her on some of those talk shows in the next week, to talk about Paul. She said it would be good publicity for her new movie. Said she was leaving here after Christmas Day and wasn't due back in Scotland until after New Year's." Bev shook her head. "Didn't sound heartbroken to me. Secret engagement? Awfully convenient, if you ask me."

"I've heard of Hollywood romances dreamed up for publicity. Maybe that was the kind of engagement Paul and Blaze had," I said.

"Maybe so. But she was milking it wicked hard."

I glanced toward the door to the hall. "So they've figured out how to rewrite the film. That's good."

"They did that early last night. Since then they've been planning some other film." Bev came close to me. "They're talking about it being set here in Haven Harbor. You know anything about that?"

I sighed. "They were talking about that possibility when we were at the Christmas Cheer festival yesterday. They got Ed Campbell all excited about the idea, and were even talking to a few folks at the parade about hiring extras."

"Ms. West kept saying nothing was to sound like the Gardeners' story—you know, the folks who used to own this place, whose daughter was killed back in the day. But they seemed to know other stories set right here in town. Turns out some local author I'd never heard of has written books. Mr. and Mrs. O'Day have those e-readers. They were reading those stories."

"A local author?" The only local author I knew of was Ruth Hopkins. And her books—her erotica—was written under several pseudonyms. Had I told Patrick about her? Ruth was one of the Mainely Needlepointers. I might have mentioned it sometime.

But her books were fiction. Was there another author in town I didn't know? Could be. I'd been gone ten years, and a lot of writers lived in Maine.

The windows in the kitchen rattled. I'd forgotten the storm.

"I need to get home," I said. "Weather's supposed to get wicked tonight."

"You'd best be on your way, then. I'll get that bag of yours to Ms. West. I hope she and Patrick will be home soon."

"I do, too, Bev. But I don't want them to find me here."

"Will you be coming to the dinner tomorrow night?" she asked.

I winced. "I'd planned to be here. But it depends on whether the poisoned cookie mystery is solved, or Skye calms down."

"She's a fair lady," said Bev. "Give her time to think things through. Why would you poison someone you're sweet on?"

Was I sweet on Patrick?

I guessed I was.

The wind had picked up and the snow was heavier. Drifts were blowing across streets, making it hard to see. It was only midafternoon, but I had my car lights on and wipers at full speed. Gusts made it hard to steer through blowing snow on slippery streets. I felt like I was driving inside a snow globe someone was shaking.

I wanted to be home, safe and quiet, hunkered down with Trixi and a hot cup of tea.

Accused of murdering the man in my life? The one who'd been kindest to me and who'd included me in his family events?

The more I thought about it, the angrier I got. Not a good emotion when I should be focused on the roads. I turned into the street before mine and drove around Haven Harbor's Green. Should I park at Gram's?

No. In this weather I shouldn't block her driveway, or my own. If I did, the plows wouldn't be able to do their jobs. I parked in my barn, shivering as I made my way across the backyard to my house.

For better or, it seemed now, for worse, I was home for the holiday.

Chapter 42

"Numerous as are the subjects treated on in this work, there are few which furnish a more pleasing occupation than Embroidery. To this art our readers are indebted for some of the most elegant articles of dress. It may, also, afford them opportunities of displaying their taste and ingenuity . . . and an inexhaustible source of laudable and innocent amusement."

—From *The Lady's Book* (later called *Godey's Lady's Book*) in July 1830.

Trixi shook as she heard the wind coming down the chimney. I closed the flu, but the roar of the wind didn't disappear. Glass in the old windows, especially those that were hand-blown, rattled. When I was little I'd loved to look at the world through the bubbles and ripples in those windows. They'd made the world look mysterious.

They still did. Wind was blowing the lit trees on the town Green. Through the snow, it looked as though fireflies were dancing. Trixi was alternately nervous and fascinated, running from one window to another as I turned on our tree lights and window candles.

Was Patrick better? Had he been released? Could arsenic poisoning do permanent damage?

Instead of tea, I poured myself a glass of red wine, in honor of the holiday, and promised myself all would be well. It had to be well. Then I called Dave.

"Are you okay?" he asked. "Wicked bad storm out there."

"I just got home," I answered. "It's a night for blankets blocking doors and snakes on window sills."

"Mine are in place by Halloween, in case the weather turns," he agreed. "I never even heard of window snakes until I moved to Maine."

"I remember helping Gram make them, when I was four or five," I said. "I loved watching her take pieces of Mama's old clothes, or mine, patch them together in long strips, and make three- or four-foot-long bags. Then we'd go to Pocket Cove Beach and fill the bags with dry sand, and she'd stitch up the ends. I always chose ones she'd made of my clothes to put on the windowsills in my room."

"I'll admit I bought mine ready-made. They're filled with balsam, not sand, and the store called them draft dodgers, not snakes. I like the old name best. They do block drafts and help keep the house warmer."

"Dave, I have a question. A poison question."

"You haven't been cooking again, have you, Angie?" he teased. Cooking was a skill I'd been working on, but wasn't my strong suit. I could shoot and do surveillance and keep business accounts. I was learning to do needlepoint. But, cooking? I needed a bit more practice. Okay. A lot more practice. I didn't mind being kidded about it. But today my skills at cooking, or lack of them, hit too close to home.

I blurted out the whole story.

"Someone left poisoned cookies for Patrick, and Skye is blaming you? That's unbelievable."

"But it's also unbelievable that someone Patrick doesn't know laced cookies with arsenic and left them at his doorstep. He looked awful, Dave. Skye was yelling at me, so I couldn't ask any questions. But she said they'd given him an antidote. Is there an antidote to arsenic? Isn't it one of the poisons that act fast? And are deadly?"

Dave hesitated. "There are so many variables, Angie. Depends on the amount of arsenic, and what it was mixed with, and whether it was eaten or inhaled. Antidotes exist. They have to be given quickly. I'm impressed that someone at Haven Harbor Hospital was smart enough to recognize arsenic poisoning."

"Me too."

"But, you know, I may be able to explain that. Do you remember Karen Mercer? Dr. Karen Mercer?"

"She treated your leg last August. As I remember, you and she got pretty friendly!"

"A little," Dave admitted. "We've seen each other a couple of times since, in a nonprofessional setting. She was interested in my poison garden, and asked a lot of questions about it. If she was on duty this afternoon, she might have recognized arsenic."

"I didn't see her. But I didn't look at any of the doctors. Are you going to bring her with you to Skye's dinner party tomorrow night?

"We're not that friendly. At least not yet."

"Too bad. Although it doesn't look as though I'll be going."

"Skye was that upset?"

"That upset. And after Sarah found me a great dress to wear!" I forced myself to joke when I was hurting.

Dave knew me well. "Skye'll change her mind, Angie. I'm sure she will."

"She would if I could prove who poisoned those cookies and left them for Patrick. But I have no clue. Dave, you didn't answer my question about side effects of arsenic."

"Arsenic either kills or it doesn't. Since Patrick didn't die, he'll be fine in a day or so. He shouldn't have any problem attending that gala his mom is giving tomorrow night, although he won't be ready to dance up a storm."

Without warning, the lights in my house flickered. And died.

"Speaking of storms . . . my electricity just went out."

"Ouch. That means no heat or water?" Dave confirmed.

I listened for a moment. No furnace. "Right. I'm turning on a flashlight right now." Gram always left a large torch on the back of the kitchen counter and one in each bathroom. I hadn't changed her system. Few towns in Maine had the underground wires I'd appreciated in Arizona; power outages were always possible, summer or winter.

"So far my place is fine," Dave said. "Power's still on. Want to turn off your water so the pipes don't freeze and come here? At noon the Channel 7 weather guy said Central Maine Power was expecting outages all over the state. Chances are you're out for the night. Maybe longer."

Stay with Dave? I was tempted. Trixi would love seeing her brother. But this wouldn't be the time to explain my choice of refuge to Patrick. Assuming Patrick would even speak to me tomorrow.

"Appreciate the offer, Dave. And thanks for the reminder about the pipes. I'll drain them right away. If it gets too cold here, I'll go to Gram and Tom's. The parsonage has a generator, and it's closer than your place."

"Okay. Good luck with that. And with finding the real cookie monster in Haven Harbor."

"Not funny, Dave. And—Merry Christmas!"

As I turned my phone off Trixi rubbed against my ankles. She didn't care that it was dark, but she wouldn't like it when the house got cold. The sound of the gales had already made her restless.

As if to prove that, a loud gust blew under the front door and lifted the small rug in the hallway off the floor. I hadn't seen that happen in years.

Trixi jumped toward me, trying to climb up my leg. Her claws cut through my jeans. I reached down and pulled her off. She was shaking.

I held her in my arms and sat down.

I could cope with a cold and windy night, but Trixi was going to be a wreck. I pulled out my phone.

Gram answered on the first ring. "Gram, power's out here. You and Tom okay?"

"We're fine, and so far our power is still on. We'll use the generator if we need to. Pack up your nightgown and toothbrush, and you and Trixi get over here. The sooner the better. Branches are already coming down. Weather Channel says wind chill could be forty or fifty below tonight, and we'll get more than a foot of snow."

"Thanks, Gram. I'll drain the pipes and then be over."

I put the phone in my pocket. Pipes, cat carrier, a couple of overnight necessities. Gram was only two blocks away.

And, deep inside, I knew tonight I needed my grandmother.

Being grown up wasn't easy.

Plus, Gram knew everyone in town. She might have some ideas about the arsenic cookies.

I hoped so. Because I hadn't a clue.

Chapter 43

"Mother dear weep not for me
When in this yard my grave you see
My time was short and blest was he
That called me to eternity."

—Margaret Barnholt from Pennsylvania
 added this morose verse to her
 otherwise gay and brightly colored
 sampler. She pictured a man and
 woman, and a boy and girl, standing
 next to a tomb marked with two sets
 of initials—perhaps those of deceased
 siblings.

I put Trixi down. She followed close behind me as I quickly
gathered overnight necessities, turned off the now-dark
lights I'd turned on a half hour before, and unplugged my

computer. When the power came back on there could be a surge.

How long would the electricity be off? How long would I be away? I hesitated, and added my gifts for Gram and Reverend Tom to my large duffel bag. Might as well put gifts under the rectory tree tonight. I threw clean underwear and a lipstick and my black flats into the bag. And my gift for Patrick.

Maybe a miracle would happen, and I'd be attending Skye's party tomorrow night. The dress Sarah had found for me was still in my car. I hadn't brought it into the house, afraid the velvet would spot from snow. It would be safe, and Jed Fitch would plow my driveway an hour or two after the snow stopped.

Second floor taken care of. Pipes were next on my mental list, and not my favorite part of power failure protection. My cellar wasn't a pleasant place under any circumstances. The dirt floor, damp in spring and summer, was now frozen. In the nineteenth century my ancestors had stored apples and squash and pumpkins in barrels of sand on the granite slabs in the center of the house, below the chimney. They'd layered oysters and mussels with seaweed in barrels, too. Dried vegetables, fish, and meat had been hung from attic beams, reached by a ladder from the second floor. I said a silent prayer of thanks for twenty-first century grocery stores and freezers.

Trixi paced at the top of the cellar stairs and cried, not wanting to go down into the cellar with me, but not wanting to be alone. I didn't linger. All I had to do was turn off the valve that brought water from the well to the house. The pipes to the upstairs would be all right unless we were without power for days, but the kitchen and downstairs bathroom's pipes were against the northern outside wall. They could freeze, and break. They had in the past.

Upstairs again, I drained the pipes to the sinks and toilet.

The winds now were more ferocious; the house shuddered under one blast. I needed to get to Gram's before the storm got worse.

I pulled the cat carrier out of the downstairs closet and put a few of Trixi's favorite treats in it. She went inside immediately. Maybe the enclosed carrier looked like a haven.

The two blocks to the rectory were looking farther away every minute.

The car carrier in one hand and flashlight in another, my duffel bag hung across my chest, I staggered out into the storm.

Trixi cried as the frigid gusts hit her carrier. I would have cried myself if my nose and cheeks hadn't felt frozen.

Large branches wavered above us, screeching as they rubbed against one another in the wind. Small branches covered with ice and snow had already fallen. I walked in the street. No one else was in sight. Plows had been by several times, and the snow in the street was only a couple of inches deep. If another plow passed I'd step into a drift, but there was a good chance I could get to Gram's before anyone else was out on the road.

A red-ribboned wreath blew by on my left. The houses on the other side of the Green were still lit, as were those near the church. My block and houses closer to downtown were dark. Probably the transformer at the foot of the Green had blown.

What about Sarah? Did she have power?

The roaring wind was like breaking waves, rising before they hit the shore. Waves at the lighthouse would be dramatic.

People eager to see high breakers after storms were swept off Maine rocks every year.

I bent my head against stinging ice particles mixed with snow.

Either Trixi had stopped crying or I couldn't hear her over the storm. I wished I could explain to her what weather was, and how we'd be out of it soon. But she was an indoor cat. She didn't know this world.

Did I? I looked down the street, across the Green, and up the hill toward the church. I knew this place so well. Tonight it was blurred, from tears or snow.

Until now, life had been going so smoothly.

How could Skye believe I'd hurt Patrick? What had I done to make her believe that? And Patrick told her I'd made the cookies. Did he believe I'd poisoned him? Did he know she'd said I was to stay away from both of them?

I shook my head in frustration. Snow fell off my hat and hair onto my neck, where it melted.

I should move back to Arizona, where it was warm, and dry, and no one baked cookies laced with arsenic.

Walking was hard enough. Carrying my heavy duffel bag and the cat carrier made it almost impossible.

I should have stayed at home by the fireplace. Trixi and I could have slept there.

But a kitten that close to the fire? And in this wind, the house would be soon be frigid.

I carefully put one foot down, then the other, balancing my burdens and trying not to slip. The top layer of snow was now frozen.

My ancestors were hardy folks, like others who'd built their homes on the coast of Maine before there were even Franklin stoves.

I straightened up and rested a moment. The Congregational Church, its steeple lit for the holidays, was close. The wreaths on its wide doors were banging, but still attached.

I turned slightly right and waded into drifts where the rectory's driveway should be. Snow covered everything.

Gram's porch light was on, sending a welcoming glow through the swirling snow.

Tonight the rectory was home.

Chapter 44

"And must this body die
This mortal frame decay
And must those active limbs of mine
Lie mouldering in the clay.
And there to remain
Until Christ doth please to come."

—Below this verse is stitched, *"Barbara A. Baner*
a daughter of Joseph and Esther Baner,
was born in York March the 20 in the year
of our Lord 1793 and made this sampler in
Harrisburgh in Mrs. Lea Meaguier School
A.D. 1812." Barbara's sampler also includes
flowers, birds, butterflies, hearts, and a
female figure in white sitting below a willow
tree, the symbol of death.

Gram had been watching for me, as she had all my life. She
opened her front door and I handed her Trixi's carrier.

"Horrid weather. Our first serious storm since you've been back," she said as I stomped my feet on her mat to leave as much snow as I could outside. I was covered in white, from my head down, so some of it would come in with me.

"Don't worry about the snow. Get in here so we can close the door."

I disentangled my duffel bag and dropped it on the floor.

"Glad you got here all right," said Reverend Tom, coming into the hallway from his study. "It's nasty out. Not a night to be alone without power."

"Thanks for having me," I said, unwinding my long scarf. I'd already pulled off my Bean boots. Snow had fallen into them, so I turned them upside down to dry on the boot rack Gram and Tom had put conveniently near their coat closet. "It's bitter out there. Snow's a nuisance, but it's the wind that's the challenge."

"Nasty wind chill," he agreed. "Hope none of our homeless neighbors are out. The Baptist Church is keeping their soup kitchen open all night, and encouraging anyone who has no place to go to stay there."

No place to go in a nor'easter two days before Christmas.

And I'd been feeling sorry for having to walk two blocks in the storm.

"Are many people in town homeless?" I asked, as Gram returned with a thick beach towel.

"Not a lot," said Reverend Tom. "But even one is too many. And they'll be others, like you, who lose power tonight."

I nodded.

"How's Trixi? And how will Juno react to her?"

Juno, Gram's coon cat, had been queen of her household for years. She was three times the size of my feisty Trixi, who right now was cold and a little wet, despite the carrier's protection. How would she react in another cat's territory?

"Juno will hide at first. We'll have to watch them. If there's a problem, we'll close a few doors and separate them. You get those wet clothes off. You're drenched. I'll get a towel to wrap Trixi in."

I wasn't sure how Trixi would like being wrapped in a towel. But Gram had taken care of cats in all sorts of circumstances for years. I'd had one kitten for less than three months.

I stripped off my wet jeans and sweatshirt in the guest bedroom, toweled my wet hair, and put on one of Gram's robes. Then I went back to the living room.

"You take care of Trixi," said Gram. "She knows you."

I sat on the living room floor near the wide Christmas tree bright with lights and slowly opened the carrier.

Trixi glared up at me. She was damp and cold and not happy about it.

Gram put a bag of cat treats next to me. "These should distract her."

I picked Trixi up, wrapping her in the towel. At first she objected, reaching toward me with her claws. But the towel was thick, and I was bigger than she was. I wiped off her head and back, which were damp, as she looked at the room and the tree. Not only was she wet, but she was in a new place.

I scratched her head gently, opened the towel so she wouldn't feel confined, and picked up the bag of treats.

She recognized it immediately and squeaked her request. I shook several of the treats out onto the rug and she quickly devoured them. Then she looked around the room and began investigating.

"She'll be fine," said Gram approvingly. "Now we'll see how Juno reacts."

As though on cue, Juno appeared from behind the couch. She'd smelled the treats, and I tossed a couple in her direction. Trixi stopped short and stared at her. They both looked shocked that there was another cat present. Trixi took a few tentative steps toward the older cat, and Juno raced off, heading for Gram and Tom's bedroom.

"She'll be back," Gram predicted. "She needs time to accept that she has a guest."

Reverend Tom shook his head. "I'll leave you ladies to tend to the cats. I have a sermon to finish." He headed back to his study.

"Cocoa?" said Gram.

"With a touch of brandy?" I asked.

"That could be arranged," Gram said, winking. "You're over twenty-one. You keep an eye on Trixi while I heat milk."

Trixi checked out the ornaments on the lower branches of the tree and batted one, but her outside adventure had exhausted her. She jumped up onto one of Gram's armchairs, turned around a couple of times, and fell asleep.

If only I could do the same.

I joined Gram in the warm kitchen.

Chapter 45

"Better by far for Me
Than all the Spinster's Art
That God's commandments be
Embroidered on my Heart."

—Verse stitched by Mary Cole in 1759
in New England.

Gram looked at me critically. "Are you all right, Angel? What's wrong?"

"Everything," I said, bursting into tears.

"And it's Christmas on top of whatever that 'everything' is," said Gram, squeezing my shoulder lightly as she put a large mug of hot cocoa in front of me.

She let me cry for a few minutes while she got her own cup and put a box of tissues on the table. "Now, Angel, your life has changed a lot in the past six months. You've moved back to Maine, found out who killed your mother, taken over Mainely Needlepoint, were maid of honor at my wedding, and became the owner of both a house and a cat. Not to mention your making some good friends here in the Harbor. I know you carry that gun of yours sometimes, and although I'm not one to do that, I know it was necessary in your old job, and is a comfort to you now. But it can protect your body; not your mind or your heart."

I blew my nose.

"So—which is it that hurts? Your mind or your heart?"

"Both, I guess," I said, staunching my tears. "I'm sorry. I almost never cry. But everything's falling apart. And I don't know how to fix it."

"Sometimes life feels that way. I don't doubt you. But whatever it is that 'fell apart' can either be put back together or put in the past. That I'm sure about."

"Patrick's in the hospital. Someone left him a tin of cookies laced with arsenic." I held my hot mug of cocoa in both hands, warming them.

Gram put her cocoa down.

"The poor man. How is he? Shouldn't you be there with him?"

"I was there, Gram. Skye threw me out. She thinks I'm the one who poisoned him. She even called Pete Lambert and told him to arrest me."

"Is Patrick going to die, Angel?" Gran always got straight to the point.

"I don't think so," I said. "The doctors figured out what was wrong and gave him an antidote. He was asleep when I saw him. Dave said Patrick should be all right if he got the medicine quickly enough."

"Have you seen Pete?"

"He got to the hospital about the time I did. Skye told him to take me away."

"But you're here, so he didn't arrest you."

I shook my head.

"What gave Skye the idea you poisoned these cookies?"

"Patrick found them outside his house this morning. There was a note on the box: *'From your secret admirer.'* He thought that was me. He took the box to Aurora, where he ate one or two of the cookies and collapsed."

"It's ridiculous to think you poisoned Patrick," said Gram. "Skye must have been very angry, and she lashed out at you. Someone played a horrible trick on Patrick. I'm sure Pete will figure out who and things will work out."

"A trick? Someone tried to kill him! I can't think of anyone who would want to hurt him, much less kill him. Can you?"

"No, but there must be an answer. You try to relax and warm up, and maybe it will all make sense."

It didn't seem that simple.

"At least you and Trixi are here, where we have heat and light and hot water," Gram said soothingly.

"That reminds me. The power outage seemed to be in the direction of downtown. I should call Sarah and see if she's okay," I said, pulling out my phone.

"You go right ahead. And if her power's out, tell her to come here. You could have a pajama party, the way you did when you were in school. Eat cookies and pop popcorn."

Elementary school, I remembered. And only once or twice. Mama's reputation kept most mothers from allowing their daughters to come to our house.

I shook my head slightly, trying to vanquish the memories.

"I'll ask her, Gram." I picked up my phone and hit Sarah's number. "Sarah? Are you okay?"

"I'm fine. I just closed the store and came upstairs. Even two days before Christmas, no customers were around.

Who'd want to go out in this storm? I'm one of the lucky ones—my commute is an inside stairway."

"Good. I'm at Gram's. I lost power, and she said you'd be welcome to spend the night, too, if yours went out."

"Thank her, do. But I'm fine so far. I have no desire to venture out tonight. The storm's supposed to let up by morning. But it looks as though we're going to have a very white Christmas."

"It does," I agreed. "I'm hoping power's restored by morning, but I suspect that's being optimistic."

"At least you have Gram and Tom to stay with," Sarah agreed. "I heard on the news that over forty thousand Maine homes are without power already. And the storm's far from over."

"Remember, if you need somewhere to go, Gram's invitation is open," I said as Gram nodded her head.

"Got it. And see you at Aurora tomorrow night!" said Sarah.

I didn't want to tell my story again. Gram was right. Somehow it would all work out, although I couldn't think how. If not, I'd tell Sarah tomorrow.

"Stay warm," I said, and hung up.

When my phone rang almost immediately, I assumed it was Sarah again. Maybe she'd forgotten to tell me something. But it wasn't Sarah.

"Angie? It's Ruth. I want to know what's happening at Aurora. I just got the strangest telephone call."

Chapter 46

"Count That day lost whose low descending
Sun Views from thy hand no worthy action done."

—Sarah Smith of Wethersfield, Connecticut,
    stitched this in 1813, when she was eleven years
    old and a student at Abigail Goodrich's school.

"You got a call from Aurora? From whom?"

"Wait a minute, Angie. I wrote down his name." Ruth
paused.

Why would anyone have called Ruth—unless Skye was
canceling her Christmas Eve dinner. Maybe that was it. Skye
was calling everyone in town to tell them I'd poisoned her
son, and she didn't want to see anyone connected with
me. Or . . .

"Angie? I've got it. The man's name was Thomas O'Day."

"He and his wife, Marie, are screenwriters, working on
the film Skye's making in Scotland."

"Why would he be calling me, asking who my agent was, and whether movie rights are available for my books?"

"He asked what?" I was one of the few people who knew Ruth wrote erotica under a couple of names. Chastity Falls was one of them.

"You heard me. Someone told him about my books."

"It wasn't me!" I said immediately. Was there anything else someone could blame me for today? "But—wait." I felt my stomach tighten. "Yesterday I gave Skye and her guests a tour of Haven Harbor. Thomas and Marie and the director, Marv Mason, were talking about what a perfect location it would be for a movie."

"What does that have to do with me?"

"I never mentioned you, or your books, Ruth. I swear! But they were talking about the history of the town and its secrets. They asked about Jasmine Gardener, but Skye said they absolutely could not use that story. Then when I was at Aurora today—briefly—talking with Bev Clifford, she mentioned they were reading books by a local author. Are there any other authors in town?"

"Not a one, unless they're like me and hiding in full sight."

"Someone must have told them about you. I did mention your books once to Patrick."

"Angie! I've kept that secret for decades. I trusted you; you're from here, and your grandmother and I've been friends forever. How could you tell someone from away about me?"

"I'm sorry, Ruth. But it shouldn't be a problem, should it? I've only read one of your books, I'll admit, but it was fiction. A made-up story. Nothing to do with the real Haven Harbor."

Ruth didn't say anything.

"They're from the West Coast. They won't tell anyone who you are. And your books aren't . . . mainstream. If they're asking about your agent and movie rights, wouldn't that be good? You might make some money out of it."

"First, I don't have an agent anymore. I've been self-publishing. Although I suppose I could get someone to represent me if those people are serious."

"What did you tell Thomas?"

"I told him I'd see him tomorrow night, at that Christmas Eve shindig Skye is throwing."

"Can you get an agent by then?"

"Maybe. I still know people in the industry. But that's not the problem, Angie."

"Then what is?" I liked Ruth, but she seemed to be making a big fuss over nothing.

"Angie, have you ever heard the expression 'write what you know'?"

I shook my head. "I'm not into writing."

"Well, to put it straight—a lot of my books aren't exactly fiction. I've lived most of my life in Haven Harbor, and this town and its people are what I know."

"You mean, you wrote about people in town?"

"I didn't use their real names, of course. But, yes, if you must know, a lot of my books are based on people here."

"But—why?"

"Because I got bored writing sex scenes, and I had trouble coming up with new plots all the time. So I took stories I'd heard and spiced them up. Since no one knew who I was, I never thought it would make a difference. But if that Thomas person wants to film one of my books, a lot of people in Haven Harbor are going to be furious. And hurt."

"Then don't sign away your rights," I said. "I'm no lawyer, but . . ."

"You're right. You're no lawyer. And because I say no doesn't mean that man and his wife won't take my stories, change the names and the details of what happened, and set them here in Haven Harbor."

"Would they really do that?"

"My dear girl, that Thomas O'Day already told me they will. And since you were the one who got me into this pickle, you have to get me out."

Chapter 47

"Death cannot make our souls afraid,
If God be with us there,
We may walk through the darkest shade
And never yield to fear."

—Anna M. Frost of Norway, Maine,
   made this sampler when she was ten
   years old, in 1836. She married
   Osgood Perry, also of Norway, in 1848.
   They had a large farm and four children.
   Anna died at the age of seventy-seven; her
   husband lived until he was eighty-four.

Gram had left the kitchen to give me some privacy while I was on the telephone. She hadn't realized it was one of her friends who'd called.

I found her in the living room, playing with Trixi. Juno was sitting on the couch, watching them. So far, no feline fireworks.

I opened my duffel bag and put my contributions to Gram and Tom's Christmas under their tree.

"Thank you, Angie. Christmas morning should be fun."

I sat next to Juno. "That was Ruth on the phone. Patrick must have told Skye's screenwriter friends about her books. They're thinking about filming parts of them."

Gram smiled, a glint in her eye. "Which parts? That might be interesting."

"Not according to Ruth. She's really worried. She says she wrote about people in town whose stories would be recognizable."

"Let me guess. You told Patrick about her books."

"Yes," I admitted.

"I'll admit I glanced at a couple of those books years ago," said Gram. "I don't remember much plotting in them."

"Maybe she changed her style."

"Angel, you're in the middle of a lot. Let's take the issues one at a time." Gram shook her head and rolled a red jingly plastic ball toward Trixi, who chased it into a corner. "Let's put Ruth's problems on the side right now. Did Pete and Ethan figure out who killed Paul Carmichael? I have a feeling that if we knew who killed him, we'd have a better idea who poisoned Patrick."

"I don't think Pete and Ethan know much. At first they suspected an illegal deer hunter. But Paul was shot with a handgun, not a rifle. They searched Aurora, and questioned everyone, including me, but if they identified a killer, they're holding it close. Those at Aurora were the only people who knew Paul Carmichael was in Maine. The only person there who had a gun was me, although I didn't even have it with me that night. This afternoon Pete took it, to test it."

"So, he'll find out it wasn't the murder weapon. That's

good. But Skye's guests weren't the only ones who knew he was here," Gram reminded me. "Patrick told all of us at your tree-trimming party, remember? And Bev may have mentioned it to someone."

"Carly knew, too," I said, remembering. "She told me she'd heard on a television entertainment news show that Skye's movie was having problems in Scotland and she was bringing several members of the cast and crew here for the holidays to get problems resolved. Anyone listening to that show would have known."

"That opens up a lot of suspects. Millions of them. To begin with, who's Carly?" Gram asked.

"Just a Mainely Needlepoint customer. She's a Skye West fan, and a pain. But Skye's invited her to the dinner tomorrow night." I tried not to clench my teeth. "I may not be there, but she will."

"It's certainly a puzzle," Gram said, leaning back and staring into her Christmas tree. "It makes sense that Paul was killed by someone who knew him. I know a little about Skye, and more about Patrick. Tell me about the others at Aurora. You said the police didn't find any guns there. But that doesn't mean there weren't any, somewhere."

"Have you been watching crime shows on television, Gram?"

My needlepointing grandmother, wife of our town's minister, was trying to solve a crime. This was new.

But she was trying to help me, and that wasn't new at all. She'd been doing that all my life.

"A few," she admitted. "Tom says they help him relax. Ministers listen to all sorts of problems. On television mysteries, the problems get solved. I think that's why he likes them."

"Makes sense. Okay. Here's what I know. Paul Carmichael was a handsome young actor. Had a reputation as a ladies' man and a drinker. He got into a brawl in an Edinburgh pub a couple of weeks before Skye brought him here. Ended up in the hospital there, but no serious injuries."

"What about the young actress?"

"Blaze? She looks like a Victoria's Secret ad with clothes on. High heels, makeup. I can't quite figure her out. She said she was heartbroken after Paul died; that they'd been secretly engaged. But later she told me their relationship was all for the entertainment press; it didn't mean anything. Now she seems back to mourning the love of her life."

"So what did she have to gain if he died?"

I shrugged. "Sympathy? Publicity? I didn't see a ring. She's gorgeous, but a bit of a ditz."

Gram was trying not to smile at my description. "You said Paul was a womanizer. He and Blaze could have had a relationship."

"If it was serious, she's a better actress than she looks."

"Is she a flirt?"

"Sure. She wears low-cut dresses and tight skirts, and she cuddles up to the men."

"Any man in particular?"

"Thomas, the screenwriter. But he and his wife seem pretty joined at the hip."

"What about Patrick. Did she flirt with him?"

I thought back. "Maybe." I grimaced. "I should have been paying more attention."

"What about the screenwriting couple?"

"They're in their early fifties, I'd say. They seem close most of the time—even hold hands. But they argued about how the script they were working on should end, and yesterday they didn't sit next to each other on the hay wagon tour around town. So they might have some problems. Marie seemed more upset about Paul's death than Thomas did. He just seemed pained that now they have to rewrite and refilm a lot of the movie."

"Which would be expensive."

"Right. That's what Marv was worried about."

"Marv?"

"Marv Mason, the director. An old friend of Skye's, per Patrick. He doesn't say a lot and keeps to himself. I don't know much about him. He's excited about making a movie here in Haven Harbor, though."

"And they were the only people in the house, except for Skye."

"And Bev Clifford. You did a big favor recommending her to them. She's a great cook, and she's been patient with everyone. Even when their expectations were challenging."

"Like?"

"Like, Blaze seems to be a vegetarian some days and not other days. And when they first arrived, Paul asked Bev to bring his lunch to him in his room."

Gram smiled. "May I guess what she said to that?"

"Right. He got his own lunch like the others, and ate downstairs. The group (except Thomas and Marie) didn't stay together after lunch that first day. They went to their rooms to unpack and rest before Patrick was to open the bar."

"And where were you and Patrick while all this was happening?"

"I was at home until a little before five, when Patrick called and asked me to come for dinner. When I got there, we went for a walk." My neck was tight. I stretched it and tucked my feet under me on the couch. "I found Paul's body in the back field and called nine-one-one."

Trixi jumped up on the couch and pushed her nose against

Juno's. Juno accepted that for a fraction of a second and then took off, heading in the direction of Gram and Reverend Tom's bedroom. Trixi looked after her and then settled on my lap.

Gram laughed. "So far so good. Trixi has you, and Juno has a place to hide. Doesn't look as though we'll have any pre-Christmas murders here."

At least of cats.

Chapter 48

*"Nothing lovelier can be found in woman than to
study household Good
And Good Works in her Husband to promote."*

—Esther Cox, about nine years old, stitched
this on her sampler in 1793. Esther lived near
Boston, Massachusetts, and stitched an
elaborate piece with two alphabets in cross-
stitch, satin stitch, stem stitch, chain stitch,
French knot, and buttonhole stitch. Her
flowered border started in a basket in the
middle of the bottom of her work. She added a
peacock (which she must have copied from a
natural history book) at the top.

Nothing more was said that evening about Paul, or Patrick,
or Aurora.

Gram's beef stew and dumplings were delicious, the rectory shook with gusts that wouldn't stop, and our evening
was a quiet one.

We checked with Channel 7 weather several times. The storm was heading to Down East Maine and then to Nova Scotia. Power was out in many coastal communities, but Central Maine Power was hoping to have most people back on the grid within forty-eight hours.

Many families would have cold Christmas Eves and mornings.

Reverend Tom and other clergy in town agreed to establish warming centers in all of Haven Harbor's houses of worship, and activated telephone chains to let their parishioners know and ask them to check in with neighbors who might need help.

"Some towns have established emergency networks that can tell everyone in town if there's a problem like this. But that works best on cell phone networks, and not everyone in Haven Harbor has a cell phone," he explained.

Maine was one of the states where cell phones still didn't work everywhere, so not everyone depended on them.

"And those who don't have cells tend to be the older people who could most benefit from a warming center," Reverend Tom added. "I called the Portland stations so they could add the information to their weather-related scroll, and we announced opening of the warming centers on our Facebook pages and on the Haven Harbor Web site, but those who don't have power won't have access to the information. Word of mouth, and neighbors looking out for neighbors, works best."

"How many people will go to the warming centers?" I asked.

"I don't know. Probably not many tonight. Mainers are tough, and a lot of people in town have woodstoves and fireplaces. They'll bundle up and hunker down. But by tomorrow hot food and a warm room may look pretty attractive." He put on his coat and boots. "I'm going over to unlock the church. Members of the Outreach Committee are going to meet me in the assembly room and help set up cots and chairs and get coffee brewing. We have a closetful of blankets for emergencies, but we'll have to get everything out and organized."

Gram handed him a carton of food from their pantry. She included several tins of her Christmas cookies.

"I'm here for the night," I volunteered. "I'd be glad to help."

He hesitated. "We'll be fine for now. Most of the committee's members live in town, so they should be able to get to the church. I'll call you and Charlotte if we need reinforcements. For now, you both should get some sleep. We'll see how bad the situation is in the morning. Maybe we'll be lucky and Haven Harbor will be one of the towns where power is restored by then."

"I hope so," I agreed. "But know that I'd like to help."

"Thank you, Angie. I'll put both of you on the backup list."

He pulled his watch cap over his ears and headed out into the wintry night.

"I'd never thought about all that a minister does, other than preaching and keeping the church going, and visiting parishioners who're sick or who can't come to the church."

"He does a lot more. Tom meets regularly with other clergymen here in town and nearby. Ministers, priests, rabbis, imams . . . they're all dealing with many of the same issues. They compare ideas and work together on projects like food banks and warming centers." Gram watched out the front window to make sure Tom made it safely to the church. Between lights from the rectory and the church itself, she could follow his short trek to the assembly room door. "It's still snowing like mad, and the wind hasn't let up. We should take Tom's advice and get some rest," she declared.

I nodded. I was more relaxed, but I hadn't solved any of my problems. I'd have to deal with them tomorrow.

Christmas Eve was going to be a lot more complicated than the elegant dinner at Aurora I'd anticipated.

Chapter 49

"I bid farewell to every fear
And wipe my weeping eyes.
Still the orphan and the stranger
Still the widow owns thy care
Screened by thee in every danger
Heard by thee in every prayer."

—Verse included on Mary Ann Leiper's
sampler, which also included the
headline: *"August 11, 1824,*
Washington and Lafayette Welcome,"
marking the country's heroes' visit to
Philadelphia. In addition to the verse
and heading, Mary Anne worked four
alphabets and a floral and vine border.

I slept deeply, despite the raging storm. I didn't even dream,
or at least I didn't remember dreaming. Considering all that
was happening, that was probably good.

Even in a strange house, Trixi reminded me it was morning by sitting on my chest and gently, repeatedly, patting my cheek with her paw.

I threw on the bathrobe Gram had lent me and stumbled sleepily to the kitchen, where Gram had already brewed coffee.

I fed Trixi (and Juno, who appeared from one of her hiding places) and sat down.

"Have you heard from Tom?" I asked.

"He stopped home several hours ago to raid our linen closet for blankets and borrow a few board games. Then he went back to the church."

"He must be exhausted!"

"He said he'd gotten some sleep on one of the cots. Only two families came in, both with young children, so the night was relatively quiet. Tom can sleep anywhere, at any time."

"So the board games were for the children?"

"For the volunteers who had trouble sleeping," Gram said, pouring me a cup of coffee. "No problems. People were just bored."

"So power is still out."

"Around here, yes. I turned the news on earlier and they said power had been restored in Brunswick and Ellsworth and Saco. Other towns that've lost power are still waiting."

"How's the storm?" The wind had gone down. I went to the window. It was only snowing lightly, but the gusts had left their mark. Deep drifts covered parts of Gram's yard and the side of her barn. Grass was visible in other places.

"Pretty much over. Plows have been rumbling by all night. Jed plowed our drive, so I'd guess he's done yours, too."

"Good."

"What are you going to do today?" Gram asked.

"I don't know," I admitted. "I'd like to know how Patrick is. And I promised Ruth I'd try to do something about the screenplay plotting at Aurora. Skye's party is tonight, but as of yesterday afternoon I was definitely uninvited."

"First things first. Why don't you talk to Patrick?"

I shook my head. "I don't even know if he's in the hospital or at home. And Pete and Ethan took everyone's phones the other day, including his, so I can't call him."

"Call the hospital and ask if he's a patient there. That would be a start."

"Would they give that information to someone who isn't a relative?"

"Let me try," said Gram, picking up her phone. "Hello! And Merry Christmas! This is Reverend McCully's wife, over at the Congregational Church. It's good to hear your voice, too, Marian. Hope to see you at the service tonight. Six o'clock. The children have worked so hard on their pageant. Say, would you do me a favor? Tom's working at the warming center at the church today, so he asked me to check on his parishioners who're in the hospital. Is Patrick West still there?"

She held her crossed fingers up in front of me.

"Thank you, yes. That's good news. I appreciate it. And see you tonight, too, Marian!" Gram put down her phone. "He was released late last night. Wasn't even admitted—was in the emergency room until he was well enough to go home."

"Fantastic! Thank you for doing that, Gram. I forgot you were a miracle worker."

"Not me, Angel. But I'm learning being the wife of a minister can sometimes come in handy. So now you know where he is. Or at least that he's either at his house or at Aurora."

"With no way to reach him," I added glumly, pointing at my phone. "Or, even more important, knowing whether he'd want to talk to me."

"So call Bev Clifford."

"What?"

"You said the police took the phones at Aurora. Did they take Bev's?"

"Gram, you're a genius! They didn't. And I'm guessing you have her number."

"Sure do," Gram said. "Here. Even if someone else sees her phone, they'll think I was the one calling."

What if she said Skye was still furious? What if Patrick now hated me? I steeled myself for the worst. But I had to know. I pressed the button.

"Charlotte! Merry Christmas. I didn't expect to hear from you today!"

"Bev, it's not Charlotte. It's Angie. I'm using her phone. My house lost power, so I stayed at the rectory last night. Does Aurora have power?"

"All we need. Angie, girl, how're you doing, after all that happened yesterday?"

I could hear Bev moving, maybe to the solarium, so no one would walk into the kitchen and hear her talking. "I'm fine, Bev. But I want to know how Patrick is. I heard he was released from the hospital last night."

"He was. I warmed up dinner for he and his mom at close to midnight. His mother couldn't bear for him to be alone at the carriage house, so he slept in one of the extra rooms on the third floor."

"He's all right?"

"Looks a bit peaked this morning, but seems all right to

me. Ate a stack of blueberry pancakes, so there's nothing wrong with his appetite, I can tell you."

I smiled. At Bev, for making blueberry pancakes on December 24, and for Patrick, for eating them. He was a pretty good cook, but I suspected he'd never made blueberry pancakes for himself. I should learn to make them.

If we were still a couple.

"Does Skye still think I poisoned him? What does he think?"

"That I don't know. Neither of them mentioned you to me," she said. "But it might interest you to know that Sergeant Pete Lambert is here, talking to them both right now."

"Would you let me know when they're finished?"

"I'll call the minute they are," she said. "I'll be stirring and mixing and such all day, for the big party tonight."

"I'll let you go. But thank you, Bev!"

I handed the telephone back to Gram. "Patrick spent the night at Aurora. Bev says he looks fine. Pete Lambert's talking with Patrick and Skye right now. Bev promised to call when they finish."

"You go get dressed now, Angel. If she calls on my phone, I'll bring it to you. And how about oatmeal and maple syrup for breakfast?"

"That would be great." I hugged Gram. "Thank you, as always."

"No thanks necessary, but always appreciated. Now, go get some warm clothes on. Snow may be stopping, but it's still bitter out there."

Chapter 50

"We, Hermia, like two artificial Gods,
  Have with our needles created both one flower,
  Both on one sampler, sitting on one cushion."

—Helena, in *A Midsummer Night's Dream*
  by English poet and playwright William
  Shakespeare (1564–1616), Act 3, Scene 2.

Bev didn't call back immediately. By the time I'd gotten myself cleaned up and dressed, Gram had put steaming bowls of oatmeal on the table.

I hadn't had oatmeal made with maple syrup in years. Another reminder that I needed to spend some time with Gram finding out how she'd made all the comfort food I remembered from my childhood. Someday soon.

What was happening at Aurora? What was Pete talking to Skye and Patrick about? If it had been about Paul's death, Ethan would have been there with him. So was it about those cookies?

I tried to focus on breakfast, and chat with Gram about the church pageant that night, but my mind wasn't in the rectory.

My phone was the one to ring. Caller ID said it was Bev. "What's happening, Bev? I thought you'd never call."

"Sorry to disappoint you," said Patrick's voice. "But Mrs. Clifford is very involved with oyster shucking just now. I volunteered to help, but she said I have enough problems with my hands. I don't need to mess with knives and oysters."

"Patrick!" I said.

"So she suggested instead of shucking, I could return a call she'd gotten a while back from a mutual friend of ours."

"It's so good to hear your voice! How are you?"

"Alive. Very much so. And looking forward to seeing you a little later today."

"Wait. Your mother said she never wanted to see me again. She was sure I'd poisoned those cookies you ate."

"Sorry I missed that scene. Pete Lambert was just here, and he implied it must have been uncomfortable."

"Uncomfortable! Your mother called the cops and asked them to arrest me!"

"And she'll be apologizing to you later, I'm sure. She was upset, Angie. You know how mothers get."

No. But I did know how grandmothers got.

"Has Pete figured out where the cookies came from?"

"No, but he was able to check fingerprints on that tin they were in. He has yours on record, Angie—from when you applied for a conceal carry license last May."

"I remember. After that they changed the law so I didn't have to file any paperwork."

"Whatever. Anyway, Pete said there were several sets of

prints on the tin box, but none were yours. So chances are you weren't the one trying to kill me."

I felt as though I could breathe for the first time in hours. "No, the cookies weren't from me." Which was what I'd said, over and over, yesterday. "He's running the other prints?"

"So he says. In the meantime, I've sworn only to eat food I know was prepared by Mrs. Beverly Clifford."

I heard Bev chortle in the distance.

"So when are you coming to Aurora?" he asked.

"Is everyone there?"

"In person," he assured me.

"Because I do need to talk to them about their plans for a screenplay set in Haven Harbor. I'd like to do that before the party tonight."

"Why don't you come in about an hour? Everyone should be around then. We're not going to have lunch. Mrs. Clifford cooked an enormous brunch and we all pigged out, even Blaze. We've promised not to raid the kitchen again until dinner tonight. Later on I suspect naps will be taken and primping will take place. But late this morning everyone will probably be working on that screenplay."

"I'm at the rectory—my house has no power—but the streets and driveways are plowed. I'll have to clean where the plows have been by and blocked the driveway, but I can be there about eleven."

"Oh—and Mrs. Clifford wants to know if your stepgrandfather needs extra food for his warming center?" Patrick sounded confused.

"Warming centers are places that welcome people without heat or light in the winter. Reverend Tom has one at his church. Tell her they're fine now, but if the power's still out tonight, anything she could contribute would be great."

"I'll pass that message along. Angie, sorry for what Mom said and did yesterday afternoon. She got overexcited and worried."

"I understand." I didn't, actually. She hadn't trusted me. And where had those cookies come from? The situation wasn't funny. I suspected Skye didn't think it was, either.

Chapter 51

"Favour Is Deceitful
And Beauty is Vaine
But A Woman That Feareth The Lord
She Shall Be Praised."

—Ten-year old Abigail Williams of
   Deerfield, Massachusetts, stitched
   this cross-stitched Bible verse
   (Proverbs 31:30), two alphabets,
   baskets of fruit, a tree, and two crowned
   lions, within an elaborate border of
   carnations and squares, in 1740.

I left Trixi safe and warm at the rectory. No one had attempted
to clear their sidewalk yet, and I knew I wouldn't be doing
mine today. I wasn't the only one walking in the street that
now was covered with frozen snow speckled with salt and
sand. Black and white. A winter walk into a black and white
photograph.

Today was chilly, but the air smelled fresh. Walking to the rectory through the storm yesterday, carrying heavy bags, had seemed to take forever. Today walking home took only a few minutes. I checked my house. It was cold, but fine. In case power wasn't restored today, I tossed some makeup and a couple of extra changes of underwear in a bag and changed into clean jeans and a heavy wool sweater.

I didn't linger. The house's temperature had fallen to forty-eight degrees, according to a thermometer in the upstairs hall. Not a time to lounge about in my underwear.

I pushed my way through the lowest drifts to the barn. Inside, my car was as dirty as it usually was in winter, but it was clear of snow. Driving on sanded, salted roads is rough on cars. People joked that you could tell a true Mainers' car by the amount of rust on the parts of its body and frame closest to the road.

I tossed my bag in the car and shoveled out the door of the barn, where the wind and plows had deposited about two feet of snow, and the end of the driveway, which was blocked by a little less.

By the time I got into the car, I was sweating and ready for a nap.

Instead, I headed toward Aurora.

The driveway there was not only plowed out, but the front steps had been shoveled, and the pathway between Aurora and the carriage house cleared. Patrick and Skye paid Jed Fitch more than I did to keep their homes accessible.

Patrick answered the door. He was paler than usual, I noticed in the second before he opened his arms and hugged me. "I'm so sorry about yesterday," he said quietly in my ear. "I wish I'd been awake so I could have stopped Mom."

"I hope you're not apologizing for being poisoned?" I said. "Because that would be really stupid."

Patrick helped me remove my jacket, as Skye came over. She also hugged me, although not with the same exuberance as her son. "I'm sorry for what I said yesterday, Angie. Truly I am. Sergeant Lambert assured us you had nothing to do with those poisoned cookies. He's been such a help, I invited him to come to the dinner tonight. The more the merrier!" She lowered her voice. "And thank you for the pillows you dropped off yesterday. Mrs. Clifford gave them to me. They're perfect! I've already wrapped them and put them under the tree. You'll be here tonight, right? Because we open our gifts Christmas Eve, and I'd love you to see how delighted my guests will be."

Tonight? I'd have to bring Patrick's gift with me to the party. Good thing Skye warned me. "I'm looking forward to tonight," I assured her.

She took a folded check out of a pocket in her slacks and handed it to me. "Here's the money for all the work your group did. I added a little extra because they did those pillows so quickly."

"Thank you. They'll appreciate that," I assured her.

"Now, Patrick tells me you have some concerns about this screenplay Thomas and Marie are outlining." She raised her eyebrows. "I don't know if you can convince them about anything they've set their hearts on, but I'm on your side. I didn't invite them here to see a possible setting for a film. Although I'll admit Haven Harbor is a beautiful iconic town, and it would be convenient for me to do a film here."

Patrick stood in back of her, making faces and looking at the ceiling.

Whose side was Skye on?

"What I'm concerned about is their filming any of the stories in Ruth Hopkins's books," I explained. "Thomas called her yesterday asking for contact information for her agent." I turned to Patrick. "As far as Haven Harbor is concerned, Ruth's books don't exist. Very few people know she's an author, and she wants it to stay that way. She was hurt you'd told people about them."

"I'm sorry, Angie. After you told me about the Chastity Falls books I read several. I liked them, and told Thomas and Marie about them."

It was Skye's turn to look toward the ceiling. "I read one yesterday. They're erotica, Patrick."

"True. Good erotica. And I loved the stories she told about traditional Mainers—people the world imagines as puritanical and stodgy—getting involved in sordid circumstances. Ruth has a great imagination."

"That's one of the problems," I said, being careful about how I phrased Ruth's issue. "You see, Ruth didn't entirely make up those stories."

"What do you mean? She's the author, isn't she?"

"She is. But, as she explained it to me, plotting is a challenge for her, so she uses local gossip or situations involving people she knows as background for her erotica."

"You mean, those stories are true?" asked Skye.

"Some of them, anyway. I've only read one of her books, and I don't know the history of everyone in town, so I didn't recognize anyone. But Ruth's afraid that if a film is made including any of her stories, people would be embarrassed, and angry, and . . . you see the problem."

Patrick and Skye looked at each other and burst out laughing. "I can't believe it," said Patrick. "The teenaged son who finds his father in bed with his girlfriend and kills them both with a knife from his mother's kitchen? The waitress who's sleeping with every lobsterman in town? The baker who feels up all his daughter's little friends? They're all real?"

I flinched. Patrick's summary was already scaring me. I recognized myself in one of those summaries. Who knew what plots Ruth had used? How many people would be hurt by them?

I looked away from Patrick and Skye and saw Bev in the hallway, outside the kitchen. I waved, and she nodded in response, but went back into the kitchen.

"Ruth will be here tonight," I reminded them both. "I want someone to assure her that none of her plots are going to turn up in movies."

"I'll talk to Marv. I know him best, and he'll talk with Thomas and Marie," Skye promised. "But I have to tell you that if they change the names and the location and some of the details . . . If they've heard a story they like, they might use it. You can't copyright a plot unless it's an exact steal."

"Ruth never used the real names of the people involved in her stories," I said. "And she's already changed some of the details."

"I don't think she has any cause to worry." Skye patted my arm. "Don't worry, dear. I'll put her mind at ease. After all—it's Christmas Eve! We should be celebrating, and enjoying a white Christmas in Maine."

I hoped Ruth would agree with her.

Chapter 52

"Honour and renown
Will the ingenious crown."

—Stitched by Polly Turner, born February 15, 1775,
in Warren, Rhode Island. Polly's elaborate
sampler was done in many stitches, had a floral
border rising out of vases in the corners, birds
flying at the top, sheep and a shepherdess, and,
in the center, the President's House at Brown
University and ladies and gentlemen attending
a reception there. Done at Miss Polly Balch's
School in 1799.

I checked my house again before I went back to Gram's. The
power was still out, so I headed to the rectory.

Gram had left me a note. She and Tom were over at
the church supervising the final rehearsal of the pageant that
would be part of the early Christmas Eve service.

I felt guilty I wouldn't be there. But Gram had known

since Patrick invited us all to Aurora for Christmas Eve that my life was conflicted.

I hoped I'd made Ruth's situation plain. Then I thought of her trying to get to Aurora tonight. Had she shoveled out her car? How would her rolling walker work in the snow?

She answered my call right away. "Ruth, I've talked with Skye and Patrick. Skye said she'd talk to you tonight and assure you no one would know they'd gotten story ideas from your books."

"I don't want them to use my books at all," said Ruth. "Besides, I'm not sure I want to try to go to her party tonight. At my age I'm cautious about going out at night, and with all this snow, I'm not sure I'm up to it. You tell Skye I'd be happy to talk with her some other time."

"You should go tonight, Ruth! You found a dress to wear, right?"

"Nothing like those glittery dresses you see on awards shows on the television. But it'll do."

"Why don't you get yourself fancied up, and I come to your house and help you and your walker get to my car?"

"That's a sweet idea, Angie. I'll admit, I'm tempted. I'd been wanting to see what the inside of that place looks like now."

"I'll call Sarah. I bet she'd come with us, too. It would be more fun than going alone. And I could drop you right at the door, and Sarah could help you inside while I park."

"You've convinced me, Angie. How lovely that you young people would help me like that. I sometimes feel like a stick-in-the-mud, staying to home in winter. But if these old bones fell down, I'd be in a real mess."

"Don't worry about that. I'll pick you up at about five-thirty."

"I'll be ready. And, Angie . . . what food are you taking?"

In Maine, no one ever went to someone's home for dinner without contributing something. But I was sure Skye wasn't expecting her guests to bring baked bean casseroles or plates of brownies to tonight's gathering.

On the other hand, maybe I should have gotten a Christmas gift for Skye. Would she give me one? "Just bring yourself, Ruth. No one's taking anything. Bev Clifford is cooking, and you know how good she is."

"All right, if you're sure about that, Angie. I don't want to look like an ungrateful guest."

"You won't be, Ruth. I promise."

My next call was to Sarah. She agreed going to Aurora together would be best, especially for Ruth. "But also for us. Walking into a party alone is intimidating."

"You, intimidated?" I smiled. "Sarah, you've traveled to three continents, opened your own business, and are one of the friendliest and kindest people I know. I don't believe you've ever been intimidated."

"You don't know me as well as you think," she assured me. "Is there room in your car for Dave? He's going alone, too, so far as I know."

"I saw him yesterday and that was the plan," I agreed. "With Ruth's walker it'll be a tight fit, but we can do it. Pick you up a little before five-thirty?"

"It's a date. Now go call Dave and pretty yourself up. Patrick's never seen you in full makeup and a dress like that red velvet."

"That's the truth. I've never seen *myself* that gussied up."

"You're going to look amazing. I know. I had a sneak preview!"

Dave agreed to go with us. I decided to pick him up first, then Sarah, and stop for Ruth last, so we could lift her over the deep drifts if necessary.

I called Gram—my "go-to" for problem solving. "Help, Gram! The good news is I'm back in Patrick and Skye's good graces, and I'm going to Aurora for their party tonight. But I just found out they exchange gifts Christmas Eve. I haven't got a present for Skye! I thought she was going to be in Scotland."

"Thank goodness everything's worked out, Angie. We'll miss you at church tonight, but we'll have tomorrow together. I always make extra cranberry bread for last-minute Christmas gifts. Look in my freezer. The gift loaves have red ribbons on them. You can wrap whichever you choose for Skye."

"Thank you, Gram! I knew you'd come up with something. And your cranberry bread is delicious. Skye will love it!" It was food, but it wouldn't be for dinner. And it was better than having nothing under the tree.

I found the loaves Gram told me about. She'd made six extra loaves. I needed to take lessons in organization from her. I wrapped the loaf with a tag from "Charlotte and Angie." I couldn't take full credit for Gram's bread.

I went and poured bubble bath and hot water into Gram's deep Victorian tub.

Some things the Victorians knew how to do well. Bathtubs were one of them.

Chapter 53

"Christmas Corset Cover! Do it Now!" (picture of corset cover embroidered in flowers) "The Corset Cover design here shown is stamped on the highest grade of Nainsook, allowing sufficient materials for any size bust measurement. Remit 75 cents to pay for the stamped cover with cotton to embroider."

—Advertisement placed by Edwin A. Fitch,
28 Union Square, New York, in *The Modern Priscilla* magazine, November 1905. (Nainsook is a soft, fine, cotton fabric.)

I'd been in and out of Aurora since Dave's students had decorated the tree in the front hallway and Patrick and I'd woven branches along the banister on the main stairway and hung mistletoe. The house had looked spectacular for days.

But on Christmas Eve it was magical.

The fire in the living room fireplace was crackling, the

electric lights on the first floor had been turned down, and lighted candles were everywhere.

Sarah's "Wow!" covered it as the four of us walked in.

Patrick echoed that "Wow!" when he looked at me. "Angie! You look amazing. I don't think I've ever seen you in a dress. Not a dress like that, anyway!"

"You clean up pretty well, too," I whispered as he pulled me under the mistletoe for our first kiss of the night. I couldn't remember ever seeing him in a suit, either.

Sarah gleamed in the candlelight. She'd outdone herself with that silver dress that matched her hair.

Blaze, who was wearing a low-cut black dress, immediately befriended her. "Where did you get that incredible dress?" I heard her ask, as they headed into the living room.

Ruth wasn't sparkly, but assured, in a red wool sheath and pearls, and Dave looked darn good in his navy suit.

Skye herself was perfect. No doubt she'd done some shopping in Scotland. She'd chosen to wear a long red and white Stewart plaid wool skirt, topped with a white cashmere sweater and a long scarf, also in Stewart plaid. She looked as though she'd walked out of a Christmas Hallmark movie.

Clem Walker was there, talking to Marv by the fireplace. I'd hoped she wouldn't come, but when she smiled and waved at me, I waved back. It was Christmas Eve, after all. I hoped she wasn't pumping Marv for news she could broadcast later.

I added the loaf of cranberry bread and my special gift for Patrick to the wrapped boxes already under the tree, and accepted the glass of champagne Patrick handed me. As we silently toasted each other Skye opened the door for Sergeant Pete Lambert, in civilian attire, and Carly Tremont. Had they come together? I doubted it. But everyone who'd said they'd be coming tonight was now here, despite yesterday's storm.

Bev was adding dishes to an elaborate candlelit buffet set on red tablecloths in the dining room. Cold dishes were displayed on the dining room table. Pâtés and cheeses, a platter of poached salmon and a bowl of shrimp, artichoke leaves covered with a spicy cheese, deviled eggs topped with—was that caviar? I tasted one. It was. I could easily have been happy filling my plate with the mushrooms stuffed with crabmeat, raw oysters and vegetables, garlic hummus, smoked trout, and stuffed olives. Many people were doing just that, and heading for the living room to sit and enjoy all the goodies.

For those who preferred hot dishes on this cold night, Bev had covered one of the sideboards with warm food: linguini with clam sauce, *tourtière,* the Quebecois spicy pork pie that Mainers with French-Canadian roots ate on Christmas Eve or Christmas morning (or any other time the spirit moved them), a roast of beef, potatoes stuffed with cheese, lobster macaroni and cheese (Skye had wanted lobster for tonight's dinner, I remembered), vegetarian lasagna, and a basket of popovers.

"Impressive," I said to Patrick, who was watching me scoping out the food.

"Bev is terrific. She made sure we had the Maine dishes Mom wanted, plus the seven fishes Italians look for on Christmas Eve, and included vegetarian choices."

"Seven fishes?"

"Clams, lobster, shrimp, oysters, salmon, trout, and crab," he counted on his fingers. "The caviar is a bonus."

"You've got some crustaceans mixed in there, my friend," I teased.

"Shh! Don't tell anyone," he said. "Shall we each get a plate of appetizers now?"

"I don't think I can manage holding champagne and serving myself," I said, reluctant to give up my heavy flute filled with bubbles.

"Angie, why don't I put your glass, and Patrick's, on the side table between the two armchairs near the fireplace," Bev suggested, overhearing us. "They'll be waiting for you while you fill your plates."

"Thank you, Bev," I said. "I can't believe you did all this!"

She leaned toward me, taking my glass and stage whispering, "I haven't slept a lot this week." She added, "I'm so glad things worked out between you and Patrick," before disappearing with our glasses.

Patrick and I filled our plates. How would we ever be able to find room to sample the hot food later? I thought of the warming centers in town. They'd have food for the families there, but it wouldn't be anything like this feast. I suspected sandwiches and pizza would fill their plates tonight.

I'd never seen a table this spectacular except in a movie. I added an extra deviled egg with caviar to my plate and followed Patrick to the living room.

Dave had filled Ruth's plate, since buffets weren't walker-friendly, and they were chatting with Thomas and Marie. I was glad Dave was watching out for Ruth, although he was sneaking some glances at Sarah and Blaze, both of whom looked spectacular.

I hoped Ruth was letting Thomas and Marie know how she felt about their using her plots (or Haven Harbor's secrets) in the screenplay they were drafting. I wasn't sure I'd convinced Skye and Patrick her concerns were serious.

Sarah and Blaze weren't eating, but were clearly having

an animated talk—maybe about vintage clothing—and Clem had just joined them. Sarah could have found new customers.

Carly had, not surprisingly, pulled a chair over to the small table where Skye was eating. Conversation at that table might be interesting. But Skye had been the one to invite Carly.

The only person alone was Pete. He was standing, awkwardly holding his plate, near the door.

"Mind if we pull another chair over and invite Pete to join us? He looks a little lost," I suggested.

"Good idea. No one should be alone on Christmas Eve, especially in a crowd." Patrick squeezed my shoulder lightly as he went over to talk with Pete.

I was already feeling full. I shouldn't have taken that final caviar-topped egg. But how often did I get a chance to eat caviar? It wasn't exactly everyday fare, at least in my house in Haven Harbor.

Before I'd finished the egg, Patrick was back, with Pete.

"Merry Christmas, Angie. Quite a setup, isn't it?" His glance covered the whole room as he pulled his chair over between Patrick and me. Every law enforcement person I know sat with their back to the wall, in sight of the door. Pete was no exception. He was on alert, even during an elegant holiday party.

"Before I forget: You're officially no longer on the suspect list for killing Paul Carmichael. Your gun hadn't been fired in months, just as you told me. I have it at the station. You can pick it up anytime."

"You suspected Angie of killing Paul?" Patrick looked amazed. "I didn't know that."

"She was the only one here who had a gun," said Pete. "We had to check it out."

Patrick looked from one of us to the other. "She wasn't the only one. Someone else had a gun."

"What?" Pete dropped his fork, and I put my champagne glass down. "Who else had a gun? When I asked, no one admitted to having one. And we didn't find one when we searched the house."

Patrick sighed and lowered his voice. "I don't know what happened to it. But I drove Blaze and Mom home from the airport. Marie and Thomas took a cab, and so did Paul and Marv. Paul and Marv arrived here later than the rest of us. I overheard Blaze asking Paul why they were so late, and he said they'd stopped at a pawn shop on the way, for kicks. He'd seen the sign, and never been to one. She asked him if he'd bought anything, and he told her that—shh!—he'd bought a gun. He'd always thought it would 'be cool' to own one."

"Why didn't you tell Ethan and I me this before?" asked Pete.

"I wasn't there. I didn't see the gun, and I had no proof. I figured Marv would tell you—or Blaze. They both knew about it."

Pete was trying to stay calm. "Where is this gun now?"

"I never saw it. I have no idea."

"Since you didn't find it in your search, maybe Paul took it with him when he went out for that walk," I suggested.

"He didn't kill himself," said Pete. "The shot that hit him wasn't fired that close to him."

"If he was holding the gun, he could have dropped it outside. It's been snowing pretty regularly," I pointed out. "It might be out there right now, under the snow."

"Or someone could have turned his own gun on him," said Pete. "Darn. This opens a whole new line of possibilities. Patrick, why didn't you mention this earlier?"

Patrick shrugged and looked guilty. "Sorry. I didn't think it was my information to tell. I just overheard a conversation."

"Which could be the key to a murder." Pete did not look happy.

"We can't do anything about it right now," I put in. "Since we're talking business anyway, Pete, do you have any idea who laced those Christmas cookies Patrick ate? That experience has put me off cookies for a while."

"Not surprisingly," Pete said. "But, no. That typed message could have come from almost any computer and printer. We've sent the fingerprints to the FBI for identification, but the Bureau's especially backlogged with the holidays. We did confirm that the tin box holding the cookies was probably purchased locally. The gift shop downtown has several sizes of boxes this season for people to put cookies and cakes in. The pattern on the box Patrick got matched one of theirs. But they've sold twenty-seven of those in the past month, and most people paid cash. No record of who they were."

"I assume they don't have a surveillance camera, either," I said.

"Right. No cameras. The only place in town that has one is the pharmacy." He shrugged. "Usually there's no need, even with all the tourists in the summer." He went back to eating. He must like shrimp. His plate was covered with them.

"Should I put a camera in my gallery?" asked Patrick. "I haven't thought a lot about security. But having a camera there might discourage anyone tempted to steal. I have some pretty valuable paintings."

"Paintings aren't exactly something you could slip into a pocket," Pete pointed out. "But a camera or two for surveillance when the gallery isn't open would be a good idea. It might discourage a potential thief. We at the station appreciate having a picture of a robbery."

"Understood," said Patrick. "I'll check into security systems in January."

We were quiet for a few minutes, eating and drinking. And thinking.

"I must say, no one here seems too concerned that their friend was shot a few days ago," Pete commented, looking around the room. "Someone in this room had access to a gun that may have killed Paul Carmichael. Ethan's the homicide detective in charge of that investigation, of course, but I'll let him know. We already knew not everything was roses between Carmichael and his colleagues, but without a weapon"—he glanced at Patrick—"or a witness, we were at a dead end. I'm concerned Ethan may not figure out who the killer is before these folks head out of town. When will they be leaving, Patrick?"

"Last I heard Blaze and Marv were planning to leave the twenty-sixth to fly out to the coast for a few days to see friends and family and celebrate the New Year. The O'Days are going to hole up here to work on the screenplays they're writing. They and my mother will fly back to Scotland January third or fourth. Of course, all plans are subject to change." He shook his head. "I still can't believe all that's happened in the past week. I'm looking forward to the peace and quiet of a new year."

"And to not having to talk about murders and poisoning in the middle of a party like this," I said.

"A-men to that," Pete agreed. "Tomorrow I'll call Ethan and we'll get the snow in the backyard dug up to try to find that gun. In the meantime, I don't know about you guys, but I'm off duty, and I'm going back for more food. I heard a weather forecast this afternoon saying the wind was going to pick up again tonight. With all the ice and snow out there, that could mean more outages. I'm on call, in case there's an emergency. Christmas Eve means family issues colliding with alcohol. I want to taste a few more of those goodies before anyone decides they need me."

Pete got up and joined several other people now in the dining room, including Blaze, Sarah, and Clem, who'd put their discussion on hold.

"Want more?" Patrick asked.

I shook my head. "I took more than ample the first time around. Although I'd like to sample a couple of the hot dishes in a while."

"I suspect they won't all disappear in the next few minutes," he assured me. "But I'll warn you, Mom will want us to take a break and open gifts soon."

"If that's our only interruption, we have no problems," I said.

Well, almost no problems. I wished we knew who'd killed Paul and who'd poisoned Patrick.

"I'll refill our glasses," Patrick said, picking them up and heading back to the corner of the dining room he'd set up as a bar.

I looked around the room, from the fire and candles to the pine boughs and people, many of them my friends. A year ago I could never have dreamed of being a guest at an evening like this.

Not exactly perfect. But darn close.

Chapter 54

"Remember I was born to die."

—Stitched, along with four alphabets,
in eyelet, queen, and cross-stitch
with a strawberry border, in 1765
by Ruth White, aged ten, in
Newburyport, Massachusetts.

I was feeling warm and relaxed when, as Patrick had predicted, half an hour later Skye announced it was time to open gifts.

Dutifully we all headed to the front hall, where the gifts were under the tree.

Patrick made sure that the needlepoint set he'd chosen for Skye was one of the first gifts opened. She exclaimed over the needles and scissors and stiletto and places for other tools, and went right to the dining room to set it behind the food on the sideboard, just as Patrick had hoped.

He was pleased with her reaction, and Sarah was thrilled.

Patrick wasn't as pleased when he opened his gift from his mother, although it got a lot of laughs. Skye had bought him a kilt and vest (she called it a "waistcoat") and a sporran, a purse to be worn on a belt. "I never dreamed I'd have one of these," he managed to say gamely. I wondered if I'd ever see him in that outfit.

"We'll have to go to the Scottish Heritage Day celebration next summer," I said, quickly conscious I was assuming we'd be together then. Patrick didn't seem to notice. He was still examining the kilt.

The personalized needlepointed sachets were, as Skye had predicted, a hit, and she made a point of thanking each of the Mainely Needlepointers in the room, which was a nice touch. She promised she'd love Gram's cranberry bread.

Blaze gave each of her colleagues tartan berets, which they immediately put on. Marv gave them mittens to match; they must have coordinated their purchases. And Skye gave everyone in the room, including Bev, who watched the proceedings from the kitchen doorway, cashmere scarves from Scotland. She must have bought dozens. The one she'd picked for me was a plaid in several shades of blue. ("A Princess Diana tartan," she explained, as I unwrapped it.) It was soft and luscious, and I loved it. Even Pete got a scarf. His was dark maroon, and he grinned and draped it over his shoulder rakishly.

Thomas gave Marie a stunning Scots Victorian pin of different shades of agate and granite set in sterling silver, and Marie gave Thomas an engraved cell phone case.

Patrick drew me aside as other gifts were being opened and exclaimed over. "I saw you'd put a gift for me under the tree. I have one for you, too. But I'd like us to exchange them later, in private, if that's all right."

I nodded. "Better than all right." I hoped we could slip

away in a little while. I was dying to know what Patrick would say when he saw the pillow I'd stitched for him.

After the gifts, Patrick and I served ourselves small plates of hot food. Bev's *tourtière* was delicious. I hadn't tasted any since I'd left Maine. The roast beef was rare, the way I liked it. (Blaze made a face at it and served herself a small portion of the vegetarian lasagna.) Patrick's favorite was the lobster mac and cheese. Pete took a little of everything.

We hadn't finished eating when a loud boom resounded through the house and the lights flickered and went out. Blaze screamed, and Pete headed for the door. The room wasn't completely dark. The fire had been refreshed during the evening, and most of the candles, set out for atmosphere, kept the rooms from being pitch-black.

"Mrs. Clifford? Would you bring us some flashlights from the kitchen?" Skye called.

I followed Pete, who'd gone outside for a moment and returned. "Sounded like a substation blowing," I said.

He shook his head. "Wind took down a large maple across the street. It took wires with it. That blew the power."

I turned back toward the room. Patrick's back was to me; he was gathering dishes to take to the kitchen. Bev was coming into the living room with several flashlights.

Carly, who'd been quiet the whole evening (Skye had even given her a scarf), was standing, walking toward Patrick. That's when I saw candlelight reflected in something silver in her hand.

"Pete! It's a gun!" I didn't wait for him. As Carly raised her weapon I threw myself on her back, knocking her (and a table) over.

All I wanted was to get that gun. She was stronger than I anticipated. We rolled on the floor, knocking over a lamp and two candles. Someone rushed to stamp out the candles before they started a fire. Someone else screamed, but I was focused on Carly's hand holding that gun.

Pete stood over us, yelling that she should drop the weapon. She didn't. I was on top of her, holding her wrist, when suddenly she twisted; then she was over me. I tightened my grip and twisted her wrist. A gun fired. I didn't know if it was Carly's or Pete's. Then Carly's gun rolled toward the fireplace.

Suddenly the room was silent.

Thomas said, quietly, "I'm bleeding."

Pete was still looking down at Carly and I. "Get up, slowly," he said. "Both of you." He picked up Carly's gun and handed it to Patrick, who held it away from his body as though it were a dangerous animal.

"You shot me," Carly said clearly. "I'm getting blood all over my cashmere scarf." I managed to pull myself up. I was fine, just bruised. Carly's shoulder was bleeding. It didn't look critical, but she stayed on the floor, trying to get the scarf she'd tied around her neck away from her wound.

Pete took control. "Who else said they were bleeding?"

"I did," said Thomas. "My side." He held up his hand, which he'd been pressing to his right side. It was covered with blood. "Was I shot, too? Or stabbed? What the hell is happening?"

Chapter 55

*"Remember Thy Creator in the days of thy youth
Before the Evil Days."*

—Small sampler decorated with strawberry
border. Undated and unsigned, in the
Newport Historical Society collection.
Quotation based loosely on Ecclesiastes 12.

"I'd like to know, too," said Pete. "Bev, would you get some clean dishcloths from the kitchen?" Bev started for the door.

"Don't let her leave the room," said Thomas. "She's the one who stabbed me."

"What?" said Skye. "What would she stab you for?"

"Because he was about to ruin my life, that's why," said Bev. "He was about to tell my story to the world. Ruth, I didn't even know you wrote until I heard Ms. West talking to Patrick and Angie yesterday. She said Mr. O'Day would change everything. That no one would know. But everyone in Haven Harbor would recognize what happened, and that's the only world I care about."

"Your story?" said Skye, obviously confused.

"My son was the one who killed my husband, on Christmas Eve, a few years back. It was a nightmare of a scandal, and I had to live through it all, with everyone in town watching and saying they were sympathetic. I knew they all thought I'd messed up both my marriage and my son's life, or else he'd never have done it. I've lost my husband to the grave and my son to state prison, and finally my life was coming together again. And you two"—she pointed at Thomas and Marie—"you were going to turn my life into a movie, and Haven Harbor into Peyton Place. I couldn't take it anymore. I've been cleaning up after you rich folks and cooking for you and coming when you called, and in return you were going to ruin my life."

"Bev, what did you stab him with?" Pete asked, calmly, moving back so he could see both Bev and Carly. "Where is it?"

She dropped the stiletto from Skye's Victorian needlepoint tool kit on a table. "Here it is. And I'm not sorry!"

"I know how you feel. I do. Only you struck a true blow, where I've now failed three times." Carly was still sitting on the floor.

"Get up," Pete told her. "Angie, would you call nine-one-one and get an ambulance out here? And police backup?"

I went to the hallway and called. Looking back at the candlelit room, I felt as though I were watching a play.

Carly pulled herself up and sat on a chair. She was sobbing and using her skirt to dab at her bleeding shoulder.

"So what's your story? Who were you trying to hurt, and why?" asked Pete.

"Skye's son. I wanted him to die," Carly blubbered. "I

wanted to make Skye suffer, the way she made me suffer. I thought I'd killed him a few days ago. In the dark, I couldn't see clearly, and I shot that other man. It was a mistake."

"She shot Paul!" Blaze blurted.

"I did! I'm a damn good shot. I just didn't shoot the right person. Then I borrowed the kitchen of the B and B where I'm staying and made those cookies for Patrick. But he didn't eat enough of them. And now—I've failed again."

"Who are you?" said Skye, going over to stand protectively next to Patrick. "How could I have made you suffer? I'd never seen you before yesterday!"

"You may not remember me, Skye West, but you probably remember my husband. Ben Prince was the name he used. He acted with you in the cast of *A Day Too Long*."

"Ben Prince. I haven't thought of him in years."

"You thought a lot of him back then. You led him on, made him believe you loved him, and then you dropped him. He followed you from Texas to California. Do you remember that? He begged you to stay with him. But you were having none of it."

"Ben was your husband," Skye repeated, as though she was trying to remember. "Where is Ben now?"

"Dead. He left me for you and drank himself to death. You ruined his life and mine. I wanted to ruin your life by killing someone you loved. Dying is easy. Living with the pain of losing someone is forever." Carly burst into tears, crying into her now-blood-soaked cashmere scarf from Scotland.

Chapter 56

"Adam alone in Paradise did grieve,
And thought Eden a desert without Eve,
Until God pitying of his lonesome state
Crowned all his wishes with a loving mate.
What reason then hath Man to slight or flout her,
That could not live in Paradise without her?"

—Mary Gates stitched these words in 1796
    New England.

As if on cue, Aurora's lights came back on.

"The generator most have kicked in," said Skye. "Thank goodness for generators."

A few minutes later the police and ambulance arrived to take Thomas and Carly to the emergency room and Bev to the county jail. Pete assured Carly she'd be joining Bev there as soon as the hospital released her. Marie borrowed Patrick's car and followed the ambulance to Haven Harbor Hospital.

"Poor Bev," said Ruth. "It's all my fault. If I hadn't

written her story in one of my books, this never would have happened."

"Poor Bev? She stabbed Thomas!" said Blaze. "Maine is a crazy place. I'll be glad to get back to the sanity of Los Angeles in a couple of days."

Skye stood, confused about everything that had happened so quickly.

Clem had left. No doubt we'd be on the eleven o'clock news. She had an exclusive.

"Let's get this place cleaned up," said Sarah. "There's enough food in the dining room for several days. Come on, Blaze. We'll cover the food, put it the refrigerator, and set aside some to take to one of the warming centers tomorrow."

"The dishes can go into the dishwasher," said Blaze, joining Sarah. "Growing up, my sisters and I were always the ones who had to clean up after big dinners like this. I'm an expert."

"We didn't even get to the desserts," said Skye, sitting next to Ruth on the couch.

"Mom, everything's okay," Patrick assured her. "I'm fine, Thomas will be fine, we've all had plenty to eat, and drink, and Angie and I'll help Sarah and Blaze clean up. You sit and enjoy the fire. Relax."

"You could have been killed," she said to him.

"But I wasn't," he pointed out. "And we can begin the new year with all mysteries solved."

Dave went to help the kitchen crew. "I'm an expert at washing pots that don't fit in the dishwasher."

Patrick pulled me aside, behind the Christmas tree, and held me. "This party was a little more dramatic than we'd planned," he said, not letting me go. Despite his soothing words to his mother, he was shaking. Carly had tried to kill him three times. Thank goodness she'd failed.

"As soon as things are cleaned up, I'm going to take three of your guests home," I pointed out. "Before the snow gets heavy again. So would you like your Christmas gift now?"

He smiled. "I would. I put both our gifts in the coat closet back here." He picked up my gift to him and shook the box the way a little boy would. "It doesn't sound like marbles, and it's too big for diamonds," he teased, as I smiled, crossing my fingers.

"Open it."

He pulled off the wrappings, and the expression on his face was worth all my hours of stitching. "I don't believe it! How did you manage this? It's a perfect copy of my painting!"

"You once said you'd like a needlepointed pillow in your living room. I took a picture of your painting and made a pattern," I told him. "I'm still slow at stitching. It took me a couple of months."

"I love it! It's perfect." He held me and the pillow for a few minutes and kissed me. Then he put the pillow on the hall table and reached into the closet again. "This is for you."

My box was also large, and light. I opened it carefully.

It was a painting of Haven Harbor, showing Sarah's shop, and the wharf where I'd worked in my teens, and Pocket Cove Beach and the Light. "Did Ted Lawrence do this?" Patrick owned Ted's gallery now.

"No," Patrick smiled.

I looked carefully. "It's realistic. Or—almost realistic. It's like Robert Lawrence's work." Robert Lawrence had been Ted's father. And one of the most famous American artists of the twentieth century.

"You know how to compliment a guy," said Patrick. "But Robert Lawrence was an influence."

Then I saw the initials, PW, in the lower right corner. "You painted it!"

Patrick grinned. He turned over the canvas, where he'd written, *"To new beginnings, in art and in life. For Angie, with love from Patrick."*

Love. We'd never used that word.

It didn't look like the painting I'd copied. That painting was brighter; modernist, he'd once called it.

"You painted this?" I repeated. "You're painting again!" I still couldn't believe it was true—and he'd been able to hide it from me.

"And I'm going to paint a lot more in the new year."

The painting slipped slowly to the ground between us as we kissed.

I heard carols outside the front door. Reverend Tom had sent the church choir, just as Skye had wanted.

This *was* the most perfect Christmas ever.

Bev Clifford's *Tourtière*
(French-Canadian Pork Pie)

Tourtière is a classic French-Canadian dish made of pork, or a pork and beef combination, served either Christmas Eve or Christmas morning. Families have their own traditional ways of preparing it. Although Bev uses seasoned breadcrumbs, some people use mashed potatoes, and some meat and spices alone. A traditional *tourtière* is, of course, made with homemade pastry, but Bev, like many busy cooks today, uses a frozen pie shell.

Ingredients

2 pounds ground pork
1 cup diced yellow onion
2½ cups apple juice or apple cider (apple cider makes the pie sweeter than apple juice)
½ to 1 cup seasoned breadcrumbs
3 teaspoons allspice
2½ teaspoons cinnamon
½ teaspoon ground cloves
2½ teaspoons sea or kosher salt
2 teaspoons ground pepper
1 nine-inch frozen pie shell (both top and bottom)

Day before Serving

Brown ground pork in large skillet, then add diced onion and apple juice or cider and mix thoroughly. Reduce heat to medium-low, stir occasionally, and allow to cook until mixture is moist, but not watery. If liquid remains in the skillet after an hour, mix in enough breadcrumbs to absorb moisture.

Remove from heat. Mix spices together and then add to pork and stir well. Refrigerate mixture at least 12 hours—preferably overnight.

Day Served

Preheat oven to 450°F.

Fill pie shell (homemade or defrosted) with pork mixture and cover with pastry. (Don't forget to poke holes in top of the pastry to allow steam to escape.)

At this point the pie may also be frozen and cooked later.

Bake for 40 to 45 minutes, or until crust is golden and filling is sizzling. (May take longer if your *tourtière* has been frozen.) Bev serves her *tourtière* warm, but it is also good at room temperature, and her recipe is easily doubled so she can have one pie now, and one in the freezer for later.

Acknowledgments

A special thank you to my agent, John Talbot, and editor, John Scognamiglio, without whom no one would be reading about Haven Harbor. Shout-outs also to the production and art departments at Kensington Publishing, who provide wonderful covers, copy edits, and proofing . . . and to Megan Eldred, who gets the word out about the Mainely Needlepoint series.

Thank you to Leslie Rounds, Executive Director, and Tara Raiselis, Director, of the Dyer Library and Saco Museum in Saco, Maine, for their expertise and extensive collection of samplers from New England, which inspire me.

Thank you to my husband, Bob Thomas, who, despite a challenging year, continued to run errands and cook (including *tourtière*!), enabling me to focus on writing. And, most of all, for his patience in listening to me untangle plot points, being my first reader, and telling me he loves me, even on days when my mind is in Haven Harbor. Love you back, always and ever!

To the Maine mystery writers who blog with me at http://www.mainecrimewriters.com, you are my kitchen cabinet and support system on good and bad days, and with whom I often speak at libraries, bookstores, and conferences. (Thank you to everyone who's invited us!) A special thank you to Kate Flora, for opening her home for a small writers' retreat, which gave this manuscript a boost along the writing way.

Unending thank-yous to the many fans who've written to tell me about their family samplers and needlepointed treasures, and encouraged me to learn more about their fascinating history, and the people who created them.

To JD and Barbara Neeson, neighbors extraordinaire, who supplied friendship, encouragement, snacks, and even the laptop this manuscript was written on.

Thank you to Tom and Marie O'Day, screenwriters in *Thread the Halls* and, in real life, stalwart supporters of mystery writers and of Malice Domestic, a special conference for readers and writers held annually in Bethesda, Maryland. If you love traditional mysteries, it's the place to be! (See you there?)

Thank you to Paula Keeney and Ann Whetstone, very special mystery fans who run Mainely Murders, a bookstore in Kennebunkport, Maine, who've told countless people about Angie Curtis (and Maggie Summer, of my Shadows Antique Print Mystery series). Love you guys!

Thanks to Henry Lyon, who keeps my Web site up to date, to my sister Nancy Cantwell, needlepointer and second reader, and, most of all, to everyone who buys, reads, and reviews my books. Your support keeps me writing.

Please friend me on Goodreads and Facebook so we can keep in touch, and check my Web site (http://www.leawait.com) for a printable list of my books and links to prequels of the Mainely Needlepoint series. And send me an email at leawait@roadrunner.com with your e-mail address if you'd like to hear when my next book is published! See you then, if not before!

Lea Wait

Books by Lea Wait

Connect with U s

Visit us online at
KensingtonBooks.com
to read more from your favorite authors, see books
by series, view reading group guides, and more.

Join us on social media

for sneak peeks, chances to win books and prize packs,
and to share your thoughts with other readers.

facebook.com/kensingtonpublishing
twitter.com/kensingtonbooks

Tell us what you think!

To share your thoughts, submit a review,
or sign up for our eNewsletters, please visit:
KensingtonBooks.com/TellUs.